Praise for James Grady and
HARD BARGAINS

"Rankin and his Washington have the same intensity and atmosphere as Raymond Chandler's Philip Marlowe in Los Angeles. . . . *HARD BARGAINS* is a novel that has rich ties to the detective masters of the 1940s and '50s, but this is a new world, with new villains, new passions, and a new hero to deal with them."

—*Richmond Times-Dispatch*

"Rankin, another product of the 1960s, comes close to being the perfect fictional hero in this well-written suspense story."

—*Library Journal*

"Grady knows how Washington works . . . the grid where prostitutes ply their trade, the clubs where lobbyists and lawyers cut their deals, the Senate offices where compromise is never more than a wink or a handshake away."

—*Washington Post*

"*HARD BARGAINS* combines the savvy elements of the thriller with startling poetic images and deeply realized characterization. . . . A beautifully written tale, with a jolt on every page."

—*ALA Booklist*

Books by James Grady

Hard Bargains
Runner in the Street

Published by POCKET BOOKS

HARD BARGAINS

James Grady

PUBLISHED BY POCKET BOOKS NEW YORK

This novel is a work of fiction. Names, characters, places and incidents are either the product of the author's imagination or are used fictitiously. Any resemblance to actual events or locales or persons, living or dead, is entirely coincidental.

POCKET BOOKS, a division of Simon & Schuster, Inc.
1230 Avenue of the Americas, New York, N.Y. 10020

Copyright © 1985 by James Grady
Cover photo copyright © 1987 Mort Engel Studio

Published by arrangement with Macmillan Publishing Company
Library of Congress Catalog Card Number: 85-11481

ISBN: 0-671-62990-5

First Pocket Books printing April 1987

10 9 8 7 6 5 4 3 2 1

POCKET and colophon are registered trademarks
of Simon & Schuster, Inc.

Printed in the U.S.A.

for Bonnie,
for Rachel.

1

SHE STROLLED INTO THE CROWDED BAR LIKE A COOL ASSASSIN CASUALLY searching for a target, spotted me at the table for two set against the mirrored wall and came my way.

"John Rankin?" she asked in a husky voice.

"Yes," I answered, starting to get up. She pushed her palm toward me to forestall such courtesy.

"I'm Cora McGregor." She didn't offer to shake hands as she sat down.

"I wasn't sure I'd recognize you from your description," she said. "Not quite six feet tall, lean, brown hair, mid-30s. Blue eyes. Not a particularly distinctive image."

"That's why I wore the blazer," I said, touching my brown suede sports coat. "In this crowd, I figured there'd only be one. We wouldn't have needed to worry if you would have come to my office—or let me come see you."

"I'm sorry, but neither of those choices was convenient."

"It would have helped if I'd had a description of you," I said.

She shrugged. "I wasn't sure how I'd look."

Sure you were, I thought. Or at least you could have been. She looked bizarre—beautiful, but bizarre.

1

We met in a slick Capitol Hill bar full of mirrors and lush green plants, bamboo chairs and chrome-legged, marble-topped tables on a blond hardwood floor, California decor three blocks from the United States Senate office buildings. Friday, January 27, 1984: a new year barely begun. Winter had been brutal, gray months of freezing winds. That day nature gave us an unexpected preview of spring: before nightfall, we'd reap 70 sunny degrees with clean blue skies.

The weather called the Capitol Hill crowd out of hibernation. This café was normally busy during the noon hour. Today it overflowed, with a waiting line at the door and bodies three-deep at the bar. Friday's customary revelry was doubled by this first taste of spring. No one believed it would last, but no one wanted to miss it. The bartender had a tape of 1960s Motown hits blasting through the sound system: Diana Ross and The Supremes chanting *"Where Did Our Love Go?"* Laughter from a dozen voices floated above the music, echoed through the cigarette smoke and stale beer smog forming by motionless ceiling fans. With few exceptions, the men wore conservative suits and ties. The women aped such acceptable fashion with their own brand of "business" suits and bow ties or high-necked blouses, sweater and skirt combinations. Most of the crowd was white, somewhere between young and late-middle-aged. Everyone projected the hard, comfortable shell of success, savvy professionals who'd earned this pinnacle and planned on never going back.

The woman named Cora McGregor waltzed through them like a shark gliding through a school of fish: everyone was aware of her from the moment she hit the door. They parted to let her pass, tried not to stare—or at least not to get caught staring.

She wore extremes effortlessly. She could have been 30, she might have been 40. She had to be at least 25: nobody was that tough and together without at least a quarter century behind them. Her hair was a rich auburn perilously close to red. That day she'd pulled it back in a severe, head-nurse bun. She wore glasses with huge chameleon lenses that colored themselves according to the light. They never cleared enough to show the color of her eyes; only hinted at their width and depth. Her face was heavily madeup, as artfully and thickly as a stage actress's. The paint job made her flesh pale, sticky. She had high cheekbones the shellac couldn't hide, a fine, slender nose, a clean, long jaw and the best mouth I would see in my life: wide, lush lips with a perpetual allure, no matter what her mood. She'd painted them scarlet.

Like other women in the bar, she wore a blue pinstripe suit, but her jacket was snappily cut, all angles and plunging lapels, shoulders padded in a 1940s style. Her white blouse had a high collar, with every button buttoned except the top one. The neckline hinted at the vulnerable ''V'' at the base of her throat. Her clothing made it impossible to judge her breasts. The skirt ended at her knees, without a slit to show off those long, dark-stockinged legs. She wore shoes with a spike heel that added inches of illusion to her stature. If her bare feet hugged the floor, her eyes would need to look up to mine, but not by much. Outfits like the one she wore are seen only in chic New York ads, the kinds of clothes real people wouldn't buy even if they could afford them, because they make their owner stand too far out of the crowd—and *that's* never acceptable fashion. Her perfume sweetened the air as she settled in her chair, an enticing musk that drop for drop cost more than blood.

Nothing about her seemed right, yet everything seemed to work.

''Have you ordered lunch yet?'' she asked.

''Just coffee,'' I said, nodding to my half-full cup.

''Perhaps we should. I don't want to take up any more

3

of your time than necessary. Besides, my schedule is rather tight."

She glanced at the food list in front of her.

"Are you ready?" she asked a moment later.

"I've seen this menu often enough to know what I want."

"Hmm." She turned toward the door where a brunette waitress in a white blouse and blue apron chatted with the blond hostess while they counted every breath my companion took. The waitress answered her summons in less than five seconds.

"Order first," said my companion. I did, a cheeseburger that sold for four times what a fast-food place would charge and was only twice as good.

"Just coffee for me," said Cora McGregor. Her hands were long, graceful, with trimmed nails painted to match the crimson sheen of her lips. Those hands were steady and sure as they passed the menus back to the waitress. Cora McGregor wore no rings. "And could you please ask the chef to rush his burger? We're in a hurry."

"Sure," said the waitress. She bustled away to do royalty's bidding.

"I appreciate your meeting me," said the woman who'd called me three days earlier. "Of course, lunch is part of my bill." She smiled. "You should have had more than a cheeseburger."

"There's always dessert."

"Whatever you can get," she said.

"I suppose you're wondering why I called a private detective like yourself," she continued.

"I use the term 'investigator,' " I cautioned her. "I'm not a traditional hired hand."

"I've never been much for tradition either," she said. Her smile softened, and curled around me in a conspiratorial embrace. "May I call you John?"

"Please," I said.

"John, I . . . I haven't exactly led an exemplary life."

My shrug said *who has?*

"Don't get me wrong," she continued, her voice even, sure, the tinted lens of her glasses fixed squarely on my face. "I'm not ashamed of who I am and what I've done. I may not have played by the official rules, but I played fair. I've always been honest about who I was and what I was doing. No pretense. I pay my own way and I don't worry about the rest. Life is hard enough without picking up guilt because of other people's judgments and narrow minds."

"That's easier to say than to do," I told her. "And there are a lot of 'what abouts' conveniently left out of your formula. Besides, it must not have worked so well for you, or why would you need me?"

"You're smart. That's good. I don't think I need too smart a man for this, but I like smart men."

"My being smart isn't going to help either of us if you don't tell me what you want."

"No, it won't, but I'm glad you are, because that makes it easier to trust you, and I've got to trust you. This is a delicate matter. I'm glad I picked a smart man like you."

"How did you pick me?"

She shrugged off the question. "Just lucky I guess." She smiled, sweet and slow. "Sometimes I'm very lucky." Her smile drooped. "Sometimes I'm not.

"I left Washington a number of years ago, John. When I did, I left my past behind me. I got a lucky break, established myself in a new city—in a new life. One, ah . . . more in keeping with those traditional and official rules. One that no one condemns me for. I made a clean break with the past. I have no regrets—about who I was, about leaving it behind me. My life now is better than I could ever have imagined, and I want to keep it that way.

5

"You asked why I need you if I'm so lucky, so smart and successful at doing what I do. What I've done isn't my problem. What's been done around me . . . Circumstances trap the smartest people in the world—and luck has the loyalty of a dog in heat.

"For years, I was able to survive my circumstances fairly well—all things considered. Then luck betrayed me.

"One of my . . . former acquaintances was murdered."

"I'm sorry," I said.

The waitress put a cup of coffee in front of her, walked away. Cora McGregor picked up the cup with both hands, braced her elbows on the table and leaned forward. She blew steam off the dark, tangy liquid, silently sipped its brew.

"It happened a long time ago," she said. "I shed no tears for him. He wasn't a man worth mourning. The police never arrested anyone for his murder."

"I don't like standard criminal cases," I told her. "I've worked a few, but not many. I don't want to hunt down a killer. That's the cops' job, and they're touchy about their turf. There's never much profit in murder for me—and usually a whole lot of trouble."

"I don't want you to chase the murderer, John."

"What do you want?"

"When I left my old life, the one loose end was that murder. What I want you to do is find out if the police have any new leads or even new interest in a case they couldn't solve seven years ago. If there are going to be any 'developments' as they call them in the newspapers. Or if there have been any recently."

"Do you think there have?"

She shrugged. "I have no way of knowing. If I did, why would I hire you?"

"Why do you want me to do this?"

"I explained that to you."

"You told me a lot of not very much."

For the first time she seemed flustered, nervous.

"Yes," she said, "I suppose you're right. Please forgive me. I know I sound overly cautious, but . . . I'm asking you to trust me."

"You're also asking me to work for you."

"I need you."

I shrugged.

"Look, if I'm in any way linked to this dead man, this murder, my new life could crumble. I'd be right back where I was when I walked away. Only now there'd be less chance I'd ever get out of . . . Besides me, someone innocent might suffer. If the police have new leads, or are going to take this to the grand jury, maybe even arrest someone, then there's a chance I'll get dragged into it. Maybe they'll show up at my door just to ask a few questions. I probably wouldn't even be called to testify—though maybe I would, maybe the defense attorney would want me to tell the jury what a louse the victim was. How this murder comes back to haunt me doesn't make any difference, just that it does. All that has to happen is for the link to be made. Seven years ago that didn't matter, that was the life I'd chosen, that was the cost, that was fair. But now, if I get ambushed, saddled with my yesterdays . . . well, then I can kiss today good-bye."

"What about tomorrow?"

"Tomorrow takes care of itself."

"Somehow you don't seem the helpless damsel in distress."

"I'm no damsel, Mr. Rankin. And I'm not helpless. I help myself. That's why I decided to call you. I am in distress, I have a problem, some trouble. Taking care of such things is what you say you do for a living. If you've lied . . . well, my mistake for believing you."

Even as she neatly dragged me over the jagged edge of

her words, she gave the impression she wasn't far from tears. I wish I could have seen her eyes through those glass lenses, but just then the light made them an impenetrable amber.

"Understand me," I told her. "I believe you've got trouble, but for all I know you could have killed this person yourself, and now want me to find out how well you covered your tracks."

"Do I look like a killer to you?"

I stared back, and she smiled.

"Nice to see you don't believe in polite lies. Neither do I. I didn't kill him, John. Or anybody. I've done bad things in my time, but murder isn't one of them. And no policeman anywhere wants to arrest me for any other crime."

"I hope not," I said. "But I'm still . . ."

"Like I said," she interrupted, "you're smart. I appreciate that—and I do understand. I . . ."

"Here we go," said the waitress as she put a plate with a cheeseburger and chunks of deep-fried potatoes in front of me. "Will there be anything else?" She raised the coffee pot in her other hand. "Refills?"

"Yes, thank you," said my companion. She smiled, and the waitress filled our cups, scurried away to serve less intriguing customers.

"Please, eat while the food is hot," Cora McGregor told me.

"As I was saying, John, I understand your concerns. I don't want you to do anything illegal or unethical."

"That makes two of us," I said as I lifted the burger off the plate.

"Could you do this?" she asked. "Could you find out if something has happened in this murder? You'll discover I'm not a suspect. Nobody will be hurt by you doing what I want, finding out what I need to know. If there is some change, if the police are about to do something . . . well, then I have another set of problems and choices, ones I must face on my own. If nothing has changed . . . then I can go on as I've planned. But either way, John, I've got to know the truth so I know what to do. That's all I'm asking. Help me know, help me so I won't make any foolish, ignorant mistakes."

"The police don't casually give out information about a homicide investigation."

"But you could find out."

"Maybe. It's a long shot."

"But you can make it. You're good enough. That's easy for anybody to see. You're smart."

"Don't sell me on myself," I told her. "You're the one I've got to buy."

She smiled. "And do you buy me, John?"

"How much of that very little you told me was true?"

"Enough," she said.

"Hmph."

I took a big bite of the burger, chewed it and thought. She let me ponder without pulling or pushing. She knew she either had the hook in me or she didn't.

"Who got murdered?" I asked.

"Does that mean you've bought me? That I'm your client?"

"No names for free, right?"

"Can you blame me?"

"Damned if I know." I swallowed some coffee.

"Tell you what," I said. "I don't know if I can do what you want—legally or practically. But I'm willing to give it a shot. No guarantees, and if it looks wrong, I'll throw it right back at you."

"Thank you! I knew I could trust you, I knew you'd help!"

"Sure you did," I said. "But we've got one more thing to settle."

"Your fee. Don't worry, I pay a man what he's worth."

"I'll bet. For something like this, the least I charge is $50 an hour."

"You're expensive."

"I'm not cheap. I want a two-hour retainer, in advance. This will either be something I can get fairly quick or not at all. I might not need that much time, but that's the minimum fee—and I keep it even if I have to walk away from this. What you want might cost more, maybe as much as four hours. I'll take expenses too, though I doubt they'll top 20 bucks."

"Plus today's lunch."

"Since you insist."

She took a white envelope from her chic black purse.

"I assumed you wouldn't start work until my check had cleared your bank, so I took the liberty of bringing cash. Do you mind?"

My mouth was full, so I shook my head. She'd come well prepared: less than half the load of bills left that envelope to make a stack between us on the table.

"That's $250. Fee plus expenses."

"That's more than twice the retainer I quoted you."

"I trust you to refund the balance. Now, do we have an arrangement?"

"Now you're my client," I said.

"Wonderful!"

"Who was murdered?"

"A man named Parviz Naderi. Someone shot him in 1977."

I waited, but she said nothing else. I got out my notebook, clicked my pen.

"Could you spell that for me?"

She did.

"And?"

"And what?" she asked.

"And what else? Who was he, how did you know him, why was he shot, how were you involved?"

She shook her head. "You have all you need to do your job."

"You mean all you'll give me."

She shrugged.

"Please forgive me," she said, standing. "I know it's rude to leave while you're still eating, but I have a very busy schedule. You'll take care of the check out of that retainer."

And you've stuck me here in midmeal waiting for it while you walk away alone, haven't you? I thought.

"Wait a minute!" I said, stopping her exit. "I don't have your phone number, your address. How can I reach you when I'm ready to report?"

"I'll call you from my hotel. You won't have anything before Monday, will you?"

"Maybe not until Tuesday. If your hotel is downtown or on the Hill, we could just as easily meet."

"Yes, that might work out nicely." She gave me her most dazzling smile of the day. "I'll see you soon, John."

Then she pivoted, waltzed through the crowd with a sweet hip-twitching walk, leaving as coolly in control as when she came.

2

"I T'S ABOUT NOW WHERE YOU TELL ME
THERE AIN'T NO SUCH THING AS A
free lunch," said homicide detective Nick Sherman. He
nodded to the scrawny waitress. Her answering nod was a
promise to fetch him another Bloody Mary.

"You knew that before you came," I said.

"Yeah, but hell, I was hungry."

And we'd eaten, he'd drank. We'd joked about this and
that, politics and the police force, old times and old friends.

We met that Monday at the Fraternal Order of Police
club, a cavernous corner bar and restaurant across the street
from the football-stadium-sized, sandstone FBI headquarters. Those two centers of law enforcement border the jumble of government office buildings, department stores and
shops that passes for downtown Washington, D.C.

More than a dozen armed bureaucracies police this city.
Most of them were represented in the FOP that afternoon,
detectives and uniformed officers scattered at tables through
the darkness, laughing, eating, staring sullenly off into nowhere, some drinking, some not; some on duty, some not.
Most of the patrons were men, a few accompanied by dates
or female civilians from the courthouse or city hall. An
ebony-skinned woman wearing the light blue shirt and sil-

12

ver badge of the city force sat at a table by herself, a half-empty glass of beer going flat in front of her. I recognized a lanky, sultry black-haired woman lawyer who confined her romantic affairs to married cops. She was sitting at a table with her latest catch, a stylishly suited detective lieutenant from Robbery Squad with gray hair and the look of a man just past 40 who should have known better. His wedding band was a dull gold in the dim light. Half a dozen hand-held radios periodically squawked, punctuating the jukebox's country and western serenade of lost love with reports of incidental evil. A squat, officious uniformed sergeant bustled through the front door, shiny visored cap crammed on his head, his radio turned loud as he pranced through the room pretending to joke with his fellow officers while he checked to see which cops on his watch might be there. No one seemed to care about him one way or the other. He left three minutes later, as unappreciated and unsatisfied as when he arrived.

"I've got a problem with murder," I told Nick.

"Me too," he shot back, and we both laughed.

"No," I said, "a particular murder, and I've got a client."

"You keep telling me you don't like doing those kinds of jobs," he said, "and you keep ending up doing them."

"They seem to be what I find out there."

"Ain't that the truth."

"I don't want to get stuck in a bad situation again," I said, and he nodded for me to continue. "I don't know what the potential is here. The odds are there's no problem, but even by asking you . . ."

"Don't forget who you are," he said. "Don't forget who I am."

For a moment I thought he was only cautioning me, then he smiled encouragement, said, "Friends like us don't worry about too much."

"Yeah, well, aiding and abetting a felony, accessory to a murder . . . little things like that tend to trouble me."

Nick's gaze was warm, solicitous.

"What I've got is this," I said, then without mentioning any names told him about Cora McGregor and what she wanted me to do.

"Can you help me?" I asked. "Could you find out which detective is handling a particular homicide, whether or not it's going anywhere or going to go anywhere? And do it without either of us stepping on our Johnsons?"

"Maybe," he said. "But I'd want your client's name—just in case, you understand."

"Her name is Cora McGregor. She said the homicide victim's name was Parviz Naderi, and that he was shot in 1977."

Nick blinked. I felt him withdraw into himself. Then he smiled the slow, chipped-tooth grin he used as both shield and sword.

"You sure you got that name right?" he asked.

"I might have pronounced it wrong, but that's it. Do you want me to spell it for you?"

"No." He shook his head. "No, that won't be necessary. What was this Cora McGregor like?"

"I wish I could tell you," I said. "She's the kind of woman you never forget, but you can't pin down anything about her and believe it. She's smart and tough and lets you see only what she wants you to see—and that might not be her at all. It's like trying to capture perfume. The day I met her, she wore musk."

"How'd she seem to you? Afraid?"

I shook my head. "Worried, but not really afraid. At least, she doesn't show fear."

"Do you buy her story?"

"She lied to me about something: who doesn't? I don't buy her as killing this guy—not because she couldn't or wouldn't, she's rough enough for that, but she's too smart to have killed someone and then put herself in jeopardy by making this play with me. She'd calculate the odds, realize it could backfire on her, and find some other way of getting what she wants.''

''Maybe she's outsmarted herself. Do you trust her?''

''I don't know. I think you could trust her, if . . .''

''If?''

''If she wanted you to.''

''Did she tell you how she hooked into Naderi?''

''No. All she said was that somebody killed him.''

Nick chuckled. ''Oh yeah, that's what somebody did, all right.''

''Sounds like I lucked out and found the right cop.''

''Let's hope so.'' He smiled again, only this time it was genuine. ''Naderi was my case. *Is* my case.''

''And?''

''And you pick the good ones, don't you, cowboy?''

''Does she ring a bell with you? Could she have been tied in with this Naderi guy?''

''A whole lot of women were tied in with him. I can't recollect her right off the top of my head.''

We both knew he didn't forget.

''What about it?'' I asked. ''Can you help me? Will you?''

''Well now, I'd have to think about that.'' His eyes drifted away. The scrawny waitress caught his gaze; her smile asked if he wanted another drink. Nick shook his head.

''Yes sir, I'd have to think about that. Go back to the office, refresh my recollections with my notes and the case jacket.''

''Nick, if this is going to cause you trouble . . .''

''I'm always ass-deep in trouble, cowboy. That's my job.''

15

"You know what I mean. Who was this Naderi guy, anyway?"

He laughed. "That's a good question. Yes sir, that's a real good question. Let's puzzle on it another time. When is this Cora McGregor going to get back to you?"

"Maybe today, probably by tomorrow."

"I'll call you this afternoon."

3

AFTER I LEFT NICK I DROVE ACROSS TOWN TO A MEN'S CLOTHING STORE at the upper end of Georgetown to pick up a check from the owner, who'd been smart to suspect an old friend in their new business deal. My client's partner had been bleeding cash out of a small bar they bought together by doctoring phony expenses and contract-laborers in the books. I didn't know what he had done with the money, though I had a couple good ideas: the three times I saw him when I visited the bar pretending to be just another customer he had a bad case of the sniffles. They'd get worse every time he visited his private office or the bathroom. That was none of my business, though. I gave my client what he needed to go to a lawyer and have that other hired gun get him out of the mess he was in. My client gave me my check with mixed feelings: now he knew he really had trouble.

Driving back I took the scenic route, caught Pennsylvania Avenue and followed it to Constitution. There are quicker roads to my Capitol Hill office-apartment, but few as impressive—and that year, none more telling.

This used to be an open city: 1984 changed that.

As I drove past the White House, front-end loaders

moved the last of the waist-high concrete barriers in place. They circled the grounds of the Executive Mansion, which was already surrounded by a six-foot-high black steel picket fence. The new gray barrier covered the center strip in the street, blocked any straight path into the White House grounds for a charging car bomber. Earlier in the winter, garbage trucks filled with sand had been used as roadblocks in the driveways. Later that year, the concrete wall would be moved from the center strip to the sidewalk curb: less obtrusive but just as effective. On Capitol Hill, where at one time anyone could freely roam the office buildings and the Capitol itself, staffers, lobbyists and reporters were now required to wear their picture IDs clipped to their clothing or dangling from their necks like military dog tags. The rest of us gambled that our identity of *citizen* was enough to let us get where we wanted to go. Metal detectors filled all the entrances, and the once-lackadaisical Capitol police force was extremely serious about enforcing their new rules. The backs of chairs on the Floor of the House of Representatives now contained bulletproof steel plates.

Fear won a round in D.C. that year. Paranoia became institutionalized, with a weary, resigned acceptance of our fate by all the powers in the city. That year's *they* were terrorists: unspecified, anonymous, the embodiment of all evil and problems in the world, ghosts cast as the second most dangerous foes of our fragile democracy. The communists (a philosophical mob led by the Soviet nation) still held first place in that contest.

That some "they" was out there was undeniable: someone bombed the Capitol in November 1983, the second time since 1971. In 1971, the "they" had been revolutionaries. Now the names had changed, but not the bombs. There'd been fear in 1971, too, and massive paranoia, but shock had dominated the city, as it had after each political attack, from 1954, when Puerto Rican separatists opened fire at congressmen milling around the House Floor, to Dallas in 1963, and later to the rainy afternoon in 1981 when an arrogant creep gunned down the current president and three other public servants.

But by 1984, the city was more numbed than shocked by political violence. It didn't matter much anymore who the enemies were. They were there, that was enough. Protection came first, understanding second. Solutions were probably impossible. *They'd* always been there, they always would be. That year we called them terrorists, and they seemed to be wherever someone didn't like us: Lebanon, Latin America. The streets of D.C. We let fear in, locked doors on hope, put up barricades against anger, doubled the guard on our dreams.

I got lucky, found a parking place for the Porsche on Seventh Street just off Pennsylvania Avenue and around the corner from The Eclectic building. Before I climbed the stairs to my third-story office-apartment I walked inside Rich's store to see if he had picked up my mail.

"So," he called to me as the door swung shut behind me, the echo of the entry bells faded, "home is the hunter. How's tricks?"

"Not bad. How's business?"

A man and a woman dressed like congressional aides who hadn't yet found and lost their first adult love affair giggled about the greeting cards in the back corner of the store; a gaunt, white-haired man with dandruff on the shoulders of his faded blue suit and a bulging, dilapidated briefcase leaned forward on his umbrella as if it were a cane, frowned as he stared at one of the old 8″ × 11″ landscape prints in a box on the glass shelf.

"Could be better," Rich said with a shrug. He rested a hand on the cash register. "Could be a whole lot worse. What I wouldn't give for another mindless craze like Pet Rocks! Remember them? I sold 43 of those suckers one afternoon, $3.50 apiece, plus tax. Paid my utility bill. Those were the good old days.''

"Sure they were," I said. "Anything for me?"

He shook his head. "Not even a 'Dear Occupant.' "

"At least I didn't get any bills."

"Life can be good," said my landlord. He smiled. "I'll send you a postcard so you won't feel neglected. I've got some rejects."

He leaned across the counter, whispered through his beard. "I lost another half pound!"

"Terrific! How many more to go?"

Rich sighed, shook his head. "Too many. Too many."

The digital counter on my phone message machine upstairs showed zero: no one had called, not even a wrong number who didn't say anything. I turned off the machine, walked back into the apartment to start water boiling for a cup of coffee I didn't particularly want, came back to the office and sat at my desk, writing the right numbers in the right place to record my latest fee in my computer.

The *Washington Post* and *New York Times* for the last few days made a hefty stack in the corner. I read the news every day, oh boy. Forests in the Volga were dying because of pollution, and a California teenage TV addict killed himself rather than suffer withdrawal. His note read, "In my heart, I will take my TV with me." The world's third largest oil company wanted to gobble up the petroleum corporation in 14th place. A congressman and a former Cabinet-level official had been sentenced to jail in unrelated corruption schemes. The U.S. launched a multibillion-dollar research program to enable Uncle Sam to wage war in outer space, and half a million children of American poverty were believed to be suffering from malnourishment. Journalistic and political sages were trying to drum up interest in the year's presidential sweepstakes, in which eight Democrats were pecking at each other while the incumbent Republican sat comfortably secure in the White House. The wise ones around town claimed the Democratic race was all but over already, with that nomination already locked up by a former vice president steeped in party tradition and promises to every special-interest group that smiled his way. The smart bet also said none of that made any difference, because the current president was a shoe-in come November.

It was one of those days. I felt off-center, out of kilter. I tried to blame it on ennui, but I knew more than weariness and boredom put me where I was. I had this funny feeling that someone had sewn strings on my back, but I didn't know who held the other ends. Anger ran not far beneath my vague unease, anger and apprehension. And it all flowed back to Cora McGregor.

The phone rang.

"John Rankin."

"Looks like you're free and clear," said Nick Sherman.

"How so?"

"Nobody named McGregor, nobody named Cora shows up in any of my recollections on that matter we discussed." In the background of his voice I heard telephones, the chatter of the Homicide squad room. "Couldn't even find anybody with initials like that—leastways, not anybody who looked like you said she does."

"Does that mean you can help me?"

"How?"

"Nick . . ."

He laughed, though with little humor in his tone. "You can tell your client that it is reasonable to assume there will be no sudden developments in the matter, nothing pending beyond what's always been out there."

I assumed there were other detectives close by, listening. Why else would he be so oblique?

"In other words, the case is dead."

"Naderi is the one who's dead."

"OK, the case is still under investigation. But it's not bubbling in the active file."

"That's fair."

"Thanks, Nick."

"Now let me ask a favor. You heard from your client yet?"

"Not a word."

"When you do, after you explain to her there ain't nothing going to be happening that she needs to worry about, why don't you tell her that the policeman who's handling the case is willing to meet with her and reassure her personally? Off-the-record, all smiles and helping hands."

"That's a hard line for me to buy, Nick. I don't think I could sell it to her, either."

"It's a damn good idea, buddy."

"I'll try, but I'll bet it's no sale. I'm not even sure I'm going to tell her I gave you her name."

"Why not? Hasn't made a bit of difference. If she doesn't want to get together with me, do me another favor."

"What's that."

"Tell me when and where you're going to meet her."

"Nick, you're asking me to bend a professional confidence."

"That seems to be what friends do, doesn't it?"

Neither of us spoke for a long time.

"Let me think about it, Nick," I finally told him. "I figure you want to know who and what and why she's messing in your case. I can't promise what I'll do, but . . . I promise I'll try to set something up."

But I didn't need to worry how to keep that promise to Nick. My office phone rang at 8:30 the next morning, when

I was only half a cup of coffee into the day, just finishing the *Post* story about the latest American Marine killed in Lebanon.

"Mr. Rankin?" The telephone made her voice seem huskier, lower. "This is Cora McGregor. I'm sorry to call so early."

"Don't worry about it."

"Were you able to help me with my problem?"

"Yes, and fairly cheaply too. I . . ."

She interrupted me. "What did you find out?"

'This is more appropriate to discuss in person. Besides, I owe you a refund on your advance."

"Oh yes, the money. Please, John, we can take care of those details when we meet. I don't worry about the telephones, and I must know: Is anything going to happen? Are the police . . ."

"Officially, it's an open investigation. All unsolved murders are. But nobody is doing anything about trying to close it, nobody expects anything to happen."

"Thank God! And thank you, John."

"Look, I only used up the $100 retainer. Expenses weren't much, lunch with a homicide detective. I figure I owe you $120. I can meet you with a check and an expense statement, a typed report, any time today or . . ."

"That won't be necessary. Thank you for your time and trouble."

"Wait a minute! What about the money I owe you? Besides, I can tell you more, maybe give you more . . ."

"You've already given me all I need, John. As for the money . . . consider it a tip."

"That's a hell of a tip."

"I told you: I pay a man what he's worth."

And then she hung up, ended it quick and clean, left me holding my schemes and questions and the dead, buzzing phone receiver.

4

Two months passed before I saw her again.

Winter reclaimed Washington with weeks of bitter winds and damp snow before spring firmly pushed its way into town. The cherry blossoms were blooming by that April afternoon. Those slender-limbed trees with delicate pink petal leaves colored the city. They circled the Tidal Basin and the Jefferson Memorial, lined the grass median of Pennsylvania Avenue on Capitol Hill. A living pink cloud covered Stanton Park two blocks east of the Senate office buildings. Often a single fragile cherry tree stood alone amidst barely budding elms and oaks in a private yard or on a plot of public earth in the brick, glass and steel canyons of downtown D.C. Each year we here in Washington wonder and wager how long the season's splendor will survive the elements and the onrush of time. Even the callused eyes of a burnt-out case in a three-piece suit or junkie's Salvation Army rags can't ignore April in this city. But the cherry trees' petals fall quickly, are replaced by the summer's mature green leaf. The blossoms become a memory almost before they are a moment. Their scent is subtle, soft, and must be sought in the air.

I'd had a good year so far since meeting Cora Mc-

Gregor. Three more law firms began using me on a regular basis. Several other clients strolled through my office door bearing interesting as well as lucrative assignments. There'd been two lovers who hadn't worked out like I'd hoped, but those encounters had been relatively blood free.

That morning had been spent in a law office not far from the White House reviewing documents to be filed in a discrimination case I'd worked on. One of the lawyers wanted to buy me lunch, and I let him. He said such business was his only excuse to leave the office and touch the world beyond the glass of his high-status, hermetically sealed window. We ate Chinese, then said good-bye on the street. He walked back to his climate-controlled warren filled with ringing phones, piles of paper, complicated schemes creating momentary victories. I watched him disappear in the crowd.

The sun warmed my back and my brow. The air was clean, fresh in spite of downtown traffic. There were no clouds, and the sky was a deep, bold blue. Some ghetto blaster radio beat out an irresistible cadence. All the people in the street marched to the music. Energy surged through our human river. I drifted up I Street to a small triangular park facing Pennsylvania Avenue, found an empty bench and sat down. Two lovers nuzzled each other on the bench to my left. Her hand rested on his thigh. A frail old lady in a tightly buttoned tan raincoat perched on the bench across from them; she tossed popcorn from a small brown paper bag to a half-dozen pigeons pecking the concrete at her feet. A scraggly blond-bearded fat man wearing a filthy white T-shirt and even filthier blue jeans presided from a bench off to my right, leering at everything and everyone with crazed but harmless omniscience. The magnolia tree behind him was about to bloom: its thick perfume drenched this tiny corner of the city.

Something inside me yearned to soar. I felt wonderfully

powerful, alive and free. I stretched my arms wide along the back of the bench, gripped the rough, weathered wood slats and pulled. My chest wanted to burst. I closed my eyes, tilted my face to the heavens. Five, ten minutes later I lowered my head. As the sun spots burned away I focused on the street corner and saw her standing there, waiting for the light to change.

She wasn't the same woman, and yet she was.

Gone was her aura of extreme drama, though she was still beautiful, men still turned to stare at her as they walked past. She ignored them. Her carriage spoke of grace, power, purpose, though today her stance lacked the challenge she'd dared the world to accept when we'd met. She wore a simple blue shirt, and its masculine cut accented her sensuality. Her slacks were tan, khaki. I couldn't see her shoes. That auburn hair hung free to her shoulders, curled up at the ends; it floated with the slight breeze. As far apart as we were, I could tell she wore much less makeup and the same glasses.

Reason played no role in what happened next. I was on my feet and moving by the time the light on the corner turned green, part of the crowd crossing the street behind her before the light changed again. I slipped my sunglasses out of my blazer, hid my eyes behind their smoked blackness. If there'd been any doubt before, watching her walk banished it: there was no mistaking that firm stride, the twitch of her narrow, taut hips. I could have caught her in a moment, but I hung back, ready to dodge behind some other moving body in case she turned around. She never looked back.

We walked that way for four blocks, a secret parade she didn't know she led. She turned down a side street behind George Washington University to a small corner parking lot. I stood at the opposite corner while she paid the attendant, waited while he scurried down the rows of parked cars. She was cool and calm, unhurried and unafraid that fine afternoon. I was ready to duck behind a parked delivery van, but she never looked my way.

Three minutes later the attendant braked a sleek black BMW to a halt beside her, left the engine running and climbed out. She slid behind the wheel, rolled down the window but didn't bother with a seat belt before looking both ways for cars—and not seeing me. She turned left out of the parking lot, headed west in the lane on my side of the street. I peered around the back end of the van and memorized the BMW's Maryland license plate as that black car rolled away in the traffic.

I've got you now, Cora McGregor, I told myself. *I've got you now.*

5

SHE RODE A DAPPLE GRAY HORSE OUT OF THE WHITEWASHED BARN.

I'd been leaning on the white rail roadside fence half a mile from a rambling, ivory-hued mansion, using binoculars to scan the house's curtained windows, when suddenly her figure on that horse filled my lenses. Her auburn hair was tied back from her face. She wore a simple tan windbreaker over a white blouse, khaki jodhpurs, sleek brown riding boots that reached her knees. For a moment I considered climbing back in the silver Porsche, firing up the engine, nudging it off the grassy strip between the fence and the black ribbon road that had led me here. Driving away. So far no one had seen me, so far nothing had changed since yesterday when I'd spotted her downtown.

I stayed and watched.

Few images surpass the beauty of a woman riding on a cool spring morning. I lowered my binoculars, not wanting to distort the vision. Time seemed suspended. The early morning light was as clear and clean as bottled water. A wispy mist lingered in the freshly budded trees surrounding the meadow, growing along the fence. The grass glistened with dew, and its tingling, damp green fragrance mingled with the moist rich soil under my feet. The long wooden

28

rail beneath my arms felt smooth and solid. The air was absolutely still, quiet, as if life were mute. Birds ceased to sing, no cars whizzed by. The horse's hooves pounded over the meadow in total silence. This could have been a movie without a soundtrack, a dream.

At first woman and horse lumbered; she coaxed and urged her reluctant mount to awaken. They turned this way and that, a tight "S" pattern winding away from the buildings with ever longer loops. Then what began as labor for both horse and rider magically evolved into a celebration of effortless rhythm and rhyme. She rose and fell in the saddle, rose and fell, at one with her mount. They merged, flawless as a memory put right; loped over the lawn, first to the left, then to the right. Graceful, certain, they criss-crossed the long stretch leading to the fence, free of all purpose except the ride.

They were midway between the buildings and the fence when I sensed her notice my figure. Rider and horse tensed, curved into the next loop with caution. On the return swing she abruptly turned the gray animal my way, slowed it to a trot, then a walk, headed straight for the fence and the man she'd soon recognize as me.

She'd told me her name was Cora McGregor. According to the Maryland Department of Motor Vehicles, she drove a car belonging to J. Emmett Sloan of 12933 Persimmon Tree Lane, Potomac, Maryland, a suburban area of winding, treelined roads connecting country estates situated roughly 20 miles from the Capitol dome. Horse country. Money country. Six Mercedeses, two Jaguars, a handful of BMWs, a Porsche newer and far cleaner than mine and about a dozen lesser cars that probably belonged to maids filled the parking lot in front of the Safeway at the small, tastefully designed village shopping center I passed through on my way to scout out J. Emmett Sloan's address.

She rode close, reined the horse steady, still. The animal's head stopped only a few feet from where I leaned against the fence.

"My, my," she said, a hard smile on her face, a harder edge in her words. She wore no glasses. Her eyes were large and nicely spaced, two blue sapphires. "John Rankin. Imagine that."

"I was in the neighborhood."

"And you just happened to bring your binoculars."

The mare whinnied, clumped three steps closer and nuzzled my arms on the fence with her forehead. She smelled damp and heavy. Her lashes and whiskers were stiff and white; her brown eyes seemed sad. She whinnied again, and spray from her lips hit my cheek. I stroked the hard bone between her eyes.

"Nice animal," I said.

"We call her a horse." The woman leaned forward, patted the horse's neck. "Oh, Molly, you never learn, do you? She's an Arabian. Sometimes that breed is more like a dog than horse. So friendly. She'd trot a mile to be petted, wouldn't you, Molly? Arabians like people, even though they're such smart horses. We're too deep in their blood for them to ignore. Legend claims that in the desert, sheiks slept with their horse inside the tent, kept their woman outside."

"Probably safer that way."

"For everyone but the horse."

Molly jerked her head upright, stiffened, her ears flicked straight. Something deep inside her chest rumbled. She danced a stiff few steps, bunched herself into a tight coil. Her eyes turned wild.

"Easy, Molly, easy!" The woman pulled the slack from the reins, patted the horse's shoulder as she soothed the animal. "It's OK, girl, it's OK. Not now. Don't worry, not now. I'm here. It's OK."

"I didn't mean to scare her," I said.

"You didn't."

Molly calmed down, lowered her head to eat the grass at my feet.

"Nice of Mr. Sloan to let you ride here."

"Yes, isn't it."

"Is he a friend of yours?" I asked.

"I've known him for a long time."

"Really?"

"Really."

"Did you and Sloan become . . . *friends* before or after your days with Naderi?"

"Sometime soon I assume you're going to tell me why you're here, aren't you, Mr. Rankin?"

"I came looking for you," I said, the simple truth.

"Lucky you," she said. "You've succeeded and it's not yet noon."

"I didn't like the way you ended our business," I told her. "Come to think of it, I'm not sure I liked our business."

"We're not required to like things in life, Mr. Rankin, just to do our part. You've been amply rewarded for yours. You've got no complaints."

Molly whinnied, picked up her head and looked back to the house.

"That's how you figure it?" I asked as Molly went back to feeding.

"Yes," answered the woman. "That's how it is."

Again Molly raised her head, looked back toward the buildings. This time her rider and I looked back too.

A sleek black car purred toward us over the private drive connecting the public road to the estate's buildings. The woman's hard blue eyes met mine. She stared at me for ten, fifteen seconds as the car drew nearer.

"Listen to me!" she said, her words quick and urgent. "Trust me, do as I say!"

"Why . . ."

"Just listen! You've got nothing to lose. Consider it honoring our bargain. I kept my word and paid you, you've pushed it. Now you can set it straight and lose nothing."

The car slowed as it neared the intersection with the public road. The machine was a closed, black Mercedes convertible with a man behind the wheel. The woman on horseback didn't wait for me to answer.

"You're a friend of a friend of mine," the woman hissed. "Her name is Tresa, Tresa Hastings. She's in Europe now, Paris. Vacation. Somebody thought I was involved in a car—no, thought I witnessed a car accident, one you're doing something on, lawsuit, I don't know what, that's your business. You and I met once before—with Tresa. You didn't want to call me, get me tangled up with the lawyers, so you came out to see if I saw anything. I didn't and I can't help and this will be the end of it."

She ran out of breath as the Mercedes turned onto the grass beside my car, parked. The driver swung out of his car to join us.

He was long and lean, elegant as hell in a gray summer suit, blue shirt, and stylish striped tie. He moved like a recently retired dancer. His hair was black, cut almost Marine short and brushed flat with no effort to hide its slight recession above his temples. His tanned face was handsome, with prominent cheekbones, smooth skin. Those eyes were large, gray and smart. The nose hooked ever so slightly, giving him a not unpleasant hawklike cast. His mouth was thin-lipped but wide. When he smiled, his teeth were even, perfect and white.

"I say, excuse me!" he called as he strolled up to me, an apologetic grin on his face. "I thought you were Doc Wyatt—he drives a car like yours. Do you know him?"

"No," I confessed.

"Damn good veterinarian," he confided to me. He stuck out his hand. "Emmett Sloan."

His grip was firm, confident and dry. He was stronger than he looked, yet made no effort to prove it.

"John Rankin," I said.

He beamed at me, then turned to the woman on the horse.

"Good morning, darling," he called. "Sorry I missed you at breakfast. By the time I woke up, you were already out and about."

"Hello, Emmett," she said.

"Well." He smiled from her to me back to her, then beamed forth at the world in general. "Isn't it a simply glorious morning?"

"Yes," I said.

"John is a friend of mine," said the woman.

"Thank God!" Emmett told us. "Then I don't need to run him off the old homestead, right?"

He and I chuckled.

"John is a private detective," she said, and smiled ever so slightly.

"Really!" answered Emmett, turning to me with absolute fascination on his face.

"Really," I said.

"You might say he's doing me a favor," said the woman. Then she told him the lie she'd concocted moments before.

"I say," he told me when she'd finished, "that is decent of you. Driving all the way out here to see Barbara in person, spare her nonsense with lawyers and the law. So you think there's no reason for her to be involved at all?"

"I didn't see any of the accident," she said. "I just happened to be nearby. Evidently someone got my license plate and description, thought I'd make a good witness."

"That you would, darling. You never miss anything.

33

"Well," he said, turning to me, "except, it seems, just this once."

"Maybe she's slipping," I said evenly, looking at him.

"Oh no, not our Barbi!"

He and I chuckled again.

"I've got a marvelous idea!" he said. "You're such a nice chap and I know so few of Barbara's friends, we should have you for dinner!"

On the other side of the fence, Molly shifted a few steps.

"Yes," he said. "That's a great idea—isn't it, Barbara?"

"Terrific," she said.

"Lucky I drove up just now and thought of it!"

"Sure is," I said.

"Let's see . . ." He frowned, wrinkled his brow in thought. A black Cadillac whizzed by on the main road. A breeze blew a whiff of lilacs past me. Molly raised her head, looked around. Emmett moved closer to me, like a confederate planning some grand scheme.

"We can't have you with next Tuesday's crowd, they're mostly conservatives and you know how paranoid some of them can be. Dropping a private detective in their midst without more advance warning would give them gas and that's never pleasant at dinner. Thursday is out, of course. We're booked solid with a batch of Democrats and they always show up with somebody extra in tow. We're already pushing it, what with that being Maundy Thursday, which is also why we can't schedule anything next weekend—bad form, Easter and all that.

"I've got it!" he said, then frowned, lightly touched me as if to implore my forgiveness in advance. "That is, if it's not too much of an imposition on you. I damn well understand if you've got a conflict. Why not tomorrow night? My wife is getting a new mount and we're hosting a small, very informal celebration dinner. We'd love to have you and your wife come. Are you married?''

"No," I told him.

"Well," he said with a sly grin, "I know I don't need to worry about lining up a date for a chap like you!"

My smile was polite.

"It's settled then," he said. "You'll come. Isn't that great, dear?"

"Great," she said from horseback.

"Is that your car?" he said, nodding to the Porsche. He started to walk toward his Mercedes, and the question pulled me along with him.

"Yes," I said.

"Wonderful machine," he said, ran his eyes over the dirt-caked silver paint, the nicks in the front bumper. He squinted, and I knew he was rating the worn leather seats. "Looks like it's been through the wars, though."

"It gets me where I need to go."

"And that's all it needs to do," he said, opening the door of his mint-condition Mercedes.

"About tomorrow night," he said before he slid behind the wheel. He looked at my nylon windbreaker, open shirt collar, blue jeans. "You might feel more comfortable in a tie, but it's certainly not necessary. Some of the men there may not even have jackets."

"I'll kick in a buck so they can buy one," I said.

He laughed.

"Barbara and the cook are still hassling over a time," he said as he climbed in the car. "Give her a call later, she'll let you know when to show up. Do come. Bring a friend and help us say good-bye to Molly and hello to the new horse."

I whirled, stared at the woman and Molly.

"Oh, didn't you know?" he said, turned on his car. The engine hummed to life. "Poor old Molly. She's to be put

down. Today. I expect that's why Barbara was up early—
a last ride. That's why I thought you were Doc Wyatt, he's
coming to help.

"You know what's even more remarkable?" he said,
and when I turned to look at him I found mirror sunglasses
hid his eyes. "My wife, my beautiful, sophisticated wife,
insists on giving Molly the injection herself. Isn't she
amazing?"

"Yes," I said, turned again to look at that woman.
"Amazing."

"Do you know what they do with the body?" he asked.
"After all, that is a lot of flesh to shove in a hole in the
backyard. They give the corpse to the Hunt Club—for the
hounds."

He smiled. "See you tomorrow night."

His taillights were over the hill before I turned, walked
back to the fence.

"You lie quick and well," I told the woman.

"So do you," she replied.

"What about Cora McGregor?" I asked.

"You can forget about her," she said. "All about her."

"I'm supposed to call you later, find out what time to
drop by tomorrow night for a friendly, civilized meal. Who
should I ask for?"

"My name is Barbara," she said, pulled the reins so
Molly raised her head to stare at me one last time with
those soft brown eyes. "Mrs. Barbara Gracon Randolph
Sloan. My husband calls me Barbi. When you call, ask the
housekeeper if you may speak to Mrs. Sloan."

Then she flicked the reins. Molly turned their backs to
me and trotted off toward home.

6

WHAT THE HELL ARE YOU DOING, RANKIN?'' DEVON ASKED FOR perhaps the tenth time as we drove through the night. I didn't answer. She folded the sun visor down, flicked on the ceiling light above her door and stretched her face this way and that, checking the results in the small mirror on the visor's back.

"I'm just going to have to do," she said as she folded the visor back up, settled herself in the Porsche's passenger seat. The lights of Georgetown glowed behind us, fading in the night.

"Besides," she continued, "you can't complain, can you, Rankin? It's not easy scrounging up an acceptable date for a big dinner party with only a day's notice."

"I guess I got lucky," I said.

"I was surprised you called," Devon said. "Then when you tacked on the 'sort of a professional favor, business evening' bit, your little joke about how I was a safe and presentable escort . . .''

"You're not mad, are you?"

"No." She smiled. "I got over being mad at you a year ago. If you'd have called then . . . well, that's that, then is over. Now I'm sort of flattered you asked me to help out. And intrigued.''

"I really appreciate this, Devon."

"So who am I supposed to be? Just another woman lawyer you picked up stalking the streets of Washington?"

"Just be who you are, Devon, an old friend."

She leaned closer as we drove over the dark, tree-lined highway. The moonlight streaming through the windshield was bright enough to make her lips glisten as she smiled, teased me with her voice. Her fingers brushed my thigh.

"How good a friend?" she whispered.

"Pretty good," I said, flicking my gaze from the road to her. "An old friend."

"Ah," she said, leaned back in her chair. "I see." She sighed. "What the hell, Rankin. I always wanted to help out on one of your cases."

"You know, someday somebody will call me by my first name, and I'm not going to know who they're talking to."

"Forget it, darlin'," she said. "You're one of those people born to be one thing with one name, and Rankin says it all."

We said nothing for a mile. The Porsche hummed over the black ribbon road without a tremble. Devon's perfume was sweet, like summer roses, but had a tang to it I didn't like. She glanced at the clock.

"What time are we supposed to be there?" she asked.

"The housekeeper told me dinner was at eight."

"Jesus! We're going to be on time! This is Washington, nobody shows up on time!"

"I don't want to miss a thing."

"Who are these people?"

"They're rich," I said, flipping the blinker on for a right-hand turn, nosing the Porsche down the private drive leading to the huge white house bathed in floodlights.

"No shit," whispered Devon when we still had about

an eighth of a mile of private road left before we reached the circular driveway and multicar parking area. "No shit."

The heavy wooden door swung inward and the Latin maid who'd answered our ring bowed us inside.

"I say, John, good of you to come," called our host as he bounded down a long staircase at the end of the hall. The maid disappeared as he grabbed my hand, shook it firmly and smiled straight into my eyes. "So glad you could make it!"

"Wouldn't have missed it for the world," I said. His eyes flicked to Devon. "Emmett Sloan, Devon Leary."

He took her hand, held it just long enough to show he liked the chance. His eyes sucked up Devon in her print spring dress with its narrow, plunging slit neckline strained by her heavy breasts. He logged every detail, from her thick brown hair to her makeup and jewelry, the pattern of her stockings, the strap of her high heels, all without seeming to stare.

"Devon, I had no idea John had such classy friends," he said.

She laughed, thanked him, uncharacteristically had no retort as he turned and led her toward the living room.

"You must meet my wife. Darling!" he called out. I followed behind them. "Here's someone special you should know."

That woman turned from a sideboard and a crystal brandy decanter, glasses. Her hair fell to her shoulders in carefully brushed waves. She wore a simple spring blue dress that highlighted her sapphire eyes, fit her perfectly and probably cost more than Devon's and my clothes combined. Her makeup was artful, understated and unnecessary. She wore no jewelry other than a huge diamond engagement ring and her wedding band.

"This is my wife, Barbara," said Emmett as the two

women shook hands. He beamed at them. "We all call her Barbi."

"Nice to meet you," said the woman of many names. Her eyes swung over Devon's shoulder, locked on mine.

"Devon is John's friend," said Emmett. "Isn't he lucky?"

"Yes," said his wife. "Very lucky."

"Your home is spectacular!" said Devon, gazing around the vast living room with its couches, its stuffed chairs, its wood paneling and marble fireplace, the original oil landscapes on three walls and the floor-to-ceiling bookcase full of all the right titles on the other.

"Thank you," said our hostess.

"Got a great idea!" said Emmett. "Let's split this couple up. You show Devon around, and I'll take John in tow."

"All right," said the wife. She turned, walked toward one of the other doors, ignored me as she said to Devon, "Let me show you the downstairs library."

"We'll go upstairs," Emmett said. He led me to the hall. "That's where the bedrooms are, you know."

But we didn't go to the bedrooms.

"I think you'll find this interesting," he said, guided me beyond a closed door to the room overlooking the front lawn.

"I'm so glad you showed up early," he said as we walked inside. He flipped the wall switch that turned on the desk lamp and carefully obscured indirect wall lights. "Gives us a chance to get to know one another better.

"I use this as a den," he said. "Not that I do much work here, but it's nice to have some place for such things in your home, right?"

"Sure," I said.

"I must confess," he said with a boyish, shamefaced grin, "I looked you up in the phone book. There's only one listing, and it's for an office. I thought you lived in the District, too."

"My apartment is behind my office," I told him.

"Damned handy, isn't it? Probably beats going to a huge building like I do every day.

"Look here," he said, pointing out the floor-to-ceiling windows behind the desk chair. "Isn't this lovely? Quite a view. Of course, it's dark out now, but in the light I can see all the way to the fence and the road, sometimes even farther than that if the foliage is cleared away. I can see everything."

"That's wonderful."

"Yes, it is, isn't it?"

Framed photographs covered the wall opposite the fireplace. They seemed out of balance with each other, though their historical montage fit in this room with its grand, flattop desk that cost as much as a small house in Kansas. I walked between the two heavy wooden captain's chairs and the leather sofa that faced the desk. My host fell in behind me like a hungry shadow.

The photographs off to the right were of this charity ball or that do-good commission. Three black and white group portraits filled the most accessible space on the wall. The first showed about 50 solemn suit-and-tied young men posed in rows on the steps of a grand building with round stone columns. Black lettering across the bottom read, "William and Mary College Beta Sigma Delta Class of 1969." The second photograph also showed a cluster of men posed in front of a building, but this group of 20 college-age males smiled at the camera with the relaxed, innocent pride of young victors. The caption read, "Oxford Exchange Class, 1968." The third photograph was the only casual picture of the lot, a quickly staged snapshot of six attractive women sitting in a half moon around an outdoor table covered with glasses and coffee cups. My host's wife was the second woman on the left, between a grim-looking blond with short hair and a laughing woman with long, black curls cascading down her shoulders.

"Yes," said Emmett Sloan, "I thought you might notice that. Barbi with our friend Tresa next to her. Of course, that was before Tresa cut off all her lovely black hair. Shame she did that."

"Yes," I said. The woman with the long hair was pretty—though nowhere near as stunning as this man's wife.

"They're at the Club, you know," he said. He reached around me, straightened the picture ever so slightly. It still seemed off-balance; the frame didn't quite match the others, seemed cheap.

"This was taken just before Tresa's troubles. Divorce is such a nasty business."

"Yes," I agreed, "it is."

"I expect you see a lot of such things."

"I don't handle domestic problems."

"Really?" He frowned. "What do you do? Chase murderers and such?"

"No, mostly white-collar crime, civil matters. Some vaguely political stuff."

"Ah, I see. I assumed you met Tresa in the course of her difficulties."

"No. We're personal friends, not professional."

"Old friends?" he asked.

"We know each other reasonably well."

"Ahhhh." This time his sigh was sly, longer. He circled around from behind me, a frown on his lean face, his eyes cast down. When they rose to meet mine, they were shrewd and as strong as steel.

"Don't take me wrong, old chap," he said, his voice quietly insistent. "Certainly don't think I'm casting any aspersions or making judgments—on anyone. I know a man of your . . . sophistication and street sense certainly doesn't need advice from me, but . . .

"You must be careful—very, very careful—with women like Tresa. They're intriguing, entrancing really. But involving yourself with them professionally is hazardous enough. Mixing with them personally . . . well, there is no profit in such adventures, just complications and trouble for everyone. You get yourself into jams you can't possibly resolve without getting hurt far more than you imagine. Everything becomes extreme. If I were you, I'd consider her a chance too dangerous to take."

We stared at each other for almost a minute, like boxers at a weigh-in, each waiting for the other to speak. Downstairs, the doorbell rang.

"Ah!" he said as he became the smiling host once more, "more guests. Come down when you're ready."

I glanced at the pictures on the wall again, followed the echo of his footsteps. I heard him glad-handing people at the door as I turned into the living room. His elegant, slim wife was mixing a drink at the side bar.

"Nice to see you again, Mrs. Sloan," I said when I stood next to her.

"You have a charming friend," she said. She raised her glass, and with a so-what smile and shrug said, "Well developed."

"Remember our other mutual friend—Tresa?"

"Yes?" she said.

Footsteps and laughter filled the hall, headed our way.

"Is she a pretty brunette, bright-eyed? Had curly hair down to her chest that she cut off not long ago?"

"Tresa's a blond, short hair, barely covers her ears. Always has been."

Devon came into the room from one door, back from the powder room. She smiled nervously at me. Our host led two laughing couples into his salon.

"Nice picture of you and Tresa in his study," I said. "A group shot. Touching of him to hang it . . ."

"Picture? Where?"

"Your husband knows we lied," I told her.

"Barbi!" he called from across the room. "Look who's here!"

"As long as he doesn't know the truth," the wife whispered back. A smile lit her face as she waltzed across the room to greet her guests.

Eventually, there were 14 of us, just an ordinary cluster of strangers and acquaintances at an ordinary American dinner party.

The beefy, balding man who didn't wear a jacket over his chain-store cotton pullover was worth just under two billion dollars. He was famous for driving an American station wagon to polo games and horse shows where mere millionaires arrived in chauffeured Rolls-Royces. His wife was dainty, petite, with sparkling eyes. Both of them had lovely tans. Everyone else in the room watched them carefully and pretended not to; listened hard to every word the billionaire muttered, laughed uproariously at everything he said that was remotely funny. He survived the extraordinary attention gracefully by ignoring it whenever possible.

"It seems we're the biggest strangers here," he said to me as we drifted to a corner of the room. We stood with our backs to the wall, watching the others pointedly not watching us.

We introduced ourselves, shifting our chilled glasses to our left hands in order to shake with our right. I'd switched to club soda after the second round. The hired young man in the white jacket who smiled as he mixed the drinks dropped an empty bottle of expensive gin into the garbage can beside the portable drink tray. The gin jug clanked against an empty bottle of imported vodka. The bourbon bottle on the bar would soon join them.

"You're not from around here?" I asked the man who was worth more than many American towns.

"No. We live down in Middleburg. Hunt country." His eyes roamed over the men, all of whom wore at least sports coats. "We're much less formal down there when it comes to dinner. But I guess I should have known: Washington dinner parties."

"This isn't quite Washington," I said, surveying the room.

"Really?" he asked, genuine surprise and interest in his voice. "We have so little to do with Washington I really don't know much about it. What's it like?"

This man owned the umbrella that covered a hundred American companies, a score of multinationals. Heavy industry, computers, agribusiness, stocks and bonds, banks, his touch was everywhere in the economy. Platoons of lawyers and lobbyists spun countless schemes through the halls of Congress, the federal bureaucracies, even the courts, all that his empire might flourish. Yet his question was guileless.

"Washington is a city of myths," I told him.

He grunted. "You can say that again."

"How did you end up here? I mean, at this party?"

"Well, it's for the horse, isn't it? The Sloans bought their new horse from my stable. When I found out it was for her, I was reluctant to sell it to them. Spirited beast. Not one I'd have chosen for her, but then . . . Mr. Sloan— Emmett, isn't it?—He insisted on buying from us. Well, what could I do? The horse trader told me there was no quibbling over price. And when he invited us here tonight to honor the horse . . . well, I wasn't overjoyed at coming, but we all have our obligations."

"Yes," I said, "we do."

He glanced at his drink, excused himself and wandered to the bar. I watched the young man reach for the bourbon

45

bottle, hear the billionaire's request, and reach instead for the bottle of Coke.

"Don't I know you?" asked a woman wearing a dark burgundy dress designed to conceal the pounds she'd gained with each year she lost. One hand held a smoldering cigarette, the other a glass of ice and amber liquid that smelled like Scotch. Her blond hair was thick but brittle with an expensive metallic sheen, combed back and up to accent her legendarily striking, go-to-hell face. She still had the look that made men's eyes linger, but a pallor waited beneath her makeup, and the slight sag of her flesh beneath her chin showed gravity was finally winning that tug of war. I wondered how soon she'd buy the knife, or if she already had.

"We've met a couple times," I said. "I'm a friend of some people at the *Post*, Cliff Palefsky, couple others. John Rankin."

"That's right," she said, smiled, nodded. Her eyes stayed on me while she flipped through her mental Rolodex, crosschecked me with the A, the B and C lists. Somewhere she made the connection, and all was right and ready for her again. "You were one of Ned Johnson's reporters, and now you work for lawyers."

"Close enough," I said, and she laughed. She didn't bother to introduce herself: everyone knew who she was.

She came to Washington in the late 1960s, bright, beautiful and ruthless. She used her press pass as her ladder, and climbed her way up the chic power circles of this city from a lowly society news researcher for the *Post* to a first-string feature writer with a flair for breathless prose, a keen eye for the enviable and a complete disdain for any substance that wouldn't sell. Her looks opened doors and her talent let her pass through them and survive. To become somebody she attached herself to people who already were and wrote about them until finally she became an institution, a celebrity unto herself: aloof, elite, clever, in-the-know and an arbiter of what the masses should aspire to be. Washington's blood is newsprint, TV and radio waves, and she'd become part of our great creation.

"So good to see you again," she cooed, touched my arm with the hand that held her cigarette. "I haven't heard much about you in the last couple years."

"I lead a quiet life."

"Really," she said, her enthusiasm cooling as she calculated just how true that might be.

"I see you have a new conquest," I told her, nodding to the three-piece suited escort who'd walked her through the door. "Professional or personal?"

"Oh, that," she said, feigning annoyance at my interest. "We're just good friends."

His was one of the names I'd recognized when Emmett Sloan had announced the couple from the doorway, then left them to mingle and meet the rest of us. He'd been an ambassador for two previous presidents, representing America in small countries burdened with oppressive governments and destined for bloody revolution. His overseas service did nothing to upset the status quo. The ambassadorships came to him because of his generosity with his family's wealth in political campaigns. Although he was nowhere near the level of the billionaire, his father and grandfather had built a lucrative empire based on newspaper chains in the Midwest. In a parody of the family tradition, their scion bought an economically disastrous but moderately prestigious foreign affairs magazine published in Washington—which drained his legacy but gave him an acceptable reason to stick around the capital while waiting for his patrons to return to power and reappoint him to another honorable government post.

"We have a lot in common," she said. "Run in the same circles."

"Yes," I told her. "I suppose you do."

A low chuckle from the billionaire briefly caught our attention.

"Isn't he simply marvelous?" she said. "I saw you talking to him for such a long while and had to come over—to say hello, of course. Catch up on old friends and old times—seems like there's more of each of them every day, doesn't it? And compare notes."

She noticed the long ash on her cigarette, frowned. There were no ashtrays near her, no one raced to bring her one. Her eyes scanned the crowd, made sure no one who cared was watching, then she flicked her refuse to the floor without missing a beat.

"Isn't it wonderful how down to earth he is—considering *who* he is?" she said, nodding to the rich man. Her head bobbed slightly, and I heard an "h" attach itself to the end of her "is." Her Scotch supply had disappeared in great and frequent gulps. She handed her glass to the Latin maid who circled through the crowd with a silver tray of hors d'oeuvres.

"Another," said the media star. She didn't specify what; didn't need to, for the maid brought her a tall Scotch on the rocks.

"Yes," I replied, speaking of the rich man. "He seems nice."

"You're a friend of Barbara's, aren't you?" she asked, carefully enunciating each word, her eyes locked on me as she waited for my answer.

"Actually, I know Emmett better."

"You're lucky," she said, a slur marring her enunciation. Her eyes shifted from side to side, she leaned closer. "She's not really who you think she is."

"Really?"

"Barbara Gracon Randolph Sloan," said the reporter.

"My ass." She chuckled at her clever, sophisticated epithet.

"Sure, she's a Gracon—by birth and just barely," said this woman who'd learned society's rank and file with the passion of a newly accepted convert. "They're the right Gracons, of course, but her father was the family fool, a lush."

She poured an inch of the amber liquid down her throat.

"And she'd have never been a Randolph if her mother hadn't remarried Austin Randolph when he was 60 and lonely and remembered the mother as a cute kid he met during World War II. Gracon was his Air Corps buddy. Cute kid, my ass."

The hand with her cigarette touched my arm.

"Her mother was a nobody from nowhere. And Barbara, shit—a would-be actress who never made it in New York. Probably didn't fuck the right people. Bitch has a stone for a heart and ice in her veins. How she landed a fuckin' prince like Emmett, I'll never know."

I said nothing.

"Want to know a secret?" she said with a leer.

"Sure."

"When old man Randolph died, everybody figured that set Mom and the Ice Queen up for life. But you know what? I'll tell you what, I'll let you in on a little secret. Randolph died damn near broke, just that big old house down in Charleston and that big old family name and a big old zero in most of his bank accounts. Then Barbara married Emmett, the poor sap, and Mama gets to keep her house and live like a real grande dame—which she isn't! Doesn't that beat all?"

"I guess so."

"Ain't life a bitch?" she said, neither of us realizing how history would prove her wrong. "You can't ever get what you want. There's no such thing as justice."

"I didn't know those were the same thing."

"If life worked out perfectly, they would be."

"What can you expect?"

"Hell, at least a little excitement or something. Some scandal. Isn't that kind of thing your department?"

"No."

"Oh." She squinted at me, felt the burning glow from the stub of the cigarette smoldering between her fingers. She held it up between us, stared at it in wonder for a moment, then met my eyes. Somewhere behind her glazed stare she sought words, found nothing, shrugged and walked away.

She wobbled across the room to her hostess, where they flashed so-happy-to-see-you smiles at each other, laughed and exchanged pleasantries. In route, the cigarette fell to a silver tray, smoldered, went out. Not far from them Devon stood earnestly talking with the third name I'd recognized, a silver-haired lawyer for one of D.C.'s megafirms more famous for its political fixes than its legal practice. Devon reached into her purse, gave the man her business card and took his. The lawyer's wife silently watched them from across the room.

"Nice party, isn't it?" said a wispy-haired, portly man in an ill-fitting blue blazer.

"Interesting," I replied.

"I'm Harry Wyatt," he said.

We both moved to shake hands, realized we'd need to shift our glasses, shrugged, grinned, and vetoed the effort. I told him my name.

"I hear you're a hell of a vet," I said.

"Not bad," he grinned. "You must have been talking to Emmett."

"When he told me about Molly."

"Yeah," said the doctor, "shame about her. Sweet little mare. But they're getting a fine piece of horseflesh to replace her. A good gelding. Thoroughbred. Looked him over myself. Mighty fine. Bit hot, but . . .''

He shrugged. Our hostess strolled by us, smiled, walked on to chat with the billionaire and his wife, who stood together in the far corner, smiling politely.

"Speaking of fine horseflesh," said the vet, almost under his breath. "Hot-blooded, spirited and sweet!" He licked his lips, talked on, almost as if he'd forgotten I was there. "She holds her reins so tight, but if she loosens up a bit, lets her head go . . .''

The vet suddenly flushed, looked back at me.

"Of course, she's a fine woman."

"Fine woman," I agreed.

"Emmett's a lucky man." He looked her way again. "One hell of a lucky man.

"They're probably all just rumors," he added, dismissing thoughts he hadn't spoken. "You know how people love to gossip.''

"Sure," I said.

He smiled weakly, drifted off.

"You look like you've had one too many or not enough," said the gorilla-sized man who replaced the vet at my side.

"Could be," I told him.

We exchanged names, shook hands.

"Don't think I know you," he said. "You don't belong to the Hunt Club?"

"No."

"Do you ride?"

"If I had to, I probably could, but no."

"Oh." He thought for a moment. "I figured even if you didn't hunt you might have been a rider, gotten to know Barbara that way."

"She hunts—foxes, right?"

"Best sport around, though you couldn't prove it by her.

Can't get her to come on a hunt. She said once she'd go if we ever used a drag—you know, where you lay down the scent. They do that a lot in places where they don't have many fox.''

He grinned. ''Around here, there's plenty of natural prey for the hounds.

''She'll ride in competition—the point-to-points, shows, that kind of thing, or go on Club trail rides. She does so little with the Club I often wondered why they belong. Good horsewoman, but she seems to just ride the country around here by herself, hacking around. I guess that's fun. As far as hunting goes, though . . . I don't think she likes blood sports.''

''Don't be so sure,'' I told him.

He laughed.

''How about Emmett?'' I asked. ''Is he a big hunter?''

''Hell, I don't think I've ever seen him on a horse! He joined the Club for Barbara.

''Don't get me wrong, though—old Emmett, he's a competitor. Fierce. I watched him at a charity skeet shoot over in P.G. County, and let me tell you, that man likes his sport. He likes winning even more.''

''Do you know him from business?'' I asked.

''No, just the Club connection, and do-gooder stuff. I run a construction company. Built a lot of the interstates around here, a few dozen buildings. Emmett teases me about letting him manage my finances and investments with that consulting firm of his downtown on K Street, but I tell him I'd rather pay for my own mistakes. Hell, between his old man's money, the clients he's got, and all the outside farting around he does, I tell him he doesn't have time for a country boy like me.''

We laughed. The maid came into the room, whispered something to our hostess, who in turn nodded to her husband.

"I say, everybody!" Emmett called out over the chatter. "Dinner is served!"

We sat around a long table, Emmett at the head, Barbara at the far end. I was stuck in the middle, between the wives of the lawyer and the veterinarian.

"I've been dying to talk to you!" said the lawyer's wife to my left. "You're a private detective, aren't you?"

"Yes," I said, wondering which of a dozen stock questions would come next.

"What I want to know is"—she looked from side to side, then whispered—"where do you carry your gun? I mean, in a shoulder holster or in your pants?"

"I don't carry a gun."

"Oh. But you do have one, just in case?"

"No," I lied.

"But . . . But all the private detectives on TV have guns!"

"Life is a lot different than television."

"Oh."

"And thank God for that!" said the veterinarian's wife on my right.

For the rest of the meal, I chose to talk to her.

"May I have your attention, please?" our host called out shortly after the housekeeper poured the wine. "As you know, tonight we're celebrating the purchase of a grand animal from the justifiably famous stables of that shy man on my wife's right."

We all chuckled appropriately.

"However, as fine and joyous an event as that is, I think we owe ourselves a serious moment. To mark that moment, to give us all a pause for reflection, I propose a toast."

J. Emmett Sloan, master of the mansion, raised his crystal glass of red wine. All around the table, his guests politely did the same. Our host spoke his words clearly, cleanly, powerfully.

"To Molly, who gracefully paid the price for no longer being able to fulfill her purpose in life."

His words jarred us, but not enough to forestall the automatic reaction: we all drank the thick red wine. All of us except his wife. She set her glass down, discreetly untasted. Her blue eyes focused on nothing.

After dessert, after coffee which I accepted and brandy that I declined, after another round of more drunken and less serious chitchat in the drawing room, I convinced Devon to say our farewells.

Our host and hostess walked us to the door. He gushed over Devon, insisted that she call his office for the name of the wine she said she'd liked. Better yet, he said, call and leave her address so he could send her a bottle.

"It's been a terribly interesting evening, Mrs. Sloan," I said. Neither of us extended a hand.

"Yes," she answered, "it has."

"I'm so glad you came," said Emmett. He shook my hand.

"Me too. Thanks."

"Good-bye," he said, and shut the door.

"My God, Rankin!" said Devon as we drove back to the city. "Do you realize where we were?"

"We ate with strangers."

"We ate with the fuckin' gods! Mr. Billionaire, and the Sloans! What an incredible couple! He's something else. And me, a flunky junior associate with a so-so law firm, hobnobbing with a senior partner from Wilson, Stern and Heifetz! We're going to have lunch someday! Can you imagine that? Me and Wilson, Stern and Heifetz!"

"You're not going to be eating with a letterhead, Devon," I cautioned her. "You're going to be meeting with a man. Watch yourself."

She stared at me before replying.

"Don't worry about me, Rankin, I know what I'm doing and I can take care of myself. Worry about yourself."

"What do you mean?"

"Oh come off it! What was this little charade tonight, huh? What are you doing? I figured you took me for a reason, and now only a fool couldn't figure it out."

"I don't understand."

"Give me a break! Maybe nobody else noticed—though I doubt it, those people aren't deaf and blind, no matter how drunk they get. You and Mrs. Sloan. Call me Barbara. Barbi to her friends, they tell me. The atmosphere between you two was so thick you could beat it with a baseball bat. You two did a great job of ignoring each other. I'll watch myself, but you're the one staring at trouble."

"It's not like you think."

"Oh yeah? Well, I've been there with you, and I know what I see. And if I'm not seeing what I saw, then how come we ended up there tonight? What brought you and the Sloans together, huh? You don't exactly run in the same social circles."

"A dead man." I glanced over at her, saw her frown, puzzle over my words. She was drunk, but not that drunk.

"A dead man brought us together," I said.

We rode in silence. I turned down Wisconsin Avenue, headed for her condominium building.

"What are you doing, John?" she asked. "What are you doing?"

"I'm driving," I told her.

All the parking places in front of her building were full, so I pulled into the yellow unloading zone in front of her all-glass entryway.

"Don't shut off your engine," she said.

She opened the door, stepped to the curb. She had to shout her good-bye words over the warning buzzer that sounds when the door isn't closed tight.

"Maybe I don't know what's going on," she yelled. "But I know one thing. You better be careful, old friend. You're playing out of your league."

The light shone above the pay phone at the all-night gas station three blocks away. I pulled in, parked the Porsche, not caring about anything except doing something about it and doing it now. I called his office first, but he wasn't working that midnight, so I dropped a quarter in the slot for the second call: so what if I paid a nickel too much? He answered on the fifth ring, groggy and only half awake.

"Nick? It's me."

"Do you know what time it is?"

"Yeah, I do. It's time you told me everything you can about Parviz Naderi, and how he got murdered."

7

"YOU HAVE TO REMEMBER HISTORY IF YOU WANT TO UNDERSTAND ANYthing," said Nick Sherman.

"Of course, times have changed since then," he said. Then laughed.

Usually we'd meet in the FOP bar, my office or sometimes even the Homicide squad room when we wanted to talk, but that next day Nick insisted on a quiet neighborhood tavern in upper Northwest, a middle-class section of the city neither of us frequented. We huddled in the shadows of the far corner booth while five men, all about 50, occupied every other stool along the bar. The white-aproned bartender perched behind the bar on a short stepladder he'd ostensibly set up to wash the mirror. He ignored that chore, used the ladder for a chair. Those six men stared at the Saturday afternoon sports show flickering in the color TV mounted high on the wall at the other end of the bar. They didn't speak, paid no attention to us.

"Do you remember 1977?" asked Nick.

"I was here then, reporting for Ned Johnson's column."

"And you don't remember Naderi?"

"There are a hundred names I should remember and

don't," I said, shrugged. "A thousand I should have learned and didn't. A name like Naderi . . ."

"So you don't know anything about how he got hit?"

Mark Twain once said the difference between the right word and the wrong word is like the difference between lightning and a lightning bug. As strong a word as "murder" is, the street specification Nick used for Naderi's fate was lightning that flashed through my memory.

"Wait a minute!" I told him. "Until now, nobody's said anything about . . . Naderi. Naderi. He was . . . a waiter or something? Right? Shot in a car."

Nick grinned. "I was wondering when you'd finally come to the party."

"I still don't remember that much," I said. "I remember a couple sources telling me how I should chase some story there, but when I pressed them, they couldn't or wouldn't tell me more. You know how that goes, you hear it all the time—they got something they think you ought to do, but they can't or won't help you. They don't know who can, or even if there's really anything there. You can run yourself into the ground chasing other people's phantoms. A couple of my associates poked around the thing, I think, but I don't remember Ned running any kind of story on it in his column."

"He did, but it wasn't much of a story," Nick said. "One of those vague 'authorities privately suspect' stories that sounds like more than it says, and I know how he got it. I can't remember which of his reporters like you did it. No big deal. The guys from the *Post* busted their ass, got a little more."

I shrugged. "You can't get 'em all."

"Yeah, well, nobody got Naderi's story, though not 'cause they didn't try. I ought to know."

"What can you tell me?" I asked.

"Seven years and a lot of blood, sweat and tears later?"

He smiled, drained his glass of beer. The bartender had his back to us. Nick walked across the room, got the bartender to do his job and returned with two more drafts. He walked back with slow, careful cowboy-booted steps, didn't spill a drop of beer. He waited until we'd sipped the foam down, then said, "What do you want to know?"

"Everything—and how it all makes sense."

"Then you're really in trouble," he said. "I better tell it my way. Some of this . . . some of this I know to be true and can prove, some of it I believe to be true, but can't prove. A lot of it is good guesswork, de-tecting."

He took a long swallow of beer.

"Like I said, you've got to remember the times, 1977. This town was fast and loose back then. Everything was out there on the streets. The games weren't new, but there was so much arrogance they seemed like it. Watergate was supposed to be over, but a whole lot of shit oozed out of that mess that never got cleaned up. Remember Koreagate? The Korean CIA bribing folks on the Hill and playing political dirty tricks? The House Investigating Committee was just poking into that back then. The GSA contracting scandals were up around the bend, and somewhere somebody in the Bureau was getting the bright idea to try the AB-SCAM stuff. Your old friend Martin Mercer was stealing right and left with his Senate job. He wasn't the only one. America had a lot of *players* back then, a lot of dirty games. Parviz Naderi slithered through the heart of it all.

"Parviz Naderi. Everybody called him Pasha. An Iranian born on the right side of Tehran's tracks who came to this country in 1968 when he was 21. On his immigration card he listed the Naval Intelligence School in Arlington as his U.S. residence. The Navy informed me it has a *policy* of never commenting on intelligence matters, including who did or didn't go to their schools. A little matter of murder didn't dent that policy, so I don't know what that card means.

"Pasha enrolled at University of Maryland, took a few courses, business, a little political science. He married some sad little girl from Iowa, who smartened up and got a divorce six months later. If nothing else, the marriage helped Pasha get a permanent resident alien status. He was working on his citizenship when he died, but not too hard. Maybe he didn't want to risk a background check, maybe he knew he didn't need to worry about getting shipped home.

"Back then, we were asshole tight buddies with the Shah of Iran. Pasha was in solid with the Iranian community here, the Embassy people, the students, the businessmen, even the exiles and dissidents.

"The most important Iranians in town were the Savak, the secret police and spy agency. Savak was everywhere. You know those brown-skinned guys who walk around Georgetown, go into all the expense account restaurants with baskets of roses, one dollar to make the pretty lady happy? One of them was a Savak agent. His going in and out of all the chic places helped Savak keep track of who was socializing with whom. The Iranian Embassy was ass deep in Savak agents, and there were others all across America.

"The Shah was our buddy, right? We put him in power. The CIA even created Savak for him. Allies. We had a lot of good friends like Savak back in those days. Guys like the Chilean secret police, who sent a hit team to car bomb their country's ex-ambassador and a couple of Americans about half a mile from the White House in 1976."

"And that's who Naderi or Pasha or whatever you want to call him was?" I interrupted. "A Savak agent?"

"Don't go looking for simple and quick answers," said Nick. "You might find them, but you'll probably end up stumbling all over yourself. Besides, nothing was simple or sure about our buddy Pasha, except that he was as smooth as a cobra.

"I'll give him this: he worked hard. He started out in college, bartending and waitering all around town, country clubs, private parties, joints downtown, wherever he could get work. He spoke English without an accent, had a quick wit and an eye for faces and names. They tell me he was a handsome son of a bitch, black hair, brown eyes, kind of New York Jewish or maybe Italian looking. Tall, thick through the body. A little soft when he died. Only time I saw him he was meat for the medical examiner's slab. Nobody looks good then.

"In 1974, one of the town's high rollers took a shine to Pasha and made him headwaiter, then maitre d' at a nightclub he owned called the Forum."

"I remember that place," I said. "Bar, restaurant, a funny kind of layout. One big room . . ."

"There were half a dozen smaller private rooms down the hall," added Nick.

"Never saw them. I remember the place as like the inside of a pentagon, with a pit for tables, bar along one wall, more tables on the balcony around the pit. Piano somewhere, wasn't there? A stuffy place, serious drinkers and talkers. Not a 'fun' place."

"One of the *Post* reporters did me a favor while trying to pump me," said Nick, "and pulled the clips on the Forum. There was a magazine story once about power broker bars in D.C. Some congressman took his wife to the Forum. They ran into a bunch of his congressmen buddies. The next day, a couple of them came up to him on the Floor and told him that wasn't the place where they took their *wives.*"

"Wasn't a place I hung out," I told Nick. "Professionally, maybe I should have, but . . . the air in there was a little foul.''

"Pasha fit right in. Hell, Pasha gave the Forum its snap. This is where we get into the 'real sures'—I'm real sure about some of this stuff, but I can't prove it now any more than I could then.

"Our boy done himself proud. He stepped off the plane as a student and within a few years he was presiding over the snazziest den in the city. Anything and everything happened at the Forum, a joint tucked away in a dead-end residential alley two blocks from the Senate office buildings. You wanted to meet somebody on the sly, the Forum was the place to go, Pasha was the man to see. Maybe he'd even arrange the rendezvous for you, one friend to another to another. He'd sure as shit know who you were seeing, and his knowing that meant he could make some damn good guesses as to what you could be doing.

"You could get anything at the Forum. If you didn't have a mistress, no problem. There were women there, political groupies, friends of friends, hustlers of one kind or another. Some were pros. They were better than street girls because you didn't need to worry about them being undercover cops—Pasha wouldn't let that happen, not in his joint. Pasha could arrange an introduction as easily as he could get you a table in the darkest corner or one next to the lobbyist you'd never been able to hit up for a campaign contribution.

"You wanted a little dope, a little grass to help you relax at the end of a hard day on the Judiciary Committee or a little coke to perk you up for that blond who finally agreed to meet you for a drink after the Senate adjourned? Go to the Forum. Ask Pasha. He'd know who to send you to at the bar, or who to call to have it delivered.

"Maybe you had other vices. Pasha understood. He had no problems with guys who wanted little boys or guys who liked to gamble. Hell, Pasha loved to gamble, handled a chunk of that business personally. There was a six-figure sports book out of the Forum, poker games in some of the private rooms. The phone records showed a lot of action, calls to bookmakers in Vegas, up in Jersey, Chicago, New York. Pasha knew who to call for what.

"He made a lot of calls for a lot of people. He was famous as a friend to his countrymen. Those were the pre-Khomeini days, when Iranians, students mostly, got fed up with living under the Shah's bloody thumb, got tired of torture and jails for anybody who complained. Remember how when they demonstrated over here they used to wear paper bags with eye-holes cut in them, hoods, so Savak wouldn't know who they were? Pasha befriended a lot of those students, helped them get jobs around town as waiters, parking lot attendants, whatever. He listened to all their troubles, their dreams and schemes, loaned them a buck or two and sent them on their way with a big smile and a pat on the back. And then picked up the phone and called a Savak number at the Embassy with all the names, dates and places he'd weaseled out of them."

"Swell guy," I said.

"Oh yeah. With some swell friends. Savak and maybe our own cloak-and-dagger boys. Guys like your buddy Martin Mercer—who's going to get out of Lompoc soon, by the way.

"Along about 1977, some of Pasha's frends ran into batches of bad luck. A lobbyist who once worked for the Nixon White House and was mentioned in all that funny money stuff in Watergate ran his car off the Parkway one night after he left the Forum. Hit a tree at about 15 mph. The guy's skull was mashed to mush, his ribs were broken, his guts all loosened up. Another guy, old-time lawyer round town who was in one of Pasha's address books, ended up falling down the stairs and breaking his neck in his downtown office building one night. Probably slipped, probably hadn't wanted to use the elevator like he normally did. Nothing they could have been but accidents.''

"Nothing," I said.

"Yeah, nothing. Our boy Pasha knew a lot about nothing, about what was and what wasn't important. He was no fool. Pasha understood that one way to get ahead in this world is to be useful without being used. Never let yourself be taken for granted, and make sure you get your due. Do nothing without a profit. Use trust as a tool. For Pasha, the world was divided up into players and pawns. He decided to be a player, so he made himself useful.

"Boy did they use him. High rollers who wanted their construction company to get a federal contract, congressmen who wanted public works projects in their home districts so the voters would re-elect them, the hustler consultant who wanted to pad a big contract out of the Treasury so he could be a legal crook, investors looking for clever schemes where suckers pick up the check, guys with hot money looking for a way to cool it down or build it up . . . Pasha ran with all of them, and all of them came to him. Asked him for a table, asked for a favor, an introduction, a good time, some 'facilitation.' He delivered, and he collected his due.

"He did favors for anybody who could help him. Uncle Sam has nightmares about revolution in the Middle East, right? Don't want to upset the oil cart, help the Russians.

"So our government does its best. We're so clever, we tolerate guys like Pasha, the friend of our Savak friends who are fighting that revolution for us. That's the real world, right? We gotta deal with him. We don't want to know about anything else, we don't care about anything else, all that other stuff isn't relevant, right? We draw our bottom line with clean hands. What goes on beyond that, we don't see.

"That makes Pasha important, that makes him strong, sets him up to do more, like arrange for heroin shipments from his buddies back home to the big-time dealers here without a whole lot of trouble from anybody in Iran or America. He takes a cut of that pie. His stateside buddies make a profit, build their business, maybe snatch some 14-year-old girl from Duluth out of the New York bus terminal, gang rape her senseless, pump her full of smack, then turn her out in Times Square as a rent-a-toy for 18 months until she's just a pair of useless, glassed-over eyes to be dumped in the Jersey swamps. Ain't no big thing, just another coin in the pot."

"So what happened to Pasha?"

"He pissed somebody off."

"Who?"

Nick laughed. "Take your pick of anybody who ever dealt with him. Pasha was popular, but I don't think many people ever *liked* him—at least, nobody who knew much of the truth about him. As for who he pissed off that much . . .

"It was such a nice spring night in March 1977. A Wednesday. Business at the Forum was slow, no big poker game going on after hours, no meetings. Pasha let his headwaiter close up, left the club and headed for home around 1 A.M.

"He lived in a townhouse condo development not far from here, between American University and Wisconsin Avenue. A two-story brick job, black oak door with a brass knocker, flower pots out front, tiny patch of grass. Not his flashy style, but he got a great deal. A long private lane curved off the main road, looped in front of the townhouses. Parking was never a problem. That night he found a space 39 feet from his front door.

"His Vietnamese girlfriend never heard a thing. She was asleep in the upstairs front bedroom, the window open less than 50 feet from where he parked his shiny new Porsche. Yours is silver, his was gold. His girlfriend was a cute little thing. Terrified of guns: she was a child in Saigon during the Tet offensive. She'd jump whenever a car back-fired, hated July and kids with firecrackers. She slept soundly that night. Until we woke her up.

"At 2:11 one of the uniforms in a scout car on routine patrol noticed the glow of the Porsche interior light, the driver's door gaping open. When they turned into the curved drive, they saw Pasha's hand dangling out of the open Porsche door, just above the street."

"And that's when you came in," I said.

"I was supposed to be off duty, but I'd done a dumb thing and switched with a fellow." He shook his head. "A real dumb thing."

He left, went to the bathroom. In the commercial on TV, everyone was beautiful, clean and happy. The sportsmen in the show were noble and rich.

"I ever tell you my great theory of life?" asked Nick when he returned. He carried two more beers.

"Which one?" I asked, and he laughed.

"The one what says there are certain people who are doomed to do things. Maybe it's 'cause of the way they look at life, maybe it's in their genes and they ain't got no choice, maybe it's because of a hundred things, don't make no difference, they're doomed. Drop 'em anywhere, find 'em anywhere, they're up to their ass in 'sich-e-a-shuns.' Like they say in the street: 'You gots to unerstan' my siche-a-shun, man.' If they aren't in one now, give them time, they'll land in one, no matter how hard they try not to. I call them shooters.

"Give that a little twist, you got the same thing from another angle, you got what the shrinks call the victim syndrome. There's people out there walking the streets doomed to be somebody's victim. Maybe it's their attitude, maybe it's their genes, don't make no difference, they're a number waiting to be called by whatever tragedy hits them first, car wreck, mugger, rapist, killer. They attract shit-storms like a lightning rod.''

''What's the difference between shooters and victims?''

''Huh.'' He shook his head. ''Sometimes it ain't much, bud. Most times . . . Most times you got to count the living to tell the difference. Shooters are more likely to end up pulling the last trigger instead of catching the last bullet.

''I'm a shooter,'' he said. ''Ain't no big thing, nothing I got any reason to be proud of, nothing I can control. I just am. Things happen to me, I keep finding myself stuck in sich-e-a shuns that so far I've survived. I'm a shooter.'' His forefinger pointed to me. ''So are you.''

''What about Pasha? Was he a victim or a shooter?''

''Well, now, he was sure somebody's victim, and he sure as shit met a shooter of some kind. But I think he was just one of the would-bes.''

''Would-bes?''

''He would be whatever he could be. Which meant getting whacked.''

''Professionally killed.''

''It sure added up that way,'' said Nick.

''There's so much bullshit believed about murder,'' said the city's best homicide detective. He jerked his head toward the flickering screen above the bar. ''Blame it on TV. They kill folks like cockroaches in that box. They took murder out of the alleys, dropped it into prime time. Only they had to dress it up, make it easy to explain in 30 seconds or less. So they take the shadows of what happens in the street, trim them down and duplicate the dummy images maybe a thousand times. They keep the slang the same so it'll play as 'authentic.' And after a while, the audience begins to believe that's what really happens. Funny thing is, after a while, the bad guys start to believe what they see on TV is real too. We all pick up the TV lingo, use it. Can't hardly help it, it hits you all day, every day, even if you don't watch the tube.

"So when it comes to real murder, we're getting more bullshit out of television, like the teenagers who hire one of their buddies for $50 to kill their folks, and call that 'contracting.' The punk who's trying to be cool thinks of himself as a TV hit man, somebody big and tough and important, not some pimply-faced 19-year-old who hides in a closet with a hammer, waiting for his spoiled buddy's mother to come home from work.

"There ain't but maybe . . . maybe a hundred true professional murders a year, murders where somebody hires a tradesman to kill somebody else—and does it without thinking of themselves as part of some TV drama. Eighty percent of those are mob killings.

"Most murders are between friends. Husband kills wife, vice versa. Usually in anger, nothing sophisticated. Then come in-the-course-of murders—in the course of a robbery, a rape, a bar fight. Things get out of hand and somebody gets dead. We got a few serial murderers cruising America, popping people because that's their thing, maybe a psycho in a tower with a telescopic rifle.

"But not contract killings. Not hits."

"Yeah," he said.

"Except for Pasha."

"Except *maybe* for Pasha. Till I *really* know, I can't say. But based on what I think happened to him—and what I know happened to me . . .

"Pasha drives back from the Forum. It's late, streets are empty. This is a roll-'em-in-early kind of town during the week because most everybody works too steady to stay out late. Come one o'clock, when he's steering his Porsche through the city, he wouldn't see much of anything but closed buildings, parked cars, lights glowing on the Capitol, the monuments. In his neighborhood, all the houses would be dark.

"He finds that lucky parking spot, backs in, shuts off his engine. Maybe he sits for a second, checks his hair in the rearview mirror, makes sure he's looking sharp for the chick he knows he's got stashed upstairs in his bed. In his locked glove compartment, he's got a loaded .38 Colt snub-nosed revolver.

"Which does him no good. He opens the Porsche car door all the way. The door is weighted and designed so it won't drift shut. Those Germans build a damn good car. The overhead light comes on. Maybe he hears something. Maybe somebody calls his name. He's starting to swing out of the car, keys in his left hand. Turns, looks.

"And somebody standing off to the side and a bit behind him shoots a .22 hollow-nose bullet through his left temple, knocks his head back against the Porsche seat. He drops the keys on the street, slumps back in the seat, maybe jerks a little, but he's already brain dead. Somebody pops him again, probably with the same gun, a .22 slug just above his left ear—to be sure, you unerstan'. Then the gunner disappears back into the night.

"Soon as I rolled on the scene, I knew I was in trouble. Some sucker gunned down in a rich car in a great neighborhood, no robbery, gun in the glove compartment, girl upstairs who flinches with every bang who didn't hear a thing, no shell casings—which means if it wasn't a revolver, then somebody took the time to scoop up the ejected ends of the bullet to keep them out of our lab. A cool, clean kill. I figured we'd need a lot of luck to break it even before I knew a damn thing about who this Parviz Naderi was.

"But I latched onto his scent like an old bloodhound. Ended up chasing it into the big swamp where you don't know where you are or how many monsters are waiting out there in the fog to eat your ass.

"Ballistics confirmed that: the bullets were mashed up pretty good, but from the markings on them, there may have been a silencer used—which fit in with the girl hearing nothing.

"If you think contract killings are rare, they're nothing compared to murders where a silencer is used. Man, those things aren't just floating around the country.

"Except in 1977. Back then, there was this wave of murders called the .22 killings—mostly mob-related hits done with .22s or .32s, lots of times with silencers. I saw a federal report on them once. Linked them to something called the Purple Gang."

"Give me a break."

"That's what I kept asking for, bud. Sounds dumb, like something out of the '30s, but that's what was there. A group of guys out of New York, took a name from a Detroit Prohibition mob that they probably heard about in the movies or on TV, and killed people for the Families. I got other sources who said maybe the gun used to whack Pasha came from the old 2506 Brigade supplies."

"The what?"

"The 2506 Brigade: those Cuban exiles we organized in the late 1950s for the Bay of Pigs."

"Which . . ."

"Which meant suddenly in a 'routine' homicide case I got reliable sources—people in federal agencies, people in the Embassy of Iran and a couple dissident groups, bad guys I've dealt with before—all talking about the CIA and right-wing Cuban terrorists and the mob and Savak. Hotshot reporters keep calling me up to play mind games. I got people telling me Pasha was number three on the list that included the two 'accidental' deaths I told you about. I got calls from investigators working for the Koreagate Committee, who in turn sent me over to investigators at the ICC working trucking scandals, who bounced me over to the FBI who said nothing—nothing! Which spooked me even more.

"Then things started happening. Coincidences, maybe. It seems I can't keep a partner or I got three of them, which means I'm spending half my time spinning organizational wheels. Then my captain takes a disliking to me and for three weeks all the cruisers are broken, I've got to use my own car or sit around the office. Let the case turn cold.

"The bad shit started after about a week. I'd heard most of the rumors and maybes and what-ifs by then. I'd talked to maybe 40 people—a classy blond hooker who looked ten years younger than she was, scumbag businessmen, Iranian Embassy types caught between Savak and wanting something good for their country, some high rollers who couldn't keep me out of their office, half the fuckin' investigators in this town . . ."

"But not me."

"Until now."

I said nothing.

"Until then, I thought 1977 might not be a bad year. Janey was in the last remission. We figured, we hoped, we told ourselves that maybe she'd licked it after all. She was talking about going back to work at the hospital. Hell, she spent so much time there she might as well have earned money nursing at the place instead of spending it as a patient.

"She called me one day at work. She wasn't scared for herself. What the hell were they going to do to her? Beat the cancer by a few months? But she didn't want me scared and she sure as shit didn't want me . . .

"Just a voice over the telephone, she told me. Some man, no accent, nothing distinctive. Calm. Steady. Who said her husband better watch his step if he didn't want to find a bomb in his basement.''

"Jesus, Nick!"

"You're telling me! That shit don't *happen!* Not in real life! I felt like I was in a nightmare, and I couldn't wake up.

"And then came my buddies in the rental cars. Noticed them about the eighth day. Different cars, same two guys. They'd pop up in my rearview mirror sometime between when I left my house in Virginia and when I parked in the lot by headquarters downtown. Where I went, they were sure to follow.

"Couple times I'd say something over the phone—our office phones, we only got six lines, my home phone—and it seemed like whatever played out next played out funny, almost as if somebody knew what I'd said on the phone. 'Course, that could have been just my paranoia, which by then was way up there, cowboy, let me tell you. I was packing two guns by then, trusting no one.

"One night I said fuck it, let's do it now. Janey'd slid back. We knew there'd be no more remissions. I'd been putting in 14-hour days on Pasha, much of it fighting the system that was supposed to help me. Those two fucks were always in my mirror. I'd stopped off at the FOP to meet a guy from the Intelligence Squad who turned out to know nothing about Pasha or much of anything else, had six drinks instead of one. It was hot, June. No moon night. I headed home, their yellow headlights in my mirror and I said fuck it.

"I rambled through the Virginia burbs like I was heading someplace special they'd want to see. Turned down a cul-de-sac. Punched it so I was up over the hill about a block ahead of them. The street dead-ended in a turnaround. I killed my lights, jerked the emergency brake and cramped the wheel for a bootlegger spin that pointed me back toward them just as they was coming over the hill. They were down in that turnaround with no place to go, me bailed out of the car and right up by the driver's open window before they knew what was what.

"I jammed my cocked 9 mm Browning automatic in the driver's ear. Hurt that boy, but he was too scared to holler. I screamed that if I ever saw their fuckin' faces again I'd splatter their brains all over the inside of their windshield. They turned white as ghosts, didn't move, and I roared off in my car."

"I don't understand all of your play," I told him.

"Understanding wasn't what it was about," said Nick. "Sometimes you just gotta *do.*"

"What did you do?"

"I got them off my ass. Never saw them or anyone like them again. And got no more phone calls."

"Who were they?"

"Odds say Savak. Or Savak doing Uncle Sam's dirty work. One of my Embassy sources called all hot and bothered the next day. 'What did you do?' he wanted to know. Seems like there was furor around that place in the night."

"What were they doing?"

"What was *everybody* doing?" he asked rhetorically.

"It all goes back to Pasha," said Nick. "He had his fingers in so many pies. So many people cared about what happened with his murder, for so many different reasons. The killer didn't want to get caught, all the players wanted to know the score, nobody wanted any more trouble. Maybe I was being birddogged by Savak to keep me in line, not blow their shit around town. Maybe they or somebody else were using me like a stalking horse, letting me flush out whoever killed Pasha so they could take care of him however they wanted to. Whatever, one day it stopped mattering to me.

"For five months I chased Pasha's scent all over this

town—hell, all over America. I learned more about my country than I wanted to know and I didn't like it. There were a hundred leads, all of them shit trails that smelled and led me nowhere but to questions nobody could or would answer. I was unpopular as hell in the Department: I couldn't close the case and wouldn't let it quietly drop, which are the only two ways the bureaucracy knows how to handle something messy like Pasha. Janey was about to go into the hospital on the no-return trip and I was thrashing around this stinking, ugly swamp where nobody cared about me or what I was doing but monsters who wanted to eat my ass.

"I took three days off, spent them all by Janey's bed at home, talking with her, going over the four-foot-thick file I had on Naderi, his notebooks, pictures, phone books, checkbooks, interviews, tips, the lab reports, the stuff I beat out of other agencies, trying to figure out what to do. She laid there in her pink dressing gown, propped up on pillows, black pupils like dimes from the morphine, mind still clear and sharp. I tried to pretend I didn't notice she only weighed 98 pounds, 15 of which was tumor, how her brown hair'd turned wispy and gray, her skin chalky. We'd both seen enough of death to know what she looked like.

"She was like that." He smiled, drifted away as he talked. "She'd be my sounding board, my conscience when necessary, my prompter. She probably put as many guys behind bars as I did, all just by listening to me.

"When I was finally all through, all rambled and what-if'd and supposed out, she asked me two questions.

" 'Have you done all your best?' she said.

"I tried to dodge the question with one of those *'Hasn't done much good'* answers. She glared at me. She cut me all the slack a man needed and none he didn't deserve. Finally I allowed as how, yeah, I'd done my best.

" 'Then what else can you do?' she said. Smiled that

74

kind of sad little know-it's-true smile she'd used a lot in those last days.

"I looked at her, said, 'Nothing.' Packed up those case files, spent the rest of the night with her talking about fishing. Next morning, I carried her to the car, her head nestled against my chest. She wore a lot of lilac perfume to cover up the sour sick smell so that's what I'd remember. Checked her into the hospital at 9:30. She died before sunset."

We didn't talk for a while. That day's news came on the television.

"And nothing is pretty much what has happened with Pasha's murder since," Nick finally said. "Every now and then I get a call, reporter or somebody, Pasha's name or the Forum comes up in a case or a question or a curiosity. The Forum closed down three months after we shipped Pasha's body back to Iran. But his ghost, that damn case, they hound me. I wish to hell I knew who killed Pasha, even if I couldn't lock up his murdering ass.

"One of those things, cowboy," he said, draining a beer.

"Thanks, Nick."

"If you want to thank me, thank me for advising you to keep your ass out of it. Don't want you ending up in that ugly swamp too. 'Course, maybe if you do, something might pop out after your ass and I'd get a chance to pick it off."

"Before or after it got me?"

"Hey, cowboy, think positive!"

We laughed.

"So the pretty lady came back to you," he said. Waited for my answer.

I gave it all to him. Once before I hadn't, and that time ended up close.

"Sloan maybe rings a bell," he said. "Her other names, maybe they do too. I'll check them out in the file at the office and"—he smiled, tapped his forehead—"the files up here.

"But the question is," he said, smiling big, flashing his chipped tooth, "what are you going to do about it?"

"I don't know yet," I said. Smiled back at him. "Guess I'm a guy trying to unerstan' his sich-e-a-shun."

8

"I DONE YOU ANOTHER FAVOR, COW-BOY," NICK TOLD ME OVER THE phone first thing Monday morning.

"What?"

"A couple years back, I met this writer. Freelancer. He had the brains to stick with his typewriter and not go off detecting like you. We worked a couple stories together, you unerstan'."

"I think so."

"I thought so. His name's Peter Denton. He's never heard of you."

"Makes it mutual."

"Yeah, well, he and I spent almost a year working on how he'd get the Naderi story nobody else in this town ever got. He never got it either, but he tied some loose ends together. If nothing else, he'll give you a different slant. He said he'd be glad to talk with you, on account of how we're friends."

"I appreciate it, Nick, but I've been thinking . . ."

"Uh-huh."

". . . and I'm not sure I'm going to chase this thing much further."

"What about your situation?"

"My situation is I'm an investigator without a client or a case. Just me. I'm curious as hell about your buddy Pasha, but then I'm curious about a lot of things. I got jacked around, but that wasn't the first time and it won't be the last."

"So you're going to let this slide." His voice turned cold.

"I can't figure a percentage in it, Nick."

"Didn't think *percentages* was what it was all about for you."

"Come on, Nick! I don't like Naderi's shit any more than you do. I'd love to take a swipe at it. I didn't come to you on a lark, I was gamed. I don't like that either, but it happens. Like you say, it's a card in the deal. I know you got your fire stoked up again by me, and I don't want to disappoint you . . ."

"Don't matter to me!"

"Sure it does," I said. Our tones softened. "All you went through, sure it does. It matters to both of us. Hell, maybe I'm tied to something that'll haunt me, something I could have made better, fixed. I'd love to be certain. But I don't think I'll ever get to know on this one."

"You ain't exactly tried too hard," he said, but his voice was free of bitterness.

"What is there to try you haven't already tried, and who is there to try it for? What difference could I make?"

"You'd have to find that out too," he said. He sighed, his argument spent.

"That's right," I told him. "And maybe if I had more of a reason, more of me tied into it . . . then maybe all those side factors would be enough for me to tackle it, but right now . . ."

"You sure?"

"I haven't walked away yet, but . . ."

"Well, hell," said Nick. "Man can dream, can't he?"

"He sure can."

"Let me know when you decide."

We chatted for a few minutes, eased the strain. He hung up, and I figured I'd call him tomorrow or the next day. Bow out. The hell with Pasha Naderi. And the hell with that woman!

She called 15 minutes later.

"John?" Her voice was husky, low. "I didn't get you up, did I?"

"I've been awake for hours."

She laughed. "I suppose I should have known. After all, it was early when you came to see me."

"That was quite a day for everybody. You. Me. Molly."

"Yes it was." Her voice turned hard and I felt petty.

"Listen," I said, "I'm sor—"

"I'm calling to thank you for your discretion at dinner."

"I don't even know what I'm being discreet about!"

"Then it doesn't matter, does it?"

"How the hell should I know?"

"That's strange, Mr. Rankin. I thought you knew everything."

"What makes you so tough?" I spat the words into the phone.

"It comes naturally," she said. "Ask anybody."

"Then you're lucky, because you'll need it in the crowds you run with."

"I don't *run* with any crowd, Mr. . . . ."

"Just along for the ride, huh?"

"Well," she said after a pause. Her voice was calm, controlled and sharp. "Well. Thank you again."

"For what now?"

"For reminding me who I called. For re-establishing who we are. Silly me, I'd forgotten, thought maybe I was calling a friend. My mistake. I make them from time to time.''

"Like with Pasha."

"Like with you, too. It appears you and he have a great deal in common.''

"Like hell!''

"No doubt time will prove that to be true, too.''

She swept me away with that one. Neither of us spoke for a moment, then she continued.

"At any rate, neither of us ever need worry about such things, as your involvement with me and with that affair is finished.''

"Maybe not.''

"Wha . . . What do you mean?''

"I mean maybe it's not finished, maybe I'm not through with your friend Pasha.''

"I don't understand.''

"Really? That's strange, Mrs. Sloan. I thought you understood everything.''

"What are you doing? What do you want?''

"I don't know," I said, truthfully. "I haven't made up my mind yet.

"You call me up for a job, I do it and do it fair, honest and right by you. I kept our bargain, and you lied to me all through it!''

"That was . . .'' she tried to interrupt, but I was rolling, wouldn't let her.

"You paid me a bunch of fucking *money!* You didn't pay me that much for my work, for being honest, you paid that much to pay me off, like I was some back-street hustler or whore! Well, you don't buy me, Mrs. Sloan! I'm not some piece of horseflesh you can fork over a few bucks for and ride around, turn my head every which way you want, make me trot when you flick the reins! *Put me down* when you're finished with me! Slip me some cash instead of a needle!''

"Oh God! You've got no right to say those . . . You've got no reason to do this! To keep . . .''

"No reason? No reason? You game me and lie to me, then your husband games me and lies to me—then you call all sugar sweet to make sure I'm in line again! Maybe all that adds up to a reason! Maybe I don't need a *reason!* Maybe . . .''

"God damn you!" she hissed into the phone. She hung up suddenly, left me holding my buzzing phone.

I slammed my receiver down in its cradle, but she couldn't hear it. For ten, fifteen minutes I paced my office, stood in the bay window and glared out at Pennsylvania Avenue three floors below. My breathing was fast and shallow, my forehead burned. Every few seconds I'd turn to glare at the phone—which didn't ring.

Anger is a powerful intoxicant. My hands shook slightly as I grabbed the receiver again, punched out the number. I got who I asked for.

"Maybe I was wrong, Nick," I told him as soon as he said hello. "About Pasha and all his fucking shit, about what I can do and what I should do and what I want to do, what other people have done. Maybe I've been thinking too much, maybe I haven't tried enough. Maybe I . . .''

"That pretty lady got to you again, didn't she?" said Nick. He chuckled.

"What's your writer friend's name?''

9

DUPONT CIRCLE IS WASHINGTON'S
REBEL ZONE, A TAME NEIGHBOR-
hood of gay male and young white street life that takes its
name from the traffic circle surrounding a park with gilded
alabaster fountain and concrete chess tables. For a dozen
blocks radiating out from the Circle the streets teem with
razor-coiffed, mustachioed men. Their smiles are relaxed,
confident. They are immaculately dressed. Lean, serious
women in their early 20s with long blond or frizzy black
hair leave small tips for the waitresses who serve them
espresso at the outdoor cafés, then shoulder their backpacks
and stride to the bookstore, to the plant store, to the natural
herb and food store, to the record store where they flip
through the classical stacks of Dvořák and Haydn, briefly
finger a hit New Wave rock album by a girl with chopped
orange hair who's famous for tough songs. They look a
lot, buy nothing. Their faces are cool, clever, profess
streetwise ways to any man who dares stare at them and
wonder. These women climb stairs to second-story dance
studios or march to the public racks where their ten-speed
bicycles are chained. They peddle off through the thick
traffic with disdain, perhaps headed north toward nearby
Adams Morgan, the congested Latino and Caribbean

neighborhood of cheap restaurants, economical apartments and gritty bars adored by the hip young singles who relish city living.

The neighborhood office buildings house a hundred lefty and liberal political causes: Ralph Nader legal reform groups, consumer rights groups, environmental federations, anti-poverty groups, anti-war study groups, population control advocates, women's coalitions, civil rights and civil liberties unions, The Fund for this and The Center for that. The Institute for Policy Studies, the liberal think tank burgled and bugged by America's law and order servants in the 1970s, takes up one corner of Q Street. Bearded men in dusty clothes hold meetings there, issue position papers and subcontract studies to counterbalance the tons of orthodox and right-wing tracts processed by rival think tanks dotting the political teeter-totter in this town.

Peter Denton lived around the corner from the IPS on 19th Street in a grand red stone mansion, a legacy that some sensible heir chopped up into apartments. A stained glass arch filled the fanlight above the front door. Moments after I rang the bell a window opened on the third floor and a man stuck his head out, yelled my name.

"Come on up," he said. "I'm on the phone."

He disappeared. The buzzer lock sounded, and I went inside.

"Just a guy looking for something," Denton said into the telephone as I walked into his apartment.

He sat at a round table by the front window. Plants lined the windowsill. An old-fashioned manual typewriter, pencils, piles of paper and the telephone rested on the table. He'd organized this room as a combination office–living room, probably used the window table for dining too. A scruffy cushioned couch ran along the wall opposite the entrance, and a hodgepodge of computer equipment—keyboard, VDT screen, a bulky several-years-behind-the-times printer—filled the corner behind me. A second sofa waited opposite the first, this one a faded fabric and scarred wood Victorian monster. The hall to my right stretched back toward a room with an unkempt bed and heaps of clothes everywhere. In the room where I waited, piles of books, boxes of photocopied articles and newspaper clippings made a canyon of the floor. The steamy odor of beef stew bubbling on the stove drifted in from the bright room off to my left. I sat on the Victorian monster, let my eyes roam over the blown-up photographs hanging on Denton's peeling white walls: the tiger caged at the zoo; black children laughing and skipping rope on the sidewalk in front of some tenement; a large, softly lit portrait of a beautiful Oriental girl with long black hair. He talked on the phone while a piano and violin concerto floated over us from the radio resting on a cheap table by his elbow; its black umbilical cord stretched to the wall socket.

Denton wasn't a bad-looking guy. He seemed closer to 30 than 40. When we stood to shake hands he was taller than me. If he'd started to lose his shaggy blond hair, only he knew it. His features were too soft to be handsome, he carried maybe ten too many pounds and he should have lost his metal glasses for any other kind of eyewear, but he wasn't a bad-looking guy. His voice was a resonant tenor.

"What you've got to do is sex up the lead," he told whoever waited on the other end of the call. "I know, that's stylized bullshit, but hey: if you don't do that, they're probably not going to print it. . . . Doesn't make any difference if it's irrelevant. . . . Worry about perspective in the body of the piece. . . . I know it's a bitch. . . . What about him? . . . Look, we've been over this: *You* know he's an idiot, *I* know he's an idiot, everybody in this damn *town* knows he's an idiot, but you can't just come out and say that, not in this piece, it's not news! . . . Can you get

any of them to go on the record saying that? . . . Not even
on background, huh? You could do the old 'private feeling
among his colleagues' bit, but . . . yeah, I know, I think
that reads lame too. Has he done anything demonstrably
dumb lately? . . . No, not stuff like that, something simple
and easy to show. . . . Nothing out of the ordinary, huh?
. . . Will they get you that memo? Can you use it? . . .
Shit! Goddamn chickenshit staff! . . . Loyal to who? . . .
Look, if you can't prove the truth, it doesn't do you any
good. . . . All I can say is you got to go with what you
got and hope they let you do it.''

He talked for a few more minutes, hung up. We shook
hands, settled down facing each other on opposite couches.

"That's a buddy of mine,'' he explained, angling his
head toward the phone. "Working on an analysis of 'the
new politicians,' the neo-whatever they're calling them.
It's a good piece for a slick monthly, but he's having trouble showing how one of the guys is a total wimp.''

"I know the feeling,'' I said.

"Yeah, Nick told me you used to be a journalist—reporter for Ned Johnson's column, right?''

"That's right.''

"Why'd you give it up?''

"You mean working for Ned?''

"The whole thing, journalism.''

"I got tired of going with what I got and hoping they'd
let me do it.''

Denton laughed. "Three thousand card-carrying jour-
nalists in this town, and that's not counting a batch of
freelancers or guys who grind out specialized stuff for
newsletter subscribers. There's so damn much to say, so
much said that isn't worth even thinking about. We throw
so much shit out there it's blinding. Us and the politicians.
We bombard the great American public that tries to ignore
Washington. The public knows they can't trust the politi-

cians, so they got to depend on us to tell them what they need to know to make the choices that dictate their lives. They need sages, and they got us."

"At least they got somebody."

"Yeah," he said. "And at least we're better than nothing."

We were reverently silent for a few moments after that affirmation of faith.

"You been doing this long?" I asked.

"Freelancing? I've been making a living at it for five years." He looked around his apartment, grinned. "If you can call this living. But I like it better than working for some factory like the *Post,* ten-to-whenever on somebody else's clock. Of course, they've never offered to hire me, but . . ." He laughed. "I don't know if I'd go. It would be tempting, be part of a number one team, there or the *Times,* but . . . I got a lot of friends over there, our age. None of them are happy. They bitch all the time—I think because they've reached their zenith and they know it: 35, 40, and nothing to do but maybe become an editor, lose the by-line for more bucks. A few of them still think about Pulitzers, getting that great story, making the big splash, but . . . 20-some work years ahead of them and they feel like they've peaked." He shuddered. "At least doing this, I figure I've got a long way I can go—either direction."

We laughed, spent a few more minutes sizing each other up, feeling each other out: we each knew this person, we agreed on that topic. I watched him slowly decide to trust me. At least a little.

"So how do you link into Naderi?" Denton asked.

"I can't be sure yet. That's why Nick suggested talking to you. How did you hook into him?"

Denton smiled. "What did Nick do? Get you psyched too, hoping you'd rip it open for him?"

"Well . . ."

"Yeah, I know the way that works.

"For me it was a speculative story all along," he explained. "In 1980 I'd gotten a magazine assignment to do a piece on trucking regulation, the aftermath of the truckers' strikes, that kind of thing. Nebulous story, but I like a broad challenge. I ended up knocking around the Interstate Commerce Commission, poking into a couple seamy messes there, some mob rumors, a story about some trucking permits granted Freddy Calossi."

"Calossi? As in . . ."

"As in son of Anthony Calossi, famous NYC businessman."

"Quite a family man, I understand."

"Or he was until he got in the way of some shotguns in a Brooklyn restaurant a few years back—after Naderi, incidentally. His son had always been distant from the mob stuff, clean enough for most business license purposes. Like trucking. Big Jersey firm, complicated ownership, though Junior had all the important titles. They wheeled and dealed in the ICC for a while, eventually got too notorious and backed off, sold the firm—I think. But they got some goodies that should have gone to a few honest truckers, and that was part of the story. Somebody mentioned that it was a shame this Iranian restaurateur got gunned, because he'd know the action in town and could have been a great source. That got me curious. I tracked down the homicide, the cop who handled it. As soon as I mentioned Naderi to Nick, *he* came after me."

"The man's sensitive on this one," I said.

"Can you blame him? Took us a while to trust each other, but after that, I 'agreed' to poke around the story.

"I filed maybe a dozen Freedom of Information requests with the feds to fish out what Nick hadn't gotten. Great law. We're supposed to be able to see all the information we taxpayers paid the government to gather. Bureaucrats have never liked that law, because it lets us see what they're doing, how they're fuckin' up. They're stuck with the law, so what they do is slow walk it to death. I'm still waiting on requests I filed four years ago—and the law says it should take only a couple months. I got in a big fight at the ICC with some Freedom of Information official who screamed that the law wasn't supposed to help me find out what I wanted to know.

"I also spent some time poking around with the truckers, sources within the ICC, investigators from the Hill, a couple crooks.

"What I came up with wasn't much. I got the immigration card where Naderi listed the Navy spy school as his U.S. residence. Nick said he told you about it. I found out everybody heard all the rumors about women and gambling and drugs, influence peddling—but nobody could help me nail them down, then nail *that* to Naderi's coffin. I found out that some of his buddies worked for the ICC, hung out at the Forum, and may have been introduced there to some mobster types, maybe even to the Calossis or their people. I found out a lot, but I never got a story anyone wanted."

"And?"

"And that was it. Nobody pays me to find things out, they pay me to deliver a story. If I hadn't gotten a grant from the investigative reporting foundation, I'd never have been able to get as far as I did. Wasn't anybody out there going to pay me to do more, wasn't a printable story I could see, so . . .

"Besides," he said after a shrug, "I got this thing where the hair on the back of my neck tingles whenever bad shit is due. My neck bothered me the whole time I was poking around Naderi. Mob or no, somebody rough most definitely didn't like the guy, and I was running around town asking why. That didn't seem smart."

"Is the immigration card the best you got?" I asked.

"I got a boxload of speculative 'we should be interested in this murder' stuff from Freedom of Information requests to dozens of government agencies. Most of it is repeats of what other agencies speculated about, circular questions and insinuations. You're welcome to paw through it."

"Does the name Sloan mean anything to you?"

"No—should it?"

"I don't know. I've got some more names . . ."

"I've got a box of them, not well organized, but . . . try a few of yours on me. I can't guarantee I'll remember anything, but maybe you'll hit a zing. You can always plow through what I've got, plus what Nick will run for you through his files and brain cells."

"How about Gracon?" I asked. "Or Randolph? A woman named Barbara, sometimes called Barbi? Cora Mc-Gregor?"

"None of them mean a thing to me.

"Tell you what, though," he said. "Besides turning my files over to you, let me send you to this guy I know who heads an independent truckers group here. He's keen on ICC scandals, what they do to his people. That's where Naderi's name surfaced for me."

"I appreciate all this," I told him.

"Don't worry about it," he said. "I figure if I can't get a story out of you on this one, there'll be another time.

"Besides, if my neck condition is right, you don't want to thank me for helping you chase this. Your widow won't be happy with me."

"I'm not married," I told him.

"Me either. You any happier about that than I am?"

"Probably not."

"I always figured on being young enough to play catch with my kids. At the rate I'm going . . . There were those couple great women who loved me lots but who I couldn't stick with, there was the one I wanted to marry who didn't want to marry me. She probably wouldn't have worked out anyhow.''

He paused, stared off into space. Finally grunted.

"Missed connections," he said, nodded toward the world outside his window. "That's all I keep finding. This is supposed to be such a great city for singles and romance. I keep hearing about all these wonderful women out there, how there're supposedly hordes of them complaining that all they meet are gay or married men, jerks or total nerds—which I don't think we are. Those women are doing a great job of hiding.

"I'm not asking for perfection," he said, "though it would be nice. Somebody smart, tough, with a fire of her own and enough spirit to keep me on my toes. Sense of humor, wit. Somebody who's kind out of choice, not just because she hasn't had a chance to knife you yet. Somebody who's been around, who's old enough not to be scared or surprised by the score. It'd be great if she were good looking, maybe beautiful—long, lean, good legs and great eyes, mouth. You don't know anybody like that, do you?''

"No," I said.

10

"SO WHAT DO YOU WANT FROM ME?"
ASKED SAM MURRAY.

He tipped his desk chair back, watched me with his hard blue glare. Crow's-feet flanked Murray's eyes, wrinkles lined his face. His skin was like leather left too long in the sun, his gray crew cut looked like steel bristles on a brush. Something had mashed his nose more than once, and he had a jagged scar on his left cheekbone. The rumpled blue suit didn't fit him, but his white shirt was clean. The knot in his tie owed its existence to grim determination, not fashion skill.

"I heard you knew something about Naderi, whether he fit into any of the funny stuff at the ICC you guys watch," I answered.

"That's what you heard, huh?"

I shrugged. "Maybe I was misinformed."

"Yeah," he said, "maybe you was."

"Murray!" The woman's voice blared over the partition between this man's office and the front reception area. She had dyed blond hair, a solid torso, and a few more years than 40. I remember her hands furiously pounding the keyboard of her electric typewriter. *"Be with you in a minute,"* she'd said when I'd walked into the office. She finished the letter, rolled it out of the machine and held it at arm's length, frowning. *"Farsighted,"* she murmured. She read the typed page for almost a minute, approved it with a nod, and only then looked at me to learn my business. When I told her who I was there to see, she gave me that same nod, then yelled back over the partition to summon this man of leather skin and steel brush hair.

"Yeah, what is it?" he now called back to her as I sat in his office.

"There's no supersaver fare to Phoenix any of those days. I got you on the cheapest flight. You might save a few bucks if you go standby, but . . ."

"Forget it!" he called. "Take the reservation. I gotta be there."

"OK," she yelled back. We heard her dial the phone, the low murmur of a conversation.

Murray swung his legs out from under his desk, propped his black cowboy boots on its cheap steel surface so I could stare at their scarred soles. The gesture tipped him back even further in his chair. His head almost touched the wall beneath the huge poster—a blown-up news photo of a long truck convoy snaking its way toward the camera over some nameless American interstate. Someone had slapped bumper stickers on the wall to the poster's right, a column of slogans like, WE HAUL THE FREIGHT, SUFFER THE RATE, TRUCKERS UNITE! and DON'T BLAME US, WE'RE ONLY DRIVING THE TRUCK!

The landlord probably didn't like that propaganda pillar glued to his rented wall. He couldn't be earning much for this second-story walk-up office stuck in a third-rate Virginia office complex 20-some miles from downtown D.C. Murray and his group weren't high-rolling Beltway Bandits—consultants or contractors living off federal projects with their headquarters in any of a hundred complexes along the interstate Beltway encircling Washington—but their landlord liked them enough to collect their rent.

"Yeah," said Murray, "maybe you were misinformed."

"Peter Denton said you were the man to talk to about trucking problems, about the ICC," I told him.

"What does that have to do with this guy named Naderi?"

"Look," I said, shaking my head, "this is getting us nowhere. I already told you, I'm looking into this murder. Denton did too. He said you were one of the guys who mentioned wondering what Naderi knew, who said he probably knew lots about trucking scams, the ICC."

"Denton said that, did he?"

"You can call him."

"I might." Murray grinned, his first real smile since I'd sat down. "Then again, I might figure to trust you 'cause of your honest face and charming manner."

We laughed.

"Yeah," he said, "I know who Naderi was. But I didn't even come to town until after he got put away. The big strike of '78, back when I was an owner-operator. Drove my 18-wheeler straight into your pretty little capital city."

"And stayed."

"The 18-wheeler went home to my oldest boy. My body was tired of jockeying the big rig around, my mind was tired of being jockeyed around by everybody and everything, from the A-rabs and the oil companies to the freight owners to the Teamsters to the big-time organizations that was supposed to be looking out for me to the mob and the fat-assed feds and every state trooper with a ticket quota.

"You know who we are?" he asked.

"Independent truckers, Teamster union dissidents."

"We're *Americans,* man, that's who we are. And we're pissed off. The strike convoys aren't rolling, the Teamsters are still on top, we ain't got as many dues cards out there now as then, so it may seem like we're all played out, but don't you believe it. We're scarier now than we were before, because now we don't have so much faith, so much belief. Maybe we'll take more shit, but when we finally say 'enough,' we aren't going to be nice about it. We may not get what we want when we start up again, but if we don't, what comes is going to be bad for everybody.''

"You talking about your group or all of the industry?''

He smiled. "Maybe I'm talking for everybody in the country. Maybe I'm just talking in general, theoretically or hypothetically or whatever word you college guys use.

"You know what TAP stands for?'' he said, nodding to a poster on the far wall urging Philadelphia truckers to attend its organizational meeting, 8 P.M., American Legion hall. "Truckers Alliance for Progress. Independent owner-operators, like me. Teamsters who'd like to take back their union from the crooks. Gypsies who can't stand the squeeze no more.

"What it's all about is rules. We got all kinds of rules in America. We got the written rules, the street rules, the bullshit rules you gotta follow, the rules nobody cares about. We got the rules the preachers and politicians scream about, and then the ones that really matter. We got so many damn rules. We got too many damn rules.

"That's what it's all about. All we want to do is play by the rules—simple rules, ones that make sense. Ones we got some hand in making. Ones that work. Ones that everybody has to play by.''

"Seems fair,'' I said.

"Smart too,'' he said. "Everybody's safer if everybody's the same before the rules, if the rules give you a fair shake.

"You take the ICC, the big rule machine with so many rules it doesn't do anything but make trouble. ICC says a trucker can only run his rig so many hours a week. That makes sense, that's fair. That rule started because nobody wants to look up in the rearview mirror and find 20 tons of steel rolling up your ass because the driver is too exhausted from overwork to keep his rig on the road.

"So what happens? You try to run a business, be a trucker. Be a good American and play by the rules. Only the freight company contractor says if you can't haul all my cargo as fast and as far and as often as I want, you don't haul any. So you gotta cheat the hours' rule. And the speed rules. And the rules that say you can't drop no Black Beauties to stay awake. Gotta cheat if you want to eat. If the ICC enforced the rules the right way, fairly, everybody from the freighters to the truckers to the moms with a carload of kids driving on the freeway would be better off. But the bureaucrats aren't fair. You do the right thing, you starve. You do what you gotta to survive, you break the rules.

"Everybody comes to this town to get rules written just for them, or to figure out ways to bend the rules, to cut the nuts off the rulemakers so the rules only work for the guys with the cutting knives. There's six pages of national associations like TAP listed in the D.C. yellow pages. Man, they didn't come here for the climate!

"And we're small fry! Hell, we can't even afford big downtown offices, high-priced lawyers, an outside lobbying or P.R. firm. We don't have a PAC, a Political Action Committee, to bribe—oops, excuse me, to make campaign contributions to congressmen who make the laws and rules and create bureaucracies who do more of the same.

"Most of the guys in TAP don't want to go that route anyway. The big push these days is on organizing. Great idea. Right idea. Carve a big enough organization out of the Teamsters, link it up with the independents and other groups, then the rulemakers will have to listen to us. Then we'll have muscle." He laughed. "Then we can become one of the fat cats, too. That'll help everybody."

"How's it going?"

"The organizing? Officially, not bad. Unofficially, lousy. I went to Philly last November. Since I went to work full time for TAP, I double up—Washington rep and East Coast organizer. Showed up at the meeting hall, saw about a hundred guys milling around, figured, 'Great, we'll really do well.' Come to find out they're goons from the Teamsters. They intimidate the hell out of the truckers who are curious and concerned but not strong enough to cross through them, take the pushing and shoving, the shouting, the threats. I call the city labor squad. They come and escort *me* out of town instead of busting the goons! Maybe they were right, maybe they hadn't been gotten to—they were good enough to warn me about 'that guy's been indicted for murder,' 'that guy did time for arson.' The written rules said I can organize all I want to in Philly. And the unwritten rules say I better not try."

"Did you ever hear anything about Naderi mixing it up with mob guys for trucking permits at ICC? Cutting any deals? Maybe with the Calossi family's trucking firm?"

"You got a one-track mind, don't you?"

"It's why I'm here."

"Who you punching a ticket for?"

"Right now, myself."

"Great work, if you can get it. If it pays."

"Do you make a lot of money?" I asked.

He laughed. "No, but I'm crazy. One of those fools who believes in shit.

"You're right about Naderi," he told me. "That trucking firm was due to be in trouble, lose their permits—which would have meant some good guys got them. I heard some boys from New York or New Jersey came to town, met with their local reps, linked up with a couple of the rulemakers down at ICC to talk about this and that and how to make a buck. Nobody mentioned who those guys were. I heard that a lot of the shit ran through a bar up on Capitol Hill, and a couple people mentioned your buddy Naderi.''

''Who mentioned him?''

He shook his head. ''Even if I remembered, I wouldn't tell you. I don't mind my shit being put out in the street by guys like Peter—hell, I work at getting it out there! That gives me a reputation, and in this town, a rep leads to clout. But I don't spread other people's shit around.''

''That's your rule?''

''That and not running down the road without a license and somewhere to go—a bit of advice you ought to think about.''

He waited, but I made no reply.

''You must be chasing this for some reason of your own,'' he said. ''I figure you'll keep going, at least for a while. But I also figure you're a realist. You say you got no client. Sooner or later, you're going to run out of good reasons to play the lone wolf.''

He frowned, stared off toward the wall. The typewriter chatter on the other side of the partition filled the silence.

''Remember how I told you most of the guys in TAP have given up on D.C.? Hell, them and the rest of the country. The idea these days is to ignore D.C. as much as possible, get rid of it wherever you can. If it doesn't work, don't fix it, forget it and hope.

''That ain't exactly my idea, but I'm stuck with it. They decided this town isn't our battleground. You're standing in an outpost, and that's all. What they give me to work with here is what you see—me and Jenny out front. We raise what hell we can down at ICC, Department of Transportation, in Congress when we get a chance. But most people ignore us, figure we're not even around anymore.

Which is real dangerous for us: if they don't know you're there, they'll run you down without blinking.''

He swung his feet off the desk, leaned across it. His hands picked up a pencil; he absentmindedly began tapping it on the steel surface.

"We got this tax-deductible Educational and Research Fund, a way our lawyers figured around the tax rules to let us do some stuff and give our members a break from the IRS on their donations. It ain't much of a war chest, but we ain't much of an army.

"I figure you for an acceptable risk. I'll make you a deal.

"You're going to keep chasing Naderi, but we both know you gotta eat, and we both know nobody takes free-lance headhunters that seriously in this town. Suppose TAP was to bankroll . . . $300 worth of your time—to research the possibility of Naderi's murder playing an influential role in trucking regulation affecting our members?''

"Three hundred dollars isn't much," I told him.

"How much are you making now? How much did you figure to be making when you walked out of here?''

"You got a point. But I have to tell you, the kind of stuff you're interested in might not be the kind of stuff I'm after. And I may not get you anything you can use.''

"Hell, man, I figure you're going to fail! At least, you ain't going to get shit on Naderi. That's dead and buried.

"That's not why I'm hiring you. I'm hiring you to stir the pot up, to let everybody know that TAP is strong enough to still handle the spoon. You're going down to ICC, poking around the wheeler-dealer circles, and you're going to be spreading our name around. Our $300 buys us an image of clout.''

"I'll be your stalking horse.''

"In a manner of speaking. You'll ring some bells downtown, so next time I call, maybe they'll take me a little more seriously.

" 'Course," he added, "I expect *you* to take me seriously. This is an up to $300 deal—no more and maybe less, if you're honest. We'll give you the money. I'll also make a bunch of phone calls, see what I can scare up for you. You work it, you work it hard and straight, you work it for us up to the $300 mark. I figure that buys us at least ten hours of your time."

"I haven't charged that little since 1980."

"So be nostalgic. This is a bonus."

Of course it was a bad deal, a paltry and jinxed offer for a doomed endeavor. We both knew that.

"I'll take it," I said.

"Jenny!" he called out. The typing stopped, and she poked her head around the partition.

"Draw up a memo or letter of agreement or whatever. The Educational Fund account to what's-his-name here, for services rendered, blah blah blah, in regard to . . ."

"I heard all about it," she said. She glared at me, then went back to her desk. The typewriter chatter started a moment later, and in five minutes she brought back a letter-perfect "Memorandum of Agreement" that spelled out the deal Murray and I cooked up in better prose than most attorneys could have drafted. While we waited, he gave me some names, some ideas. We signed on the dotted lines.

"Take it next door and get it Xeroxed, OK?" he said, passing her the sheet.

"Hmph." She left on her errand.

"Don't mind her," he said after we heard the door shut. "She worries too much. Best damn person you'll ever meet. Do me a favor. She can help you with almost anything, but don't . . . If you find out something that could be a little dicey to know, I don't want her getting mixed up in

99

it. Otherwise, dealing with her is the same as dealing with me.''

"I understand," I said as we shook hands. As I left, I heard him call some motel in Baltimore, ask about their meeting rooms.

Jenny was waiting for me in the hall. She passed me my copy of our contract. She glared at me, then her face softened. Her words were hushed, a whisper though there was no one but me to hear.

"Please don't cheat him!" she said.

She scurried back into her office before I could reply.

11

FROM THE SIDEWALK I WATCHED THE TWO OF THEM INSIDE THE STORE, laughing on the other side of the glass: Rich, my landlord and friend, leaning over the counter beside The Eclectic's cash register. Even through the window I could see the twinkle in his eyes. And Barbara Gracon Randolph Sloan. Mrs. J. Emmett Sloan. Barbi. Khaki slacks, white blouse and a wide grin, her hip cocked in a relaxed pose as she stood in the aisle, sparkling while Rich exaggerated his gestures to punctuate some story I couldn't hear.

The tinkling of the bell over the door interrupted their fun as I came in from the street.

"It isn't fair!" Rich called to me. "Look at her!"

Her smile was cautious, nervous, her manner open.

"Just look at her!" said Rich again. "I'm agonizing over *ounces*, and she's never had to go on a diet in her whole damn life!"

"Some people just can't hang on to what they get," she said.

"Not me," said Rich. "Whatever I eat clings to me. And that's not the worst of it! You guys want to know a secret?"

"Sure," I said.

Rich peered around the store to be sure we were alone.

"I'm getting shorter!" he whispered.

"It's not funny!" he insisted as Barbi and I laughed, but his mustache and beard lifted with a grin.

"My father promised me six feet. We'd measure the first Sunday of every month. I remember him marking off the closet door, a pencil line where the book said my head ended. We stopped that in junior high. Good thing, 'cause I didn't get much taller. Never made six feet, but hell, five-eight isn't bad.

"And then what happens? I turn 30, 35—yeah, I know, Rankin, *and a few more!* Anyway, I started settling. I figured it was just more fat making me feel worse than I was, but oh no! When I went on this diet and killer Marine exercise program at the health club, they gave me a physical fitness test—which I flunked—but they measured me. I'm five-seven *and a half!* I lost a half inch between here and high school!"

"Got to be the world's fault," he said.

"How do you figure that?" she asked.

"Well, what did I do to make that happen? Got to be the world pressing down on me, all those years. Pretty soon I'll be squashed down to nothing."

"I know what you mean," she said.

"Hah!" he snorted. "You children! What do you know?"

"Never enough," I said.

"And you never will," said Rich.

"Is he always this optimistic?" she asked me.

"Most of the time," I answered.

"If I'm an optimist, what does that make you two?"

"I'm just visiting," she said.

"I didn't expect you," I told her.

"That doesn't surprise me," she said.

"If you two are going to do business, go upstairs to your

own office," said Rich. "Suppose one of my customers wanders in here? You guys will confuse him."

At the door, she turned back and smiled to Rich.

"I'm glad I wandered in here when John wasn't there," she said. "I'm glad I met you."

"Me too," he said. "I'll see you soon."

She smiled again, said nothing.

We didn't speak as we walked along the storefront window, went in my street door. We said nothing as we climbed the two flights of stairs to my office and apartment. She led the way. Her hair bounced slightly with each step. She kept one hand on the railing. We were silent except for the scuff of our shoes on the wooden stairs. My eyes traced the outline of her bra through her thin white blouse: a strap over each shoulder, a thin line drawn across her back; four small bumps in its center marked the clasp. Her hips belled out toward me, round and firm, taut. They swung from side to side, a steady, rhythmic rotation with each step as she climbed higher. Her long legs were strong. She wore no perfume that day, only the fine scent of baby powder and a whiff, just a whiff, of tangy sweat.

I had to go around her to unlock the door. She moved inside my office without a word. The afternoon sun streaming through the bay windows bathed my white walls with undulant waves of pink light. She walked around the couch that folds out into a bed, stood in the tower, looking toward but not at the street below.

"There's so much out there," she said.

Nothing came to me to say.

She turned to look at me. That light made her sapphire eyes seem wet.

"This turned so ugly," she said. "I didn't want that."

"What did you want?"

"I already told you." She smiled, but wasn't happy; thought nothing funny.

"What do you want now?"

"I don't want this ugly. I don't want this at all. I feel like . . . I didn't buy a ticket on this train."

"Why did you come here?"

"You're still going, you're still doing something . . . in my life. With what I hired you to do. It's turned ugly, nasty. It's making more of itself than it was, and I can't seem to stop it. That's why I came. To see you. To get you to stop."

"It's too late now," I said. Murray's check burned in my shirt pocket. "Maybe if we'd talked more earlier . . . But it's too late now."

"Why? Because of me? Because you're mad at me? Because . . ."

"It's more than just you now. It's more than just me."

"What have you done?"

"I bought a ticket on a train."

"Naderi." It wasn't a question.

"Yes."

She shook her head, wandered around the couch.

"You can do anything you want," she said. "You can stop whatever you've started. You can walk away. You can't get anything from this. You're not in this for money, and that's all anyone else can pay you. Please, won't you do this for . . ."

"Why don't you tell me the truth?"

"The *truth!* Is that what you're after?"

"That's a start."

"You wouldn't know what to do with the truth if you had it."

"Try me."

"Can't you . . ." she started, then broke off, shook her

head. "At least . . . Promise me you'll let me know, you'll tell me what's going to happen, what you . . ."

"I could never promise that."

"Who are you doing this for?" she asked.

"I can't tell you that either."

"Oh. I see. So much for trust. What can you . . ."

"I'll tell you what I can. I'll tell you if . . . if you come in conflict with what I'm doing."

She shook her head. "Then tell me now, because I already am."

"Please, Barbi: whatever it is . . ."

"It's my problem," she said. "It's my life."

She walked to the door, stopped. She leaned her forehead against the edge of the door.

"Don't go," I asked.

"I can't . . . John, I can't do any more. Not now. Maybe . . . I'll call you."

She left without looking at me again.

The phone rang 15 minutes later.

"Look, John, how busy are you?" Not even *hello*, but then Art Dillon seldom wastes time on ordinary courtesy.

"I've been better."

"Are you busy?"

"Now?"

"Our firm just landed a big case, toxic waste poisoning from a chemical conglomerate. Our clients are dockworkers who didn't know cancer and birth defects were part of their wages. We're probably going to file suit here, and a law firm on the West Coast might join in with us. There's a hell of a lot of shit to dig out. You can bill lots of hours. Are you too busy to take it?"

"I've got some odds and ends," I said. "One main case."

"What's her name?"

"Just business, Art."

"Too bad. Don't worry about your one main case. We're just getting going on this. You've probably got time to wrap it up."

"I hope so," I said.

12

In 1984, THE INTERSTATE COMMERCE
COMMISSION'S HEADQUARTERS WAS
a giant, dirty gray concrete bunker on Constitution Avenue
across from the National Museum of American History.
The ICC's architect began his work inspired by the grandeur of ancient Greece: classic Doric columns supported
each corner of the four-story, block-long building and a
chain of cement busts depicting anonymous mythical figures encircled the outer wall beneath the second floor's
windows. The red marble columns and shiny brass elevator
doors inside the main lobby were the last attempts at such
creative extravagance: the budget for aesthetics ran out
rather quickly, leaving the builders with low bid possibilities for their task.

Murray's ICC contact was the deputy director of Regulatory Enforcement and Legal Affairs, a man named James
Doss.

"Better come today," he told me when I called him after
finishing with Art, "I've got a cold and the blues. Makes
me weak. Today I feel like talking. Tomorrow I might tell
you take a walk."

The armed guard at the main door barely glanced up
from his desk when I walked past him, paid no attention

as I loitered on the first floor killing a few minutes before my appointment. The Directory took up one wall. Across from it, mounted on a red marble column, was a glass-framed "Code of Ethics" for government employees printed in red, white and blue ink on fake parchment much like the "historic replicas" of famous documents heartland American gas stations once gave away free with every fill-up. Tucked in a dark corner was a shiny brass bell on a waist-high stone pedestal, a gift to the ICC from a defunct railroad. I didn't read the Directory or the Code of Ethics. The plaque on the bell's pedestal said, "In memory of the steam locomotive that served so long and so well."

And is no more, I thought. A sign by the stairs told me there was a cafeteria in the basement, another announced that one of the four elevators was temporarily out of service. One that worked took its time getting to me after I pushed the proper button.

The elevator doors slid open to a world of halls where the walls were either tan or pale green. Light came from mammoth white globes hung on chains from the ceiling every 30 feet. The floor was an endless checkerboard path of maroon and gray tiles. Every ten feet on both sides of the corridor were black-numbered, frosted glass doors leading somewhere where something was done. Someone had taped a Xeroxed cartoon to one of the doors: hysterical humanoid creatures laughing and rolling on the ground beneath the caption, YOU WANT IT WHEN?!!!? The air was still, stale with vanished smoke, dried ink, dust, sweat. As I checked the "You Are Here" map next to the candy vending machine, two women talked above the echoes of their heels clicking on the tiles.

". . . saw a lot of things today, so I thought I better give it to you."

"That's great."

"You're welcome."

Two doors closed, one after the other.

We met when I turned the last corner before my destination. He was the only human I saw walking those halls. He padded toward me in silent black shoes like a frightened gunfighter. His trousers were black, his short-sleeve shirt white, with a pocket for three pens. Nothing could be said about his tie other than it was dark and properly knotted. A pink hue colored his skin, as though he suffered from total embarrassment or weekend sunburn. Or both. He watched me warily as we drew closer, not sure if he should speak or even acknowledge my alien presence. We nodded to each other. He kept his face locked forward, but his eyes slid sideways to watch me as we passed. I didn't look back, don't know if he saw me turn into the office three doors before the next corner.

"You must be Mr. Rankin," said the gray-haired woman at the back desk in the pale yellow room. No one sat at the front desk. Closed wooden doors in the walls to both sides of me led to yet more offices. A blue-jeaned workman turned from handing a long electrical conduit pipe up to his partner on the ladder propped against the left wall, saw I was nobody, and went back to his task.

"He's on the phone," she said, pointing to a red dot glowing on a small gray plastic box on the empty desk. Her hand swung from the box to a black plastic chair beneath a terrible and faded color print depicting Old Faithful spouting in Yellowstone Park. The plastic squeaked as I sat down.

"Sorry about the noise," she said, nodding to the workmen as she moved a batch of papers from one file folder to another. "We're getting a new electrical outlet for some equipment."

From the hall outside came a crash of metal against metal followed by a hollow, rubbery booming sound that drowned out the soft whirring from the workmen's hand drill.

"They must be doing a lot of work everywhere," I said.

She frowned at me, puzzled. I nodded toward the clamor outside her office.

"Oh that," she said. "They're just picking up the garbage. Happens every day."

She typed a letter on an old Remington manual machine. Her phone rang. She answered it, told whoever called that some division's office number had been changed. She listened for a moment, then said yes once every ten seconds for a minute, as if her affirmation were the chorus for a song. She said no, and hung up. The red light on the empty desk blinked out. She picked up the phone again, dialed a number.

"Mr. Rankin is here." After a pause, she told me, "You can go in now."

The size of his yellow-walled office and the fact that he had a tall window (true, his view was blocked by another building in the courtyard, but he had a window!) showed he was an important official. There was enough room for a couch against the back wall, a couple chairs in front of his desk with its high-back brown plastic executive chair close to the glass, a bookcase full of law journals and selected jurisprudence tomes. A third chair waited to one side of his desk, while on the other side a small table supported in-out boxes and a framed color photograph of a pretty woman and three children. Some of the prints on the wall were standard government issue, a few were obviously personal.

"Welcome to Sunset Strip," he said as he met me at the door. We shook hands and he gestured for me to take the chair to the right of his desk. He stifled a sneeze as we walked to our seats.

"Damn cold," he said. "Weather keeps changing."

"Hope it goes away soon," I said. He waved his hand, took a handkerchief from his blue suit pants, blew his nose as we settled in our chairs. He was handsome, black, in his early 40s. His white shirt had long sleeves, his tie was distinctive, a fashionable red and navy blue striped pattern with just a hint of gray. I wondered where he'd hung his suitcoat.

"What do you mean, 'Sunset Strip'?" I asked.

"Haven't you heard?" he said. "That's the plan for this agency—sunset it, abolish it, whatever. It's the era of 'regulatory reform,' though we won't know what that really means until long after it's over. The ICC is the heart, the nation's oldest independent regulatory commission, 1887. The odds are they're going to discard it before its centennial birthday." He shrugged. "Times change.

"Not that shaking the place up is such a bad idea," he added, and we laughed.

"You been here long?"

"Since 1970, straight out of law school. I intended to stay a year or two, go back to Georgia and hang out my shingle, maybe raise some pigs and chickens, the good life. This was a different place back then. Highly structured, lots of cubbyholes, all the trappings and traps of any bureaucracy. I was only the second black attorney on staff, and there were no blacks in any position of real authority. That challenge, the chance to knock down some barriers . . .

"You spend your life bumping up against rules and regulations, policies, *the way things have always been done,* all of it coming down on you from the top. I was naive enough for the first few years to believe that I was a civil servant, not a politician. You can't play this game without being politically astute and active. You can do it without being partisan, but being partisan, one party or the other, that's just the shadow of politics. I've spent 14 years manuevering through this system to get to where I'm finally in a position where I can directly influence policy.

"And now that echelon, the whole institution, is probably doomed. Because of bad policies, because of abuses of policy and abuses of us. Because history moves faster than this city. Because there's a revolution going on out there, the pendulum is swinging."

"Like you said, times change."

"I'm not complaining about that," he said. "Hell, I spend half my time pushing for most of the stuff you hear the sloganeers complain about. We need to clean the mess up. But I'm afraid people are going to throw the baby out with the bathwater."

"Speaking of messes," I said.

He started to laugh, but a sneeze overcame him instead. "Sorry," he said. "My old gadfly buddy Sam Murray called me already, told me what he hired you to do. Sam loves to stir things up. He's told half this town about you and him by now, anybody who'd listen—other trucking associations, Teamsters, probably the few Hill staffers who'll take his calls."

"He told me it pays to advertise."

"I hope so."

"I don't know how much Sam told you, but I'm investigating the death of a man named Parviz Naderi, how it might be tied to trucking regulation scandals. Back in . . ."

"I know the story. I never knew that Naderi guy, or any of the people involved in all the accusations, but I know the story. Back then I was out in the field, working on teaching independent truckers how to get through the maze of federal and state agencies and conniving jobbers and brokers without going insane or bankrupt. I wasn't in town for most of the scandal, or even around the agency. Hell, my wife thought I'd become a trucker!"

"But you know about it now."

"The case is under the purview of this office, at least part of it. The files have passed through here. I've been head of this office for two years, which means I inherit its history as well as what we've done since I came on board. Naturally, I made myself aware of the case after Sam called and told me the issue might be hot again.''

"How did Naderi figure into rigging trucking permits?''

"Whoa!'' He shook his head, blew his nose. "That's a lot of loaded question for a member of the public to ask a civil servant. What makes you think I can tell you anything?''

"You've read the files.''

"What I know isn't the issue. What I do with it is.''

"I don't want you to do anything bad.''

"Un-huh.''

We looked at each other for a few minutes.

"Somebody was murdered,'' I said. "And his ghost doesn't seem to want to leave town. Maybe I'll get lucky, find out something to get rid of him once and for all.''

"Officially, the ICC, this office—*me*—we have nothing to say that hasn't been covered in the no-comment press releases of seven years ago. And the discipline actions taken against some ICC employees for improper conduct in what were probably peripheral matters to your Mr. Naderi.''

"Influence-peddling cases.''

He shrugged. "That was an allegation. Neither the grand jury nor the commission's investigation ever found enough evidence of that to file criminal charges. The actions taken against four ICC employees were all departmental.''

"I understand your official position and response. I'm not limited in what I'm seeking to official or even attributable responses.''

"That might come in handy, because the official and attributable responses are now complete.''

"Nobody ever got nailed.''

"People were disciplined, and they probably deserved

it. They exhibited a massive indiscretion in their personal associations.''

"There was talk of them being wined and dined by a trucking company tied to organized crime figures.''

"There was improper social contact with persons involved in an ICC proceeding—two strikes. That's as far as the proof went. There was no evidence suggesting that anybody did anything directly or successfully to improperly influence the commission.''

"What about the organized crime connection?''

"We came across evidence that one of the owners of a firm involved in a route request was a bad actor. The commission granted the request contingent upon that person totally disassociating himself with the firm. Which I believe he did.''

"And Naderi was in the middle of it.''

"His name came up, because some of the alleged improper activity took place at the restaurant where he worked.''

"What do you think of the whole thing?''

"I think the premise is shaky. If somebody was trying to influence the commission improperly, they were starting pretty far down the chain of command. Those four guys were support staff, not decision makers. They'd have to influence the decision makers. Not a very practical approach.''

"But possible. And time tested. And maybe just the tip of an iceberg.''

"Who can say? You know one of the funny things is that the rule in question is now off the books. These are the days of deregulation. We don't care about those kinds of things anymore.''

"That's handy.''

"For some people. For the ones who are big and powerful and already in existence. For the ones who had the moxie and muscle to buck the old system in the first place. For everybody else . . . Well, if you think there were sharks out there before, you haven't seen anything until—if—they get rid of all us rulemakers. We were at least something for the bad guys to trip over. We should have been more, could have been more, but . . ."

"Did the name Sloan ever pop up in the Naderi probe?"

"There was no Naderi probe—he 'popped up' in an ICC housecleaning."

"J. Emmett Sloan," I said. "Or his wife, Barbara, Barbi, maiden names of Gracon and Randolph."

"You can't have two maiden names."

"She's an unusual woman."

"No," he said after a moment's thought, "nobody of those names was involved."

I asked him the most important question for an investigator in an interview: "How do you know that?"

"I read the file."

"You mean those names don't show up in the file?"

"Ah, you're right. Did you ever think of becoming an attorney?"

"Not for a long time. How can you be sure your memory is that good?"

"Like I said, I read the file. More than once. Last time was . . ." He glanced at his watch. "About half an hour after Murray called and told me you'd be sniffing around. I don't want our office unprepared."

"As long as the file is that handy, can I see it?"

"No."

"Totally off the . . ."

"Totally *no.*"

"If you were me," I said, "where would you go next to find out more about Naderi, the whole truckers-ICC connection?"

"If I were you?" He laughed, used a tissue to blow his

nose. He wadded the tissue in a ball, tossed it toward a wastebasket under the desk. The tissue bounced off the rim, hit the floor.

"Been one of those days," he said. "I'm sworn to enforce the law. I've been up on the Hill most of the last month getting the riot act read to me by one congressional committee after the other. Those guys yell at me for enforcing 'stupid' laws, bad rules, take the credit for beating back us devils at the ICC, as if we were some band of outlaws that rode into this town and took over, forced them and all their constituents to pay up and dance to our song. Hell, those congressmen are the ones who wrote the laws that told us to do what they're bitching at us for now!

"I'm trying to save the baby and change the bathwater and wash the kid all at the same time. There are great changes that we've got a chance to make in this country, here at ICC, and I'm fighting to do them instead of seeing everything mindlessly, emotionally, *politically* savaged. In the meantime, I'm supposed to make sure my division works at full capacity on everything in sight, and they've cut my budget 57 percent. No matter what happens, I'm going to have to tell some good people they don't have a job anymore. I probably won't have one either, but I don't have time to worry about that. Next year my oldest boy, 13, will be going to a good junior high school, which means no more than 10 percent of his class will be using hard drugs I didn't even know about until after law school. My daughter Angie is worried she'll have pimples, and she's only 11, and our baby, Matt, he doesn't care about baseball or football or anything that's not a TV show or a video game. My wife is a saint, but I want her to get a little more heaven now rather than later. Me, I've got a hell of a cold and you want to know what I would do if I were you?

"What would you do if you were me?"

13

MY PLAN WAS TO TELL HER EVERY-
THING THAT RAINY TUESDAY
morning.

I'd filled four of the "up to" ten hours in my contract
with Murray, enough time and effort to predict that spending the remaining six hours would net neither of us anything new. I could keep poking around the ICC, rehashing
Nick's work on the murder, but barring a miracle, I'd know
no more than I did now. Since Doss of the ICC had told
me Murray was spreading my story all over town, telling
her would be breaking no secrecy bond. Maybe she didn't
deserve anything from me, but I wanted to tell her. Let's
be honest: I wanted to see her again, wanted her to think
well of me. Wanted to send her cleanly out of my life.

I waited until Tuesday because I wasn't sure if her husband would be at work on Easter Monday. Just keeping
my first client's secret safe, I told myself.

"You said you couldn't tell me anything," she said,
after answering her home phone.

"Times change," I said. "When can I . . ."

"Are they doing something about . . ."

"No. That hasn't changed. It's the rest I want to tell you
about."

"Can you come out here? I can't leave until I take care of something. I don't know when I'll be through.

"Emmett won't be around," she added.

The hard rain changed to mist as I left the city. Every 30 seconds the wipers *whawhumped* before my eyes, sweeping droplets off the Porsche windshield as I followed the winding, black ribbon road. The sky was a vast gray river churning from horizon to horizon. A freak earthquake shook D.C. on Easter Sunday, two days earlier. That Tuesday morning the green trees along the road swayed with the wind.

A brown horse trailer and truck stood inside the meadow fence between the house and the barn. She was one of five figures huddled by the trailer as I turned onto the private lane. I parked the car in front of the house, climbed over the white rails, and walked through the wet grass to join them.

"This won't take long," she said when she turned to greet me. Her face was grim, determined. She wore her tan windbreaker, riding gear. The squat Latin maid stood behind her, huddled like a scared rabbit inside a hooded, yellow rain slicker. Her brown eyes stared at me with a plea I couldn't understand. She kept her hands clasped tightly to her stomach. The three men were nervous, too. Their leader was about 50, weatherworn and anxious. He nodded to me, watched Barbara intently.

"Might as well do it now," she said. "Bring him out."

The chief nodded again. His two assistants hustled to the back of the horse trailer. Shuffling hooves and an occasional unhuman snort came from inside that slat-walled cage. One of the assistants cranked a winch, lowered the back gate into a ramp. After a moment's hesitation, the other one climbed the ramp, disappeared inside the trailer. He emerged leading a prancing dark horse with a halter line; we all sensed that the horse ceded the man that illusion of control out of convenience.

The animal was a great sexless beast with long legs, a strong neck supporting a huge, finely-shaped head. His black-haired tail bobbed up, bounced as the horse high-stepped over the lawn. His color was deep, rich, more a chocolate brown than a true black. The eyes were molten ebony stars. Every few steps he'd jerk his head against the halter line—lightly, just enough to let his nervous handler know he was there. The horse seemed twice his true size.

"Walk him around a little," said the chief. "Calm him down."

Barbara moved further from the truck. She was the pivot as the groom led the horse around her. Her eyes followed the beast circling some ten feet from her touch. The beast watched her.

"Are you the husband?" asked the chief as we stood together. I'd later learn he was the billionaire's horse trainer.

"No."

His practiced eyes showed no judgment.

"Wasn't sure," he said. "When I saw your car, I was hoping you were that doctor fellow."

"Does the horse need a doctor?"

He didn't answer me.

"All right," called Barbara after the third pass, "let's not waste any more time. Saddle him."

The two grooms glanced toward the trainer. He nodded. The maid reached toward her mistress with her left hand, then quickly clasped it back to her bosom.

"I don't like this," whispered the trainer.

In too little time, the horse was bridled, saddled. One groom held the halter. The other produced a small step box, placed it beneath the left stirrup. The horse waited, hooves rooted in the wet grass, burning eyes locked straight ahead. Its flanks trembled. The hot smell of its sweat on the leather riding gear cut through the morning mist.

Barbara didn't need the step, used it anyway. Slowly, deliberately, she placed her left foot in the stirrup, gathered the reins in her hand on the saddle horn. She pushed off the step, swung her right leg over the horse's back, settled in the saddle. The groom whisked the step away.

"Easy, lady," whispered the trainer. She couldn't have heard him; he didn't care who did.

The horse snorted, pranced sideways, backward, crossed its legs and shuffled.

"Steady," said Barbara, pulling back on the reins. "Whoa!"

"I told them the horse was too hot," whispered the trainer.

"Steady!" she said as the horse shuffled again.

The maid mumbled something in Spanish; her eyes were closed, her right hand jerked through a pattern on her chest.

For a moment, horse and rider were still, settled, one. Everything would be fine, *was* fine. Barbara flicked the reins. The horse bolted forward—she pulled back, tried to find her balance, her seat. The horse dug his front hooves into the ground, snapped his right flank sideways at the same instant he arched his back, a graceful, cunning move that flung her headfirst to the earth.

The horse pranced, then stood still, relaxed. The reins hung free, swayed with a slight breeze. Barbara lay face down in the grass, motionless. I started toward her but the trainer grabbed my elbow.

"Wait!" he said. "Be sure. Give her a chance."

Slowly, carefully, Barbara pushed herself up to her knees. She stood, turned toward the horse. A streak of mud marred her forehead. Her hair was disheveled, her cheeks pale. A long grass stain colored the left sleeve of her tan jacket. She walked to the horse. He didn't move. She took the reins. He didn't move, didn't move as she slowly circled around to his left side. She flicked the reins over his head, gathered them at the horn, stepped high into the stirrup.

This time he didn't even wait for her to get settled. He spun into her mount, and before she could correct for inertia, spun back the other way. She slid across his rump, crashed to the ground on her right side.

The horse stood not far away, waiting.

The trainer wouldn't let go of my arm.

She tried three more times. After the third time she was thrown, she limped to the horse, limped but went anyway. And was thrown again. She took the fourth fall on her left arm, rolled in a cartwheel that sent her stumbling to her feet like a bumbling clown. No one laughed. The fifth time she mounted him, the horse shook his head, whinnied nonchalantly. He stood still. With disdain. She waited. He stood still. She braced herself, flicked the reins. The horse broke into a trot, casually as if nothing had happened. She guided him through three short loops around the meadow. He moved beautifully. Flawlessly. Effortlessly. Like a prince. On the last loop she headed him toward us, and as soon as he realized this he loped higher than she wanted, went faster than she asked, stopped more abruptly than she ordered, all with just enough insolence to let her know he chose to play out her commands, not accept them. Her dismount was careful but quick. She tossed the reins to a waiting groom.

"There's an empty stall in the barn. Put him there, our man will take care of him."

She turned her back on us, wouldn't show her face as she limped toward the center of the meadow. She cradled her left arm in front of her.

"Ma'am!" called the trainer. She kept going. He yelled

louder. "Ma'am, this horse ain't ready for anybody! You don't have to take him!"

"He's bought and paid for!" she yelled without looking back.

"We can take him back!"

"No you can't! You can't take anything back!"

"But . . ." He turned to me; I was already moving after her.

She stumbled toward the far fence. I jogged a few steps, caught up with her. I reached to grab her shoulder, turn her; checked that instinct and bustled around to block her path. Her face was wild and wet, streaked with mud on her forehead, tears on her cheeks. She whirled around, gave me her back again, took a stutter step but saw nowhere to go. She stopped. Her back shuddered as she fought sobs.

"You're hurt!"

"I'll live," she said.

"That's not the point."

"Isn't it?" She whirled, glared at me. A thin stream trickled down from the outside corner of each sapphire eye. Her face was a maelstrom of emotions: anger, pain, fear, others I couldn't identify. "Isn't it? So tell me: what the hell is the point?"

"Barbara, let me look at your arm."

"There's nothing to see. It's just flesh. Like the rest of me."

Twenty yards away, just out of earshot, stood her servant in the yellow rain slicker and the billionaire's trainer, waiting.

"That horse . . ." I started, began again. "I don't know shit about horses, but I know some things like I know gravity, things I feel in my bones. That horse is one of them. I don't care how pretty he is, I don't care how expensive he was, I don't care if he's a thoroughbred. That

122

horse is a monster. Get rid of him. Send him back like the trainer . . ."

"You don't understand, do you?" She sniffled, shook her head. Her smile was sad. "You think you're so smart and yet you don't understand. That horse is part of the deal. Emmett bought and paid for him, picked him because of who owned him, chose him so he could do business with . . ."

"Get rid of him," I repeated, not hearing her as I should have. "Get another horse, get one like Molly. . . ."

"Oh Molly!" She lost control, sobbed. She cradled her left arm tighter to her body, hung her head and sobbed.

"I know it's rough, but Molly's dead. You had to . . ."

"What do you know about what I had to do? Huh?" Her head snapped up, she glared at me. Rage glistened in her wet eyes. "I know what you think. Molly was old and sick, lame every other day. No good anymore. No use anymore. But why put her down? Why not let her live out her time, pasture her, feed her, take care of her . . .

"Because you can't, that's why," she said, cold and bitter. "You can't. Because she's not yours. You don't own her. You don't pay for her. You don't make the decisions, you live with the deal. She's served her function. So she's got to be put down, done away with.

"And I know what you're thinking now. Look at her, crying in the rain! What a joke! What a hypocrite. Her. Crying. The stone-hearted bitch. The ice queen. The killer. The one who insisted on giving Molly the needle, on being the one to . . .

"Sure, I gave her the needle. I fed her extra oats, petted her and calmed her down. Then I took that long steel thing from that vet's creepy hands . . . I gave it to her. She barely jumped when I stuck it in her. She wasn't afraid, trusted me all the way. I stayed with her, watched her die, listened to that last sigh as she lay on her side in the stall. Her chest rose and fell, rose and fell . . .

"What would you do? I loved her and she had to die. Somebody had to . . . What would you do? Betray her? Desert her? Turn her over to people who didn't care, who didn't love her? Let the last ones to touch her, to do that . . . let them be someone who does it out of pity or for money or . . . for fun? I take care of who I love, and I don't give a damn about what you or anyone else thinks or wants or says or . . ."

"I understand," I told her.

"The hell you do!"

She trudged by me as fast as her limp allowed. The housekeeper hastened to her side. They headed toward the building Barbara called home. The maid in the yellow slicker kept reaching out to touch the wounded woman— but each time the servant knew enough to check her outstretched hand, stop short.

I looked at the horse trainer. He looked at me. It started to rain.

The memories collided as I neared the quaint suburban shopping center in Potomac. I turned the Porsche off the main road, parked in the small lot and dashed through the rain to a deli. The pay phone on the wall by the back beer cooler wasn't private, but the only other person in the store was the clerk. He sat behind the counter, dismally watching the torrent outside.

"Good morning," said the last receptionist the switchboard transferred me to. "Correspondents desk."

"Is Harry Connors in?" I asked.

"He was supposed to take a camera crew out, but . . . Just a moment," she said, put me on hold.

"This is Harry Connors. How may I help you?"

"It's Rankin, Harry."

"Well! Mr. Rankin, sir! It's been a long time!"

We'd worked together for a couple years as reporters at Ned Johnson's column, then he left to become a television reporter with a local network affiliate. Half a dozen years later, we saw each other infrequently, usually in movie lines, sometimes at parties, though our social circles gradually evolved away from each other. As small a city as D.C. is, we seldom crossed paths. I assumed that he too sometimes thought, *We should get together, I should give him a call.* But we rarely did, and when it happened, it usually meant business.

"Too long, Harry. I catch you sometimes on the news. You're still looking good."

"Tell me about it—the station manager says I better make a name for myself soon because my hair's starting to go and without a big rep I won't be worth putting on camera. Of course, he's just joking."

"Of course."

"How about you?" he asked.

"The hair is still there. Now and then I see a streak of silver."

"Ignore it. What can I do for you?"

"You went to William and Mary College, didn't you?"

"Class of '70. Would you believe *with honors?*"

"No question in my mind, Harry. Did you know a guy named Emmett Sloan—J. Emmett Sloan? Graduated I think in 1969. According to a picture I saw, he was in a fraternity."

"Who wasn't? His name sounds familiar. Got any more on him?"

"Not really. He's a local high roller."

"And you're not sure of the year, or which fraternity, right?"

"I was expecting you to help me out."

"Obviously. You chasing him for something?"

"No. I just want to know what he's like. Really like."

"Probably only sort of like he was in college. We all grow up, Rankin. Well, most of us.

"I can't help you right off the top of my head," he continued. "But I'll think about it and . . . Wait a minute! One of my old college buddies is a lawyer around town. Haven't seen him in . . . almost as long as I haven't seen you. He was in a different fraternity, maybe the same one as your buddy, what's-his-name . . ."

"Sloan," I repeated. "J. Emmett. Goes by Emmett."

"Yeah, well, tell you what I'll do. I doubt I'll remember anything. I'll give my buddy a call, see what he says. How deep and dark do you want me to play this?"

"I don't want Sloan to know I'm asking about him. That's more important than finding anything out."

"OK. I'll see what I can do. You caught me at a good time. Rainy days mean poor light, and poor light means fewer stories for us TV types. You at your office?"

"On my way."

"Be sure to check your machine."

Harry had a message waiting for me when I got to my office.

"I don't know who this Sloan guy is," he said when I returned his call, "but he sure rang a bell with my buddy. From the way he talked, I'm assuming they're far from being best of friends."

"Sounds better all the time."

"I gambled, told him your name, said you'd like to talk to him all off the record and incredibly private. He said that was the only way—and brother did he pump me about you! Since everybody knows anyway, I told you you did a lot of work for Art Dillon's firm. I got a feeling he's going to make a lawyer-to-lawyer call, ask Art about you too."

"Will he talk to me?"

"Maybe. I think so. He said he'd call me in a day or two, let me know. I told him I didn't know who your client was or what this was about."

"Thanks, Harry."

"I'm assuming, of course, that if there's a story in this you'll let me know. Remember my falling hair."

"No story, Harry, Just me. Just curiosity."

"Sure," he said. My old friend's tone said he believed I was hedging, holding some secret back. "Sure."

14

"EVIDENTLY YOU CHECKED OUT," HARRY TOLD ME WHEN HE CALLED at 8:30 the next morning. When I asked him why he was up so early, he referred me to the weather report that claimed this would be a glorious spring day. "Gotta make news while the sun shines," he said.

"Besides," said Harry, "nobody else seems to be working office hours. My lawyer friend who knows this Sloan character called me at home last night, agreed to meet you, though it sounds weird to me."

"How so?"

"He says you're supposed to show up at the Capitol Hill Squash and Racquet Club over by . . ."

"It's only a few blocks from here."

"Be there at quarter to four Friday. You have to bring gym gear—shorts, top, sneakers without dark soles."

"I'll bring what I've got. What's he planning?"

"Don't ask me, *compadre,* it's your gig. And one more thing. You're not supposed to call him—he doesn't know you and won't ever know you, if you know what I mean—which means he's 'unavailable' to strangers named Rankin who might try to reach him on the phone. It's be there or forget it."

"One more thing, Harry."

"What?"

"Who is this guy?"

"He's a John like you—only his last name is Hanson."

Everybody seemed to be up early that day. I barely had time to go back into my apartment, make myself a cup of instant coffee before Art Dillon called.

"You want to tell me what you're doing with John Hanson?" he asked when I answered the phone.

"No. What's he like?"

"Tough-assed son of a bitch, but fair, and honest as any lawyer can be."

"That's not exactly an unqualified recommendation, Art."

"Neither was the one I gave him when he asked about you. Hanson is a good guy. Gruff, hard to get to know, but solid. And smart. Don't try anything funny on him. Is this on our toxic waste case?"

"No."

"Good, I'd just as soon not oppose him. I don't enjoy beating people I like."

We talked about our business for 45 minutes. I called Murray the trucker, got his answering service. I didn't leave a message, wondered where he and his secretary were.

"Look at this!" cried Rich as he swung my office door wide open. "Will you just look at this!"

He ushered Barbara into my office with a cautious sweep of his hand. She wore another simple blue shirt–khaki pants outfit; her left arm was in a sling. Her face was slightly flushed. She had an awkward smile and her eyes darted away from me.

"I thought it was going to be a perfect day, no bad news. Outside the air is clean, the birds are singing, my bills are covered. I look up from my cash register, and there she is! Walking by my window—walking, hell: she limps when she thinks nobody's watching! Even a fat man like me has time to run outside and . . ."

"You're not fat," she mumbled, not looking at either of us.

"Tell that to the health club scale." He shook his head, nodded toward me. "I told her that if you did this to her, old man that I was, your tough guy act was going to get knocked up one side of the street and down the other!"

"You're not old," I said. "And you don't need to worry—that's not my style."

"I don't know, Rankin," he murmured, joked. "I've been around you almost as many years as I got fingers, and I've seen you rough up a lot of women."

He grinned—yet bedrock seriousness buttressed his words. "All I got to say is you better not pull any of your shit on her!"

"Don't worry," I told him.

"Worry? Me? When have you ever heard me worry?"

We all laughed—not much, and nervously.

"Except for right now," said Rich, "when I'm worried some street sucker is downstairs rifling my store!"

He started to leave, abruptly turned back and spoke to her.

"I didn't mean to grab you and steer you wrong, you know," he said. "You were coming up here, weren't you?"

"I guess I was," she said. "Yes."

"I thought so." He left, closed the door behind him.

She looked at the wall above my bookshelf and I looked at the closed door on the opposite side of the room; we stood on the edge of each other's view. I moved around my desk, she circled around the couch, stood in the bay tower, the center of a half moon of windows.

"Are you OK?" I asked.

"Oh! Sure." She turned to face me. "This is nothing."

"It looks . . ."

"No, it's fine. About yesterday . . ."

"I didn't mean to . . ."

"No," she said again. "I owe you an apology. I was upset, angry . . ."

"You were having kind of a rough day."

She laughed.

I laughed back, walked around the couch. Stood beside her, windows surrounding us.

"You came out to tell me something."

"Yeah." I smiled. Nodded. "That's why I came out."

"What . . . What was it you wanted to say?"

"I just wanted to tell you that you don't need to worry. Your friend Naderi . . ."

"Don't use the word 'friend' between him and me."

"What word should I use?"

She smiled without humor, shook her head.

"Still won't tell me." My words weren't a question, her silence was an answer.

"Anyway," I went on, "what I'm doing with him won't affect you."

"Are you sure?" Again that melancholy smile.

"As long as you're not a trucker worried about corruption at the ICC. The way I'm going, nobody who's anybody needs to worry about me uncovering anything new."

"And that's all you're doing with this."

I didn't answer.

"You won't tell me," she said.

"Things keep changing. . . ." I shrugged.

"And you still won't tell me."

"Maybe someday," I said.

"Yes," she answered, "maybe someday."

"We share some secrets," I told her.

"That neither of us knows."

We had nothing to say for a few moments.

"How bad's your arm?" I finally said.

"Not bad. I went to the doctor this morning. Bruised but not broken or even cracked. He made me wear this sling. I . . . I don't really need it."

She lifted her left arm out of the white strap.

"It doesn't even hurt anymore. Not as long as I'm careful. It looks worse than it is."

She undid the buttons at her left wrist, slowly pulled back the blue cotton sleeve. The bruise started just beyond the thin veins in her wrist, ballooned out in an ugly, swollen smear of blacks and greens that curved around her elbow.

"Oh, Barbara!" I heard myself sigh, wince. "I'm sorry."

I reached out, gently took her wrist in my right hand, turned her arm up so I could see it all.

Then stood there, unable to speak until far beyond the appropriate time limit for casual comment. When my words finally came, they weren't what I'd planned, what I told myself I wanted to say, should say.

"This is the first time I've ever touched you," I whispered.

"How do you like it so far?"

My eyes burned, met hers. Her right hand reached out, floated toward my face. Her fingertips brushed my cheek, my temple, slid through my hair; she leaned toward me for our kiss.

15

SUNSHINE STREAMED THROUGH THE SKYLIGHT ABOVE MY BED, COVERED us as we lay naked on the dark blue sheets.

"Don't worry about it," she said, her head nestled above my heart. "It's all right."

I sighed. "Thanks."

"I mean it: it's OK. It happens to everybody."

"I know all that," I said, not wanting to care how *she* knew that; fearing she protested too much. "I just . . . I don't . . ."

"Is it my fault?" she asked, her voice a whisper. We shifted, and her blue sapphire eyes looked up at me.

"Your fault? Why would it be your fault? How could it be your fault?"

"Something I did. Something I didn't do."

"No, it . . . it just happened. Happens sometimes."

"Well," she said, "at least we know your plumbing works."

We laughed; she snuggled closer.

"What's it like?" she asked.

"You mean besides embarrassing and humiliating?"

Her head nodded *yes* on my chest; she pressed her hand against my ribs in comfort.

"Frustrating," I said. I felt her gentle smile.

"What happens, though?"

"You mean why?"

Again she nodded.

Again I sighed.

"Lots of reasons," I said.

"We've got lots of time."

"I guess . . . I guess because I want you—really, really want you."

"Thank you," she whispered. "Thank you."

"Isn't that dumb? I want you so much, I'm so eager, I . . . I fix it so I don't have you. I jump to my own failure when success is merely a matter of doing what I want to do."

"It's OK," she said. "That makes sense."

"Yeah, well, I'd prefer to be making another kind of sense."

"You will," she said, stroked my thigh.

"Promise?"

"I hope so," she whispered.

Neither of us spoke for a few moments.

"Is there . . . Are there more of those lots of reasons?" she said.

"Yeah, probably."

"Take a guess at some for me." She raised up, lightly kissed my chin, my forehead, my lips. Settled back down on my left side, shifted her weight. "Don't be surprised if I've maybe guessed a few myself."

"Like?"

"Like it bothers you that I'm married, doesn't it?"

"Yes."

"Haven't you ever slept with a married woman before?"

"Two—*three* times. Maybe four if you count the all-but-divorced."

She smiled. "You're the one who counts, who cares. What was it like?"

"I didn't like it—oh, not that the lust wasn't there, or whatever. And I didn't abhor it enough to always say no, did I? It just . . . It seemed so . . . Ultimately there was no question about what we were doing, about where we were going. And we knew that the whole time. It was just what it was, so maybe that's not important, because if all it is is sex, then really who cares?"

"I know what you mean," she said, and I didn't want to ask.

"It was all so . . . cheap. So dead-end. I've got nothing against casual passion. It's not something I'm good at, something I seek anymore, but . . ."

"I've heard that for you men, after 19, you begin to lose interest."

"Are you kidding?"

"No," she said.

We laughed.

"But with them," I continued, "I had to be part of something else, something . . . Deceit. That was the one thing about it that was endless, limitless. The passion had its borders, the promises were all cut and dried, the future assured. Only the deceit never stopped.

"Besides," I said, "it was so weird."

She raised up on one elbow, frowned at me.

"Not like that!" I laughed. "It's just . . . They were all one night or weekend stands. Road shows. Never an affair, never a romance. One of the women, as she drove me back from the motel to where I was staying, told me all about her two sons, how wonderful they were. How smart. We had this ten-mile discussion about whether her oldest boy's Little League team would make the local play-offs."

"Did they?" asked Barbara.

"Probably not. They didn't have a good pitcher."

"At least you don't have to worry about that with me. I don't have any children."

She waited a moment, then whispered, "I can't.

"A kind of cancer," she said after a moment.

"Are you . . ."

"I'm fine—really, no big deal."

My arms tightened around her; I wanted to conquer the past.

"Think of all the money I've saved on birth control pills since I was 19," she said.

Neither of us laughed.

"Just as well," she added. "I never want to have children with him."

I couldn't ask.

"Besides . . . What else besides the deceit?"

"With you? Barbara, what else has there been? I have to . . . Barbara, I just can't make love with anybody, I'm not built that way. It just doesn't work. I have to know it's something. That it's personal. That it's me that you're touching and kissing. That you want *me!* That my body's name is John, that . . ."

"You don't think . . ."

"Let me finish! I need to trust you before I can let go, be right. I need to trust you and since I met you it's been secrets and lies and scams and games, more levels, more ways. . . . It's hard enough, two people ducking around each other, scared to death because they have the good sense to realize how powerful a thing it is that they're playing with, but with you . . . Barbara, forget about trust—I don't even know how to *believe* any truth about you!"

She lay frozen on my chest; not a muscle stirred. Outside in the street a car horn honked for what seemed like an hour. Someone screamed an oath we couldn't understand.

There was a hiss of air brakes and the glass in the windows rattled as a bus rumbled by. She smelled clean and fresh and good, like warm baby powder.

"You can believe I'm here," she finally whispered.

"How much of you?" I whispered back. "And why?"

Something tickled my chest hairs, tapped lightly on my flesh millimeters from the press of her face; another something warm and wet.

"All of me that can be here," she sniffled. "That's how much."

"Barbara . . ."

"No!"

She pulled off me and I turned on my side; we lay curled toward each other like parentheses, our hands clasped tightly on the sheet between our hearts.

"Don't!" she said as a tear snaked down her cheek, along her jaw, dropped to stain the blue beneath. "Please, please don't! Don't say anymore, ask anymore. I know, maybe before I didn't realize what you were . . . I know now and I care and it's not fair but . . . Please don't!

"All my life I . . ." She shook her head; began again. "All my life nobody ever really cared why I . . . was in a place like this, not as long as I went there. If they worried about anything, it wasn't why or what. Or even who." She smiled wryly. "About the only thing they ever cared about was what this cost and what it would get them. What was it worth anywhere but where we were."

"You've met a lot of wrong people."

"Oh, John!" Her fingers brushed my cheek. "How many right people do you know?"

I didn't answer.

She pulled my hands to her face, kissed my fingers as we tightly held our grip.

"I don't know why I'm here, John." She shook her head. "Maybe I came looking for trouble, like fighting fire with fire. Maybe that's part of it but that's not all of it. I know too much about trouble to believe that, and this is trouble but . . . not like that.

"I'm here because I want to be!" she said, sobbed. "I want to be here with you. All the secrets and all the lies, all the acting . . . all the rest, the yesterdays, they don't matter. Not for this. I don't have any answers, but . . . John, can't you see? Don't you know, can't you feel it? I . . . Please, *please!*"

"Yes," I whispered. Nodded to her pleading eyes. "Yes."

We pulled each other close, lay silent while her tears dried.

"I don't even know what to call you," I said.

She raised her head from the crook of my neck.

"What do you mean?"

"You've got so many names. Cora McGregor. Barbara Gracon Randolph Sloan. Barbi."

"Do me a favor?" she asked.

"What's it worth to you?"

She laughed.

"Hourly or flat rate?"

"Depends on the favor," I said, and we laughed.

"Don't," she said, tracing a pattern through the hair on my chest with her finger, "don't call me Barbi. *He* . . . I hate that name."

"Then what can I call you—Barbara? I think we're a little beyond the formal stage."

She smiled, thought a moment.

"Want to know a secret?" she asked.

"Sure."

"Promise you won't laugh!"

"Not unless it's funny," I said. "And I'll only laugh with you, not at you. Deal?"

"Deal."

"You remember my friend Tresa Hastings?" she asked. "The one who's in Paris now."

"That's the one. She is my one true and special friend." The naked woman in my arms smiled. "Until now."

"Tresa and I are the outcasts of our social set. Everyone treats us . . . Never mind all that. Anyway, we basically collided together, forged this bond. We huddle in the corner at all those society events we must go to, laugh and point at all the fools in their finery. Get drunk together.

"One day we were bitching about how we'd like to be somebody else, somebody simple, some . . . *real* person, somebody with a regular husband and a couple of kids, maybe work some regular job, too. No more Mrs. Barbara Gracon Randolph Sloan, no more Tresa Arthur Hastings. No more Barbi. She decided she'd be Sandy. I decided I'd be Bobbi."

"Why Bobbi?"

She shrugged.

"I don't know," she said, her voice soft. "I always liked my initial, but . . . It's simple."

"Will you call me Bobbi?" she asked, as serious as she was shy.

"It's nice to meet you, Bobbi."

We kissed.

"You're not so simple either!" she said.

"What do you mean?"

"What about your name? I don't know what I'll end up calling you. All different, I think. Rankin for when you're . . . business. John for when you're serious. Maybe . . . Maybe Johnny other times, I don't know."

"Work on it," I said.

"I plan to."

"Tell me more about Sandy and Bobbi."

"There isn't any more."

"What do they do?"

139

"Wouldn't just being them be enough?"

"I doubt it."

"Makes no difference anyway," she said.

"Sure it does," I said. "To me, anyway."

She smiled and something in me exploded.

"You're a fever in my blood, Bobbi!"

Her cry was wordless, almost silent. Our arms pulled us to each other, flesh to flesh, face to face. Her mouth was wet and wide and wonderful as we kissed, hungry; her cheeks were damp. My hand cupped her taut hips, pressed her closer. Thigh to thigh and she raised her knee, wrapped her outside leg around me, pushed up, rubbed. Her breasts were firm, soft, perfect pears that filled my hand, her nipples pink, hard, like nails into my palm and *she moaned* when I squeezed gently. She felt me stirring: *"Yes!"* reached down and took me in her hand, encircled me, caressed me, and this time I was fine, we were fine as she guided me deep, deep inside her wet fire. As we rocked together she cried my name and words I'd hear often, never enough:

"Fill me, John! Fill me!!!"

16

"EXCUSE ME," I SAID TO THE SLIM WOMAN BEHIND THE U-SHAPED counter, "my name is John Rankin. I'm supposed to meet . . ."

"Me," boomed a voice over my shoulder.

He was a bear of a man, 6'2" at least, thick-bodied with heavy arms and stout legs. Only a horseshoe of greasy black hair remained on his head, but his mustache was full, his eyebrows bushy above fierce eyes. The squash racket in his right hand seemed like a lollipop, the white gym towel in his left hand looked like a handkerchief. His extra large blue gym shorts and T-shirt strained to contain his bulk, and his white court shoes had to be size 12.

"Give him a towel, would you, Chris?" he said to the woman behind the desk. "And put us on Court Six."

She smiled, handed me a rough white towel and flipped a switch on a silver steel control board.

Beyond her, a wimpy-looking guy in a blue shirt, tortoiseshell glasses and white shorts juggled his squash racket while he talked into the pay phone on the wall: "I don't know if we should do a press release or not, Marjorie, but we should try and take credit for it. . . . A pretty big deal, a $32 million GSA parking garage in St. Paul or right outside there, just came out of committee. . . ."

"You been here before?" asked my host as we walked past the man on the pay phone, past the glass case with its sweat gear and squash balls for sale, up the red metal stairs to a door labeled MEN.

"Once. A friend of mine belongs to use the Nautilus machines. He's trying to lose weight and he figured if he convinced me to join too, he'd have more of an incentive to keep up his training."

"Can't make it on his own, huh?"

"He does just fine." My words were as cold as his were sharp.

All locker rooms are fundamentally the same, though this one was far from a junior high basement with exposed pipes, cold cement floors, steamy heat and towel-snapping sadists. This place had white walls, red lockers, brown carpet. The benches were varnished, bolted to the floor. There were mirrors set high on the wall for men who wore ties, the medical scale that daily passed judgment on Rich. The showers, sinks and toilets were at the back, and for this narcissistic decade, the locker room boasted a sauna and a door labeled TANNING ROOM. You could build your muscles, sweat out your fat, color your flesh, and emerge from *the club* fresh and clean and chic. But this was still a locker room, and beneath the cologne and aftershave, the pine-scented disinfectant, lay the smells of sweat and wet tiles, human waste and nervous self-consciousness.

Two other men were changing from street clothes to gym wear; they obviously knew each other. The four of us looked at each other, then looked away in the male locker room etiquette that demands you never stare at your fellow human being, especially when he's in some stage of undress.

My host, John Hanson, attorney-at-law, ignored etiquette. "Take any locker," he told me. "Dress out." He leaned against the wall, coolly watched me strip, his eyes as unblinking as if I were a side of beef hanging in a butcher shop. I stared back, gave him a good frontal show as I unbuttoned my shirt, unzipped my pants, stepped out of my clothes.

"You were supposed to wear sneakers that didn't have a black sole," he said as I tied my laces.

"They're my running shoes," I said. "They're what I got."

He grunted.

Our two companions carried on their conversation as if we weren't there. The taller one with brown hair cursed a thirtyish child of privilege and power who in the 1960s claimed the ideological crown of a revolutionary and had just pled guilty to a bank robbery during which she and her comrades gunned down two policemen, sons of the unliberated middle class.

"I didn't read the newspaper story," said the other man, the one with the walrus mustache and twinkling eyes. "It was too depressing."

As they walked out the taller guy jerked his head my direction, asked my host, "Where's his racket?"

"He doesn't need one," said Hanson. "He'll catch."

The two men laughed.

Court Six was a long white box in the back corner of the third floor of this building that had once been an undertaker's livery stable, then home for milkmen's one-horse delivery wagons. My host had me enter first, stayed behind me. I had to duck low to go through the court door. Red lines defined zones on the white walls and blond, almost mirror-like hardwood floor. Black smudge marks marred the clean surfaces, as did a curious, crusty crimson smear on the wall to my left. The light was brilliant, overruled any shadow. I heard the *thump* of racket against ball, saw a blur and *Whack!:* the black ball bounced off the far wall, whistled toward me. I snagged it with my left hand, tossed it up and caught it a few times before I threw it back to Hanson.

"I didn't come here to play ball," I said.

He grunted, smacked the ball again. This time it bounced back to him. He hit it again. All the while we talked he'd serve, smash that ball against the far wall, *whack!*, catch it, smash it again.

"So you say," he said. *Whack!*

"That's right," I told him. "And if that's all you want to do, I'm leaving."

"You asked for this."

"Bullshit. I asked Harry if he knew about a guy, he asked you, you agreed to talk to me. And that's that."

Whack!

"Harry says you're OK, but then you two used to work together for Ned Johnson, so he'd have to say that. I don't like Ned Johnson."

"He probably doesn't care that you're alive."

Whack!

"Art Dillon says you're good, too. Not that I trust him all the way, but what he says has weight."

"What do you say?"

Whack!

"I say I'm a careful man and the kind of guy you don't fuck with. I don't gossip with strangers, especially P.I.'s. That's why what we say is off the record . . ."

"Of course."

Whack!

"You're damn right 'of course.' If you think any different, remember: it's just your word against mine—and I'm respectable. I'm also an attorney who loves to sue for slander. You got no proof we did anything other than meet here. That wasn't a microphone swinging between your legs in the locker room. If it was, I'd have shoved it up your ass and all you'd be taping would be your own hot air."

"So you're tough, so you're smart. So what."

"So what do you want?"

"You know Emmett Sloan. Went to school with him."
Whack!

"Joey Sloan. J. Emmett, these days. Plain old Joe wasn't good enough for him. What do you want to know about him?"

"Everything. Not just facts. What he's like."
Whack!

"Why do you want to know?"

"I've got my reasons."

"Reasons? Not a case, not a client?"

"I've got a client."

Hanson laughed. Hit the ball against the wall lighter than before.

"Do you now?" he said. "I wonder. I just wonder."
Whack!

"Yeah, I know Joey Sloan. I've known him since we were frat brothers at William and Mary. He became a hobby of mine back then, and I've kept my eye on him ever since. Wasn't too hard. I went to Georgetown law, stayed in town to practice. He came here on some phony volunteer job for a congressman, floated around town in a couple nonsense semi-political jobs, front committees, whatnot, nothing committal, before he started playing with his family bucks and money from whatever suckers he could con.

"J. Emmett Sloan—hell of a fancy name for the son of a used car dealer, ain't it? Our boy always calls his old man a *Richmond businessman*. Says he was into real estate. Sure he was. He owned the lot he sold suckers cars off of, he owned a few shacks down by the dirty curve of the river. He played the good-old-boy, cigar-chewing, belly-

145

slapping country cracker. Natural role for him, and he loved it, especially every time he ate up some city sharpy. He made a pile of money for his little boy Joey—who wanted more, a whole lot more.''

Whack!

"Not money. Joey—I like calling him Joey, kind of robs him of all that buffed up 'Emmett' polish—Joey wants to be somebody. That's why he went to William and Mary. State school that had to take him, though I bet he had the grades to get in. He's smart enough to be sure he has the right credentials to get where he wants to be.''

Whack!

"From the day he stepped onto campus, he angled to be somebody, trying this persona, that routine. Nobody cared. We were in college, young. We were all fishing around, trying to find out who we were and who we could be. But I never met anybody who went after himself as cold-bloodedly as Joey. He didn't even realize how much like his father he was acting: the kid was after what would sell best. He was smooth, savvy enough to get in an OK fraternity, and got on honors council. Prestige post, but he got off of that when he realized he'd have to do the unpopular thing and censure other kids for cheating.

"These were the mid-1960s, a hard time in America to be sure of who to be, especially on a college campus. The antiwar stuff, the drug stuff, even the rock'n' roll, it was too soon to tell what would be cool to do, whether you would ultimately profit from being student body president or whether that would be something only for squares and no-accounts and the thing to be was one of the few guys who didn't ever wear suits and ties to class.''

Whack!

"But there were some safe bets—like the frat. And for Emmett, the Oxford exchange program. He lusted for that from the day he heard about it. If you went to Oxford, nobody would know you got your family bucks off a used car lot.''

"So he worked hard, earned his way up," I said. "American success story."

"Yeah, an American success story. That's him. He worked hard. And he got lucky. Emmett always manages to get *lucky.*"

Whack!

"And somebody else always gets unlucky."

Whack!

"Like I said, these were the mid-'60s, 1967. Back then, smoking dope was something all us cool college stars thought about, some of us tried, and nobody admitted. Your good friends maybe knew. We were so bush league: grass sold in nickel bags—remember? Five dollars for a handful of so-so shit from Mexico or Colombia or Nebraska. Remember lids? An ounce for fifteen dollars, and in those days fifteen dollars was a lot of money for a kid working his way through school. And an ounce—shit, a lousy joint of grass was a hell of a risk! The law treated grass like the scourge of all time, like we treat heroin today only worse because behind the grass smoke was a fire threatening *the way things were.* That was more dangerous to the establishment than any drug. We're talking felony, a decade of hard jail time. Prisons full of guys waiting for you in the showers. Your whole life for a lousy two-hour high. If we weren't so young, we'd have been too scared and smart to try it."

Whack!

"Every year William and Mary and Oxford exchange six students for six months. We were so proud at our frat house! Two of our guys made the exchange program for 1968, and our brother Joey, slick Joey Sloan, he made it as an alternate. Nice try for him, good show, but that second-place certificate didn't get him off daddy's used car lot.

"The exchange takes place spring semester of your junior year, the selection the spring before. 1967. Joey had a long hot summer selling cars for daddy to savor his second place before we came back to school. There was all that summer something could have happened, didn't. Nothing happened for the first part of fall semester either."

Whack!

"The week before Thanksgiving vacation. Fall is beautiful in Williamsburg. Football games, trees turning. That was the last year of college autumns that looked like *Saturday Evening Post* covers. After 1967, the protests, the drugs . . . But back then everything on the surface still looked like all the Norman Rockwell prints said it did.

"My two friends who made the Oxford exchange were Ken Smallwood and Ron Boyd. Smallwood was a whizz, the most natural brain talent that I ever met. Wanted to be a history professor. Boyd was the joker, the easygoing fellow. He didn't know what he'd do for sure, but he wanted to do something good. We all still remembered the old JFK 'ask not what your country can do for you' bit, and beneath the clowning, Ronnie believed that as only a kid in his teens can."

Whack!

"We used to call one of our campus cops the Nazi—big dumb blond guy who loved his brown uniform and spit-shined his shoes, his silver badge and little whistle. Carried a big key ring and a huge flashlight. He wanted to be a TV-tough guy, but he was just an over-the-hill ex-Marine who'd served between wars. He couldn't get a job as a real cop so he ended up stalking around our school, making sure all the lights were turned off, making sure the girls dorms were locked and nobody'd spray painted a frat slogan on the dean's house.

"One night, 'bout nine o'clock, Ken and Ron are walking cross campus from the library to the frat house, kicking their way through the leaves on the sidewalk, talking about girls. Midterms. Suddenly the Nazi jumps out from behind some trees, yells, 'Halt!' They couldn't believe it! Some sort of funny joke. Ken and Ron kept snickering: 'Yes, Officer, no, Officer.' The Nazi made Ken open up his briefcase—this was the last year for a decade that anybody on a college campus in America carried a briefcase and wasn't automatically ruled uncool. The Nazi pulled three joints out of Ken's briefcase and nothing was cool, nobody was laughing anymore.

"Ken and Ron got lucky. The Nazi wanted to be sure he didn't offend the hand that gave him his badge, so he marched them over to the dean's house rather than calling the city cops. We didn't see them again until noon the next day. The adults of this world played judge and jury with these two evil kids they'd caught. Didn't matter that Ken swore up and down that the joints weren't his, that Ron swore so too. They had them. That was that."

Whack!

"At first, the Nazi spouted some bullshit about 'intelligence sources' tipping him that these two were making drug buys, would be carrying stuff on them. The dean didn't buy any 'intelligence' nonsense from the Nazi, who finally admitted that it was an anonymous phone call. Just a man's voice, somebody who called campus security when everybody knew the Nazi was on duty.

"The dean called the local prosecutor. They huddled all night. They had two problems: what to do with the kids, what to do about saving the school the embarrassment of a drug bust.

"The prosecutor came up with the solution. He allowed as how the search might be ruled illegal, the case thrown out of court. That took care of him needing to press charges. That meant no public scandal.

"But they still had Ken and Ron waiting outside the dean's office. Somebody saw them, said Ken sobbed every now and then, had tears running down his cheek. Ron sat there, stone silent and pale as paper."

Whack!

"They got a bargain they couldn't turn down. They were allowed to drop out of William and Mary, voluntarily get off campus within 24 hours. Their folks got a call. Their rooms at the frat house got searched for more drugs. They didn't even find any matches. The assistant dean and another campus cop watched them while they packed. The rest of us barely got to say good-bye."

Whack!

"All of which meant they didn't go to Oxford. Which meant our buddy Joey Slick Sloan did. He was oh so sorry, oh so upset. Wrote both the guys a great letter—and made sure the whole frat knew he did. Came back for his senior year with that 'good chap—old boy' British talk and using his snooty middle name. He'd found who he was going to be."

Whack!

"What happened to Ken and Ron?"

"Ken lives in California, outside of San Diego. He works in a computer store, assistant manager I think. Divorced, got a couple kids.

"Ron . . . Ron got drafted two months after leaving school. Volunteered for the draft, actually, took some other involuntary number's place rather than simply join. I remember how Joey had all these doctor's letters.

"You know the black wall?" he said. "Down there by the Lincoln Memorial? There are 58,000 names carved on it, guys who got their ass blown away in Vietnam—so sorry guys, it was all a great national tragedy, a mistake. That's where Ron is."

"And you blame Emmett Sloan for that."

He slammed the ball against the wall, caught and turned to me.

"You're damn right I do. I can't prove it, I'll never be able to prove it. But somebody planted the joints on Ken and Ron. Somebody called the Nazi. Sure, they smoked dope—so what? One night before all that, when he was trying to be my buddy, Joey let me know he knew where to get grass for his friends. We were all so cool, right?"

"Emmett . . ."

"Emmett— *Joey*—wanted to go to Oxford and those guys were in his way. He could do something about it, so he did. Period. He didn't give a shit what happened to them, not as long as he got what he wanted."

"And you've stayed his friend."

"No!" He shook his racket at me; I carefully stood my ground. "I kept my eyes on him, kept goddamn good and close but out of his reach. Someday I'm going to see that son of a bitch pay. Maybe just a little. But he'll pay, and I'm going to help write his bill."

He wheeled, slammed the ball to the wall again, caught it, turned back to me.

"Why the hell do you think I'm talking to you?"

"You said you kept your eye on him when he moved up here."

"Yeah, Washington, D.C., heartbeat of America, where a smart boy can make it all come true, become somebody big and important if he plays his cards right.

"Joey had money, enough to afford doing bullshit volunteer work. He helped out on some right-wing Democrat's campaign, which gave him a foot in a couple political camps. When that campaign folded, he got a job on some token commission. Then his father died, and he came into a bigger chunk of change. Went into business for himself.

151

For a while he tried to be one of the wheeler-dealers, felt that game out. He made money, some of it . . ."

"How?"

"I don't know all the ways. Nowadays he calls himself a financial adviser or investment counselor, entrepreneur, whatever label fits the moment. He gets his money half a dozen different places. Early on he ran some deal with a shady airline company, commodities tied into it somehow. A South American consortium of some kind. I ran into him one night with a bunch of rich but greasy Latin types at a K Street bar. Joey spent a lot of time not explaining who they were and what business they had together. I remember a phrase like 'countersubversive control systems,' some such horseshit. My guess is he helped get guns to right-wing secret police governments in South America. Who knows? He ran with that wheel-and-deal international crowd for a few years, used their deals to become truly rich on his own, then started cleaning up his act, becoming more pious and legitimate. He must have figured those boys had taken him as far as they could."

"Where does he want to go?"

"Joey wants to be a star. He doesn't care about the power, he just wants the worship, the fame. He wants J. Emmett Sloan to be recognized, to be somebody big and fancy and important. Not a used car dealer's kid. And he'll do anything to get that, though he's too smart and too cagey to get caught at it. Yet."

"Did you ever hear about him playing around with a guy named Naderi, Parviz Naderi?"

"I never heard of anybody named Naderi. If he was slime, he and Joey probably got along just fine. Especially if Joey could use him at all."

"Do you know if Emmett ever hung out at a bar called the Forum?"

"No. And I got nothing else specific I can help you with,

though if you come up with anything you want checked out, I'll do all I can. As for what he's doing today . . .

"I try not to run in the same circles he does. I'm afraid too much contact might be dangerous—I'd be likely to blow up one day, turn his face into hamburger. I keep my tabs on him from a distance, quietly. That's how I stay sane. And safe. And keeping him thinking I'm an old school chum who's got nothing against him, the kind of guy he could maybe try to fuck with some day, the kind of guy he doesn't put up too many guards against.

"Hell," he said, "he even invited me to his wedding."

He smiled. "And I went. Beautiful bitch. Poor broad. I wondered how he ran into her, what she cost him?"

17

THE FIRST PHONE MESSAGE WAITING FOR ME AT MY OFFICE WAS FROM ART Dillon, a routine check-in on the toxic waste case.

The second call came from a small-business man in Ohio who'd been referred by a former client, something about unauthorized use of patents. He gave me a number to call him collect on Monday to see if I could help.

Bobbi called. "No reason," she said, laughed and in my mind I saw her shake her head, flash that wry smile. "Except I wanted to, so I guess there is a reason. A big reason. I . . . I can't see you or talk to you until next week." The tape whirred for ten, or fifteen seconds. Her final words were a whisper: "I miss you."

The last message came out of nowhere. The woman had a coarse voice, one I'd never heard. Her message started in mid-sentence, as if she hadn't waited for the beep to begin her tale.

". . . so that's why I called you, because my friend said you were asking around town about Pasha. My friend didn't know I knew Pasha, but I did. I know a lot about him I've never told anybody. I figure telling you might mean an angle for me somehow. If not, what the hell, right? Get it off my chest. Long as you keep me out of it. I won't come

154

to your office or meet you anywhere but in public. I'll be at the Madison bar until about eight tonight. Ask for Christy, I'll leave a message for you.''

Christy. The name meant nothing to me. I glanced at my watch as I dialed the phone: 6:30. Outside, Pennsylvania Avenue teemed with the Capitol Hill crowd walking their way into the weekend, ordinary life. Friday night. Dates. Movies. Dinners, maybe a play. Maybe home to the spouse and kids and family life, maybe home to rooms full of possessions and a telephone that never rang. Sunset filled my office with pink light.

"Homicide," said the man who answered my call.

"Is Detective Nick Sherman there?"

"He's on the street."

And would be until no one knew when. I had 90 minutes to make my best play down a blind alley.

"This is a friend of his, John Rankin. Would you take a message?"

"Uh . . . Long one?"

"An important one."

"OK, I got paper in the typewriter. Your name is . . ." and I heard the keys tap as he spelled it out. "Go ahead."

"I got a message on my answering machine from a woman about our friend Pasha." I spoke slowly, timing my words to the chatter of keys coming over the phone line. "She said her name was Christy, to ask for her at the Madison bar before eight tonight. The message is still on my office machine. I've never heard of her or her voice. I'm on my way to the Madison now, and I'll check in with him later tonight when I'm done. By 11, at least."

". . . will check in by 11," he said, typed the last letter. "Is that it?"

"Yeah."

"Who are you? Just curious," asked the policeman.

And I told him, "I'm just a friend."

"Of Nick's? Then good luck."

The liveried doorman at the Madison bowed, bid me good evening. Across the street and up the block from the Washington Post building, the Madison is eminently respectable, one of the city's classiest homes away from home. The thick carpet absorbed my steps, the dark wood paneling glowed with reflected light from the crystal chandelier and ten-foot-tall gilded mirrors. The lobby smelled of furniture polish. Bellhops and desk clerks smiled, tried to link me to a room number. This was the transition hour between business and pleasure, time for a drink in the hotel's cozy bar, time to relax.

The three women in the bar had male companions; a business-suited brunette with a severe page boy haircut leaned across the small table so her escort could light her cigarette. She steadied his hand with hers, both of them intent on the match's flame. Her fingernails were dark.

The bartender wore a black vest over his white shirt, used a white towel to polish a wine glass while he kept his eye on the half a dozen well-dressed men nursing drinks at his counter.

"Excuse me," I said. He walked over to me, smiled, waited patiently for a tourist question. "I'm looking for a woman." He blinked. "She said she'd meet me here. Her name is Christy."

He thought for a moment, frowned, shook his head.

"Doesn't mean anything to me."

"Did anybody leave a message for me? My name is Rankin."

"Sorry, no messages for anybody." He shrugged. "It's early."

"I'll wait over there," I said, nodding to the table in the back corner. "If she comes in . . ."

"Right to you," he said.

I thanked him, bought a draft beer.

They let me settle into the big plastic swivel chair and drink half my beer before they made their move.

He was a big man, handsome after the fashion of an ex-college jock. He wore a standard businessman's suit, didn't look dangerous. He finished his drink, detached himself from the bar, and leisurely maneuvered through the maze of mostly empty tables until he came to mine, lowered his bulk into the empty chair and flashed me a *Hello, sucker* smile. Over his shoulder I saw two other "businessmen" at the bar watching our every move. No one else cared.

"I'm afraid Christy won't be able to make it, Mr. Rankin." He had a nice voice, even, steady, strong.

"Held up in traffic?"

"Actually, there is no Christy."

"Just like Santa Claus."

"There is, however, someone who would like to meet with you about the matter she mentioned."

"This seems like a good time. A good place."

"We thought you'd think so. But, ah . . ." He looked around. A laughing couple in evening clothes stood in the light of the doorway, made a show of choosing the perfect table. "The matter is confidential, and this is a bit public."

"I like the public."

"They have their uses. But the person who wants to see you prefers privacy."

"I'm not in the mood to go for a ride."

"Neither are we—at least, not around town."

"What did you have in mind?"

He smiled, pointed toward the ceiling. "How do you feel about elevators?"

"I don't go to strange men's hotel rooms. Not on the first date."

"Come on. Be a sport. It's a lot easier for all of us that

way. Besides, what have you got to lose? What could happen? This is the Madison."

"What are my other choices?"

"You can walk away." He nodded his head toward his buddies waiting at the bar. "Nobody will stop you now."

"And later?"

"You tell me, pal. You tell me."

Neither of us spoke for a long time.

"Listen," he finally said, "if anything bad was scheduled to happen to you, nobody would need to go to all this trouble."

The chill had left my beer, the glass was dry and smooth to my fingertips.

"You talked me into it."

He led the way. His buddies at the bar looked just as respectable as he did. One of them fell in behind us, the other stayed on his stool, his eyes on the crowd, watching to see who might care about our exit.

The elevator came immediately. As soon as the brass doors slid open I stepped inside to the corner, pushed my back against the wall. My two escorts thought that was funny.

"Hold it please!"

A plump, fiftyish woman scurried on the elevator ahead of her husband. She pushed against the rubber-edged door, made it rebound back into its slot while he bustled in beside her.

"Thank you so much," she said over her shoulder to us, though we'd done nothing. "Now what floor are we on?"

"Seven," said her husband in a tired voice. Even his suit looked limp.

"That's right," she said, pushed the proper button. Her wrist was heavy with jangling gold bracelets, and a dime-sized diamond sparkled on her finger.

The doors slid shut.

"We barely have time to change and make the Kennedy Center curtain," she said as the light behind the numbers cut into the brass bar above the doors flashed "2."

"We've got an hour," he mumbled, sighed. He stood in front of me, a short man with wispy gray hairs barely covering his shiny pink scalp.

"He certainly does talk a lot," said the wife. She'd paid a lot of money to add a blue tint to her stiffly sprayed white hair.

The light flashed "3."

"Seems like a nice enough fellow," said the husband.

"I wonder if he plans on joining a good firm?" said the wife.

The light flashed "4."

"Why should he?" the husband wanted to know. "He likes his boss."

"Yes, well . . . We've never even *been* to Wisconsin."

"So we don't have to go."

The light flashed "5."

"At least he got us into the White House," she said.

"He probably gets those tickets for all his boss's constituents," said her husband. His voice was weary, flat.

"Didn't he seem a little high-strung to you?" she said. The light flashed "6." "Too . . . I don't know. Nervous or something."

"She could do a whole lot worse," said the husband. "A whole lot."

"Well," answered his wife. "I suppose."

The elevator stopped, the doors slid open.

"What should I wear on the tour tomorrow?" she asked as they walked down the hall.

The door slid shut.

None of us spoke.

The elevator stopped again at 8. My escort got out first,

turned and smiled. I followed him. His buddy slipped into my shadow. We made no sounds as we followed the corridor to the corner suite. The ex-jock unlocked the door, let it swing open on a dark room. He reached inside, flipped a hall switch and a dim gold light flowed from the room.

"He'll be along in a minute," he said. "Make yourself comfortable."

He shut the door behind me.

Too many of the possibilities were rough. The entryway light outlined chairs and tables in a room dead ahead, the suite's central living room. The closed doors along the hall no doubt led to bedrooms, the bathroom. I didn't want to leave my prints on their knobs, so I had to gamble that they were empty. My eyes adjusted to the dim light. I heard nothing, not traffic from the street eight stories below, not the babble of a television in some other rented cubbyhole. The Madison is a solid hotel. I stood at the edge of the living room. The window curtains on the far wall were open, the venetian shades down but tilted flat, cutting thin black bars across the silver glow of the city lights. I could make out the dark shapes of a couch against the wall to my right, a coffee table in front of it, an end table with an unlit lamp and large chair to each side. The vase on the coffee table was full, and the faint perfume of roses scented this rented chamber. The Madison is an elegant hotel. I sat in the far corner of the sofa, pressed my back against its solid cushion, the striped silver glow from the window to the world to my right, closed doors to my left, to my front. My breathing and beating heart were the only sounds.

A key turned in the lock, the hall door opened, closed.

The dark shape of a bulky man stood in the entryway.

"We could use more light," he said. His voice was raspy, a tenor scarred by too many cigarettes, too much talking or too much bad air, maybe all three. I said nothing.

He rocked from side to side as he walked toward me, his suitcoat swaying like a tail. I kept my hands on my knees, the rose vase an easy reach away; my feet pressed hard to the floor. He grunted when his shin bumped the coffee table. It took him almost 30 seconds to squirm his mass into the chair to my right, get comfortable, drape his right leg over his left. He reached out, snapped on the lamp and suddenly there we were for all to see.

"That's better," he said.

He had a face like a fish, gray skin, almost no hair.

"Nice to meet you," he said.

"I don't believe we've been properly introduced," I told this man I'd never seen before.

"I'm Victor Landell. I'm an attorney."

Yes he was, with a small firm in an acceptable if not quite prestigious K Street building. People had whispered his name to me before, though I'd never tell him that.

"Is this how you run your practice? Faked phone calls and hotel rooms?"

"I bought us some privacy. I'm not even here, I'm having dinner with some very respectable people. I'm sure you can appreciate that."

"How's the food?"

"Good. How's your business?"

"It's been worse."

"It's been better," he said. "I hear you're chasing a ghost all over town. A guy named Naderi?"

"Friend of yours?"

"He's dead. All my friends are alive and well."

"Good for them."

"What do you want?"

"Didn't your friends tell you? I got a client."

He shook his head. "That's bullshit. Murray is a joke.

He doesn't have the bread to buy you a decent lunch. You went to him. Why?''

"That guy named Naderi."

"What do you want to know?"

"Look . . . *Mister* Landell. What do you want from me?''

"You got nothing I want. But this Naderi business . . .

"Like I said," he continued, "I'm an attorney. I have a small practice, represent a few people, out of towners. A normal Washington representative. My clients don't have much to do with this town. But this town spills over its borders. You do your homework, you'll find out I represented a family friend of some friends who had difficulties with some bureaucrats. Everything came out all nice and legal, but there was a lot of unfortunate press. Now you're out there, poking around in that old shit pot. A guy like you, fumbling around out there . . . There's nothing happening, but you could create the appearance of something, get people excited over a lot of hot air. That would be bad for business, and business is all my clients are concerned about.

"They're not worried, you understand." His smile showed me a jagged row of small teeth. "Nothing can hurt them. But you could be an inconvenience. I'm paid as an attorney to help my clients avoid inconvenience. If there's any trouble I can't handle . . . Well, my clients have a big payroll.''

"What are you trying to tell me?"

"I know your business. What I don't know I can find out. I don't want your business to mix in with my clients'. You don't want that to happen even more than I don't. The civilized way to handle that is for us to have this little talk. I believe in being civilized.''

"Me too."

"You want to know who killed Naderi—right?"

"Among other things."

"I'm not going to be an encyclopedia. But I'll tell you this: I have no knowledge of who killed that guy or why. But I know who didn't, what wasn't involved. You've been mumbling theories around town, you and Murray." His fish face moved from side to side. "You guys are making bad guesses. Naderi was never involved enough in that trucking stuff for anybody to remove him. He never mixed it up directly with my clients, not on big business. Certainly, he was around. And perhaps you'll find some people who'll say he was connected. So what? From what I hear, he had a lot of connections. As far as my clients or their associates are concerned, they didn't care that he died, they don't care who did it."

"Do they have any idea who did?"

"Nobody cares enough to wonder," he said, and I knew at least that was a lie. "And if anybody knew, why would they tell you?"

"To protect themselves?" I ventured.

He laughed.

"You're supposed to be smarter than that," he said. "This is it, Rankin. This is the line we go to for inconvenience. Whatever else we need to do, we'll do. It can be handled with a minimum of fuss for us. You want to go further, that's your problem."

"Are you telling me to stay away from Naderi?"

"I'm not telling you anything. I'm giving you your options, advising you. That's what attorneys are good at."

"Will . . . your clients, your friends, whatever the hell you call them, will they be . . . upset if I keep chasing Naderi's ghost? If I turn up something about who killed him?"

"We all think you're stupid to try," he answered. "But as long as you don't mess around in our business . . ." He shrugged. "Chase your ghost, have fun. Be careful."

"How will I know what's your business, what to stay out of?"

"That's your problem, Rankin." He glanced at his watch. "My advice is not to make any mistakes—especially don't dump your shit in public. These days, my clients are particularly image conscious. They aren't cutting anybody a whole lot of slack."

He stood.

"Almost time for dessert." He glanced around the room, noticing it for the first time. "Nice place. Stick around, if you want. Order dinner. Close the door when you leave."

"If I have any questions, where should I call you?" I asked as he started to leave. He turned back, stared at me with those fish eyes.

"Why call me? We have no business together. We've never even met."

Then he was gone. I sat for 15, 20 minutes. The phone didn't ring. No key grated in the door. When I left, I didn't turn out the lights, and I used my handkerchief to turn the door knob.

18

"DO YOU BELIEVE HIM?" ASKED NICK. "WHICH PART?" I SAID.

We leaned against the unmarked cruiser, our arms almost touching as we stared across the street toward a row of dark townhouses converted into offices. This was the West End, a jumbled commercial and residential neighborhood between downtown and Georgetown. Streetlights and neon signs colored the night with an eerie yellow glow. Radio calls crackled out the cruiser's open window: robbery, car make and model check, request for a lab team at a burgled house and a paddy wagon to pick up a wino passed out in front of a swank restaurant. No one wanted Homicide. Not just then. Nick's partner for this shift was somewhere inside the chain hotel behind us, using the bathroom, caging a drink at the bar. He was savvy enough to leave us alone for whatever business prompted Nick to arrange to meet me after my check-in call. Citizens who strolled behind us on the sidewalk were careful not to get caught staring. They heard the radio, recognized our stance. We were trouble.

"Any part," said Nick.

"I believe he was serious."

"No question 'bout that, cowboy." His words were impatient, angry.

"Bottom line is I don't think they give a shit about Naderi," I said. "Business is all they care about, and he's not part of it. If he ever was, it died with him. That doesn't mean they didn't kill him, or don't know who did, but I don't think so.

"The way I figure it, there's something going on *now* that they don't want disturbed, something that has nothing to do with Naderi and what happened back then. They figured if I start asking a lot of questions, trying to make a link between Naderi and them, somehow their current operation might get some limelight. Could be a lot of things—some new scam at one of the agencies, some bone they're trying to rip off the ICC skeleton. Maybe they don't want any old wood added to a fire they're worried about, some new federal or city probe into . . ."

"They got nothing to worry about from the department," Nick said, shook his head.

"Maybe not." I shrugged. "They want to keep it that way. Maybe it's just election year jitters and they don't want their boat rocked, don't want anything stirred up that might get them any ink, make them an issue so somebody will be forced to try to muss their hair. Maybe some hotshot reporter around town is asking questions about who ultimately profits from porno, who bankrolls some of the big gambling operations, who wholesales the heroin for the local gangs, who lobbies to keep the offshore banking operations safe, who . . ."

"Hey!" interrupted Nick, smiling. "Don't you remember what the man said? He and his buddies aren't in Washington."

"Yeah, sure." I shook my head, watched an all-American family walking past us on the opposite sidewalk: Mom, Pop, little boy and little girl, all clean and well dressed and well fed. Healthy. The boy was about ten. He pointed to us, said something to his parents. His mother quickly pushed his hand down and father marched the family faster on its way. *Don't point, Jimmy. Don't look. Pretend there's nothing there. Pass on by.*

"I'm tired of people telling me they've got nothing to do with this town!" I said. "Everywhere I go, everybody says they got nothing to do with D.C., this city isn't their business, they don't know and don't care. But they made this town. It's a figment of their imagination. And they're all here, every last damn one of them. At least Pasha was honest about it."

"Lucky us," said Nick. "Lucky him."

"No shit," I said. "No shit."

We walked toward the bus stop where my car was parked.

"What now?" asked Nick.

"Now I'm going home. Going to bed."

"Alone?"

There was no malice in his question, no coy sexism.

"Worse than that," I told him, shook my head. "There's somebody who can't be there."

"Let me guess," he said.

"You don't need to."

"You've made some real trouble for yourself, cowboy."

"Tell me about it. Tell me what to do."

Nick shook his head. "You already know."

We stopped in front of the car. Nick pushed the front tire with the toe of his cowboy boot.

"Pasha drove a Porsche too," he said.

"Different color."

"Yeah, well . . ." He glared at me. "That wasn't a smart play you pulled tonight, going up to that hotel room. Where did you think you were?"

"The Madison."

"Don't give me that shit."

"Sometimes you don't play the smart move, Nick. Sometimes you just play it as it comes."

"When you going to start carrying your gun?"

"What gun, Detective Sherman?" I unlocked the car door, rolled down the window before I slid behind the wheel. "I don't have a permit for one, for either possession or carrying. I'm smart enough to know the law."

"Do me a favor," Nick said. He pushed my door shut. "Start being the right kind of smart."

The Porsche engine caught immediately, growled to life.

As I turned on the lights he said, "Remember where Pasha's Porsche took him."

Then he walked away into the night.

19

APRIL BECAME MAY, MAY SAILED INTO JUNE. BOBBI BECAME THE center of my universe. I cut myself free from my old world, embraced a wind that swept me through streets ablaze with a wondrous, frightening intensity. Electricity charged the air, like before a thunderstorm, and everywhere swirled currents of unasked and unanswered questions, of unspoken alternatives, of ignored consequences. Nothing seemed to matter more than the moment.

We took every moment we could steal. Work became something I did when necessary. There were time-consuming, lucrative cases I could have had that I passed by, clients who wanted to buy more of my hours than I would sell. The one client I gave full attention to was Art Dillon; our toxic poisoning case took a few hours each week. Friends who I'd formerly seen regularly called to ask what had happened, where I was. *Been busy,* I said. *Just busy.* Only Rich and Nick knew at what and with whom.

She met me almost every weekday, often staying into the early night. On days we didn't see each other, she'd call, say *Hi,* make sure I saw a cartoon in the *Post* or read a certain story. Saturdays and Sundays were catch-as-we-could treats; I spent weekends by the phone, waiting, just in case. Only twice, when he was out of town, did she sleep over, did I wake, start a day with her head on my pillow and her warm body curled close to mine, the smell of her flesh and her hair truly a part of the air that gave me life. Her visits bent around Emmett's calendar. They entertained at least once a week, went to dinner parties or fund raisers or social events at least twice a week. When she wasn't his escort, he seemed not to care where she was.

"He's seldom home," she told me. "Always meeting somebody, attending a reception or committee meeting. I don't know where he eats, what time after midnight he comes home. Sometimes I wonder if he sleeps. He told me once that he loves to drive alone through this city at night. He surveys his domain."

"We have separate bedrooms," she said, and I didn't ask more.

All our questions were guarded, mine more than hers, for my questions could be our fatal land mine: if I probed too deeply, asked too much, our fragile alliance might shatter, she might bolt. Sometimes my conscience whispered that if I learned too much truth, *I* would need to bolt. I ignored that voice, guarded my questions well. When we talked about yesterdays, I never mentioned Naderi and what had brought her to me. I waited, worried, watched as she'd take first one brick, then another from the wall around her. When we talked about today, we were careful to focus on the excitement and joy we brought each other, on the mechanics of meeting, of being, of surviving. Beyond arranging rendezvous, we tried never to talk about tomorrows, and we never, never spoke the word "love."

At least, not about each other.

Memories can never be quantified; they are too complex to be numbered and known like photographs of captured time or sculptures of captured substance. Memories are liquid. Their quality never stays constant, nor does their shape.

It's a sunny 1984 May morning, nine minutes to 11. I've been watching the numbers change on my digital watch since it beeped me awake at dawn, carefully compartmentalizing the phone calls I make, the files I read, the reports I write, channeling their demands into the best schedule we could craft. Her footsteps sound on my stairs and I'm up, moving from behind my desk as the door opens, as she comes into the room, sees me and smiles, swings her arms around my neck and pulls me close. We kiss and she tells me she missed me, cracks a joke. We make love, but that's only part of it, such a small part, such a sweet part. Maybe we go to lunch on the Hill, someplace close like the Tune Inn, a honky-tonk tavern defiantly out of place in this suit-and-tie town. We'll have burgers, maybe a beer, laugh and hold hands on the table, sit in the booth and stare at each other while clichéd country & western songs blare from the jukebox and congressional aides rub elbows with the blue-collar boys at the bar. She doesn't wear her rings.

"And nobody knows me here," she says. "Not unless some senator or congressman wanders in, which, given their schedules, isn't likely at noon. The aides aren't quite . . . I've begged off all of his routine political things in the last few years."

"All these people will remember you," I tell her. "They'll wonder what a guy like me is doing with such a classy woman, who you are."

"I'm your girl," she says, squeezes my hand.

At noon on the drizzly, cold 30th of May we walked to the west front of the Capitol for Washington's first solar eclipse in decades. Red steel scaffolding covered the white marble walls looming behind us. We found a spot next to a TV crew on the long concrete veranda, leaned against the marble railing, shivered, held each other close. The

Mall stretched out before us, a mile-long, tree-bordered grass boulevard leading from the base of Congress's building to the Washington Monument; from there, beyond our vision, to the Reflecting Pool and Lincoln Memorial. Black clouds rolled over the city like an ugly sea, parting for only seconds to let us glimpse the sun floating like a pale yellow dime in that ferment. The storm misted all light with shades of gray. The TV cameraman wore a green army rain poncho, the reporter a suit. They took turns announcing how many seconds remained before history could be filmed.

A junior high tour group scurried around the Capitol's corner, 30 kids under the weary charge of three nuns. The kids shouted and laughed as they raced down the stairs, the lucky ones not noticing the fat girl who hung back by the Sisters and didn't try so she wouldn't fail, the graceless boy in thick glasses who pretended to be interested in mere stone buildings and not the cool way he couldn't walk.

The prettiest girl called back to a nun: "If I fall down the stairs, Sister, it's on your conscience."

"No it's not," was the reply.

"One minute," announced the cameraman.

"Doesn't look any darker to me," said the reporter. Bobbi and I nodded, but he didn't care if we agreed.

"Should I pan up, try to catch the sun?" asked the cameraman, pointing to where we'd last seen its pale glow, where now was only a black cloud.

"What sun?" said the reporter. "Keep it focused out over the Mall. Get the effect. Thirty seconds."

"Crank down the iris," said the cameraman, "that'd be just as good."

We counted down the time. The shadows deepened briefly, the air chilled, but what was more noticeable than the eclipse was the return of the light.

"Talk about a non-event," muttered the cameraman as he turned off his camera, unscrewed it from the tripod.

"We've always got that congressman's press conference," said the reporter as they walked away.

"What was his name again?" asked the technician.

We never heard the answer.

When we could, we'd have dinner together. Occasionally out, but more often we'd cook in my cramped, yellow-walled kitchen. We'd laugh, talk, burn the meat or undercook the potatoes, eat it all anyway. Sometimes we'd risk a movie, a black and white classic at the Circle's matinee. Buy popcorn, Cokes.

"Just like teenagers," she said. "Only I skipped most of that stuff."

"It skipped me," I told her.

One afternoon she found my old Beatle records and we played them so loud Rich called from downstairs like an exasperated parent, made us turn it down. I introduced her to Springsteen, bought her his cassettes for her car stereo.

"Emmett never listens to music," she said. "Just the all-news stations. He'll never find the tapes: he prefers his own car."

She taught me to enjoy Scotch and water, and one day, when one of the renegades from my yesterdays passed through town, I overrode my better judgment and accepted his generosity so she could experience cocaine.

"I didn't know you did this sort of thing," she said as she watched me chop out the lines of cream-colored crystal powder.

"I don't," I said; shrugged. "Used to, but . . . It stopped being worth it."

"We all smoked grass when I was in New York. Lots of pills around. I never did them."

"Well," she confessed, with a smile, "not unless my Valium counts."

"It does. Why do you take it?"

"It helps me sleep."

"It blocks your dreams."

"Whatever. What will this do?"

"If it's as pure as my buddy says, your nose'll get numb, you'll feel . . . great, surging with ego and energy. It won't last long."

"That never does."

I snorted two of the inch-long lines, handed her the dollar-bill tube. The coke was great, as my friend claimed.

"Emmett . . ." she paused, then figured what the hell: she'd already brought his name up, might as well complete her thought. "Emmett doesn't even drink much. He says drugs—any drug—make you vulnerable."

"He's right," I said.

"Oh yes," she said as she leaned back after snorting two lines. She stared off into space, waiting, feeling the coke roar through her; smiled, shook her head. "He's always right."

We looked at each other as the chemical illusion danced through us. On the table between us lay a plastic packet with about three thimblesful of crystal magic, my open clasp knife, a quarter-sized mound of cocaine with six other white lines drawn out beside and the dollar-bill tube. I picked up the makeshift tube.

"Here's to all the Emmetts of this world," I said.

For a second we stared at each other, said nothing. Then we laughed.

And more of those lines disappeared into us.

One afternoon we spun the couch around in my office so it faced the round bay window instead of my desk. She wore one of my dress shirts, I was naked. We leaned back, our hands lightly touching as we talked and stared out over the rooftops of Capitol Hill.

"I used to sit with my father when I was a child," she said.

"What was he like?"

She smiled sadly, shook her head. "Lost.

"He was a schoolteacher at a private academy across the river in suburban Virginia. He taught literature, and never accepted a post as an administrator because he knew he couldn't handle it. He'd been a major in World War II, was a true son of the South—a distinguished gentleman with empty coffers and faith in legends about a genteel life that never existed. When he came back from the war, his father's bank had been bought out by one of the new entrepreneurs. The profits were just enough to wipe out the debt from years of family pretense.

"He started drinking before I was born. By the time I was old enough to notice, he was locked inside the bottle. He stayed sober enough to teach Sir Walter Scott and Charles Dickens to me and the rich boys who liked it when his daughter visited the school. We lived on campus, in a far grander house than we could otherwise have afforded. He spent hours sitting on the back porch swing, bourbon in hand. He was a handsome drunk, dignified. He never slurred his words, no matter how much he drank. When I was a little girl I used to sit with him and he'd tell me stories. When I got bigger, realized what he was, I still sat with him from time to time, but he had no stories for big girls. He was very apologetic, matter-of-fact about being a failure. He'd take whatever happened with that same even, disassociated smile.

"The only adult advice he ever gave me was when I was a junior in high school. I went to a good public school, was the star of the drama department, had all these illusions about college, about acting on the stage, in the movies. I got the female lead in a community theater's production of *A Doll's House* even though I was just 16. When I found out I got it I raced home, bursting with excitement. I ran out to the back porch, to Daddy sitting there in his swing, rocking back and forth, his mind drifting through his regrets and nostalgias. I blathered on about what it meant, where I was going to go and who I was going to be.

"I didn't focus on him until I ran out of breath. When I did, there he was, same old Daddy: sitting in his swing, the faint smell of whiskey sweat drifting through the lime cologne he always wore, same old sorry smile on his face, same glass of bourbon in his hand. He shook his head, smiled at me for real.

" 'Barbara,' he said, 'Don't believe too much. Don't believe *in* too much. Otherwise, you'll have too much to lose.' "

"That's . . ." I started to say, stopped, unable to choose which word.

"Sad? Pitiful? Disgusting?" She shook her head. "True? All of the above, none of the above. That was my father."

"What about your mother?" I asked.

"My mother?" She smiled. "My mother is the best thing that's ever happened to me.

"My mother came from the wrong part of Kentucky for my father's family. Her family were tenant farmers always forced to bow to some landowner. She worked her way east, somehow squeezed in a couple of years at a finishing school. Finish is right. They prepared you to either be a wife or a typist secretary. Either way your life was finished. You were an item on the market, dependent on your luck to be given a good life.

"My mother got lucky, or at least she thought so. She met my father in World War II, some USO event. He was so handsome then, so alive and full of such promise! And she had this grand, deep dignity, this heart full of love waiting to be taken. She has an infinite capacity for giving and my father had an infinite need of charity—at least that's what his need turned into. His family hated her, hated the *idea* of her. Sometimes I think the only heroic thing my father ever did was marry her.

"They made life a chilly hell for her, never let her forget who she wasn't. Blamed her for the joke my father made of his life. She was never accepted by them, or by any of their snooty Charleston and Virginia friends.

"They weren't happy with me either. Even though I came from tainted stock, there'd been some hope that the heir to the Gracon name would be able to rise above his handicapped heritage and reclaim some of the grandeur the old name supposedly had. When I was born they blamed my mother all over again: how dare she have borne a girl child!

"She was so good to me! She made up this grand fiction of how our life was that kept a child from being hurt by the truth of a drunken father. I didn't even understand that my father wasn't 'good' like all the other kids' fathers until I was almost 12—and I wasn't a stupid little girl."

"You're not a stupid big girl either," I told her.

"Sometimes I wonder.

"Mom took a job as an office manager so I could afford a shot at my dreams—and so we could afford Daddy's bourbon. Oh did the family hate that! A Gracon woman, working in a common office, where people could come in off the street and see her!

"One day my father realized he was dead and gracefully floated away. He left his body in the swing, rocking back and forth with the wind, with the spinning of the earth, dead for hours before two boys cutting across our yard from the school noticed that old Bottle Bill Gracon didn't look right. His glass was on the porch floor. No matter how drunk he got, Bottle Bill never dropped his glass and he never passed out until the last glass was empty, carefully set beside the bottle by a proper gentleman. I got the call from my mother when I was shooting a panty hose print ad in New York. I think they used one of the shots the photographer snapped while I was on the phone.

"The family was secretly delighted: a dead martyr to the tragedies of the South and a bad marriage is far more acceptable than an embarrassingly alive drunk. They thought they were rid of my mother and me forever."

Bobbi laughed.

"But they didn't get away with it! My father's childhood friend, Austin Randolph—his wife died the year before my father. Randolph was the only one from my father's old circle of friends who stayed in touch with us, who liked us, who came round at the funeral and wanted to help. His name was just as big in *the proper Southern circles* as Father's, though Austin once told me that his family had only been in Charleston since the 1890s, so they were still on probation. Austin owned a mansion behind one of the walls on Legare Street, the heart of the old South, everything my father's family aspired to—and when he married my mother, she got it all in one fell swoop.

"For the first time in her life she had some currency, something that was real and valued and true, something . . . something recognized. She wasn't the barefoot hillbilly from Kentucky anymore, she was the widow Gracon who'd married Austin Randolph and lived on Legare Street. Austin treated her like a queen, like she deserved. He gave her happiness Father wouldn't and I couldn't. Finally she could relax, she could not be ashamed of who she was and where she was, she could walk with pride."

"All she had was another image," I argued. "She still wasn't getting any credit for herself. She was still just a married name."

"But she was redeemed!" Bobbi insisted. "After a lifetime of being a nobody, of being treated like a leper and chained to a cripple, to finally have a chance to be somebody is like being handed the key to heaven!

"You don't understand how good she is, how much she did for me, how much I owe . . . ."

"Yes I do," I said, but Bobbi went on as though she hadn't heard me.

"Poor Mother!" Bobbi shook her head. "She went from my father to his friend, loved them both in a peculiar, almost maternal way. Just when she finally got what she deserved, finally got something from this life, Austin had a heart attack and she found out another husband was less than he seemed. He wasn't broke, but without him working every day in the business she thought he kept his hand in for fun, life on Legare Street was unaffordable. She'd have been thrown out in the street, out there for all those *eyes* to see, to laugh at, for the Gracons to get the final joke on. Maybe she'd have been able to get work again at 55, but as what? What could she do? Who could she be? And what about her future? I had nightmares of her in a nursing home.

"That was when I met Emmett," she said. "J. Emmett Sloan. No white knight, even then I knew that, but . . . He fit the role of savior."

Neither of us spoke for several minutes. My heart beat hard against my chest, our hands lay intertwined between us on the couch.

"He can be so charming," she said.

"I came down to D.C. regularly after I moved to New York," she said. She seemed to be talking more to the city outside my bay windows than to me. "I had few friends in the area, but the headmaster of my father's school and his wife had never shunned the wife and daughter of their drunken employee. They were like a second family to me. I babysat their little girls. When I couldn't afford to leave New York to go see Mom in Charleston, I'd take the train down here. Sometimes they'd send me a ticket.

"They were a socially prominent couple. When one of those little girls got married, the wedding was a major society affair. All the right people were invited. I was there because I was family. Emmett came as a guest of someone they knew. He always keeps his eye open for a good invitation.

"He can be *so* charming!" she said again, laughed bitterly.

"I'm beautiful," she said.

"I know," I told her, raised her hand and kissed it.

"No, I . . ." she smiled at me. "I'm not saying that to . . .

"Being beautiful opens a million doors for you," she said. "And behind most of them are monsters waiting to trick you inside. Some of those doors you make, some of them are waiting out there for all the beautiful women. Even the good doors that open to you because you're beautiful . . . it's still because you're beautiful, not because you're you. Being beautiful is such a small part of who you are, but if you let it, it can become all that defines you, it can decide everything about your life, it can . . ."

"It's better than being ugly," I told her.

She laughed. "You're damn right! I'm not asking for pity for something I wouldn't trade away even if I could. But I want you to understand . . .

"All my life men have been intimidated by me because I'm beautiful. Those who get over that discover I've got a mind and a will of my own and most can't handle it, don't like it. Maybe hate it."

"Not all men," I said.

She pulled me close, kissed me. "Oh John! No, not everyone. Not you. You're so special! So different."

We held each other until she said, "So is Emmett.

"He was the first man I ever met who didn't give a damn about me being beautiful," she said as we leaned back. "I knew that from the start, just like I knew that he was attracted to something else about me. He was charming, he was smart, he moved through crowds so gracefully. I'd never met anyone like him, and I hope I never will again.

He's beyond strong. He's never had the slightest doubt, the slightest feeling of guilt or need to apologize. No hesitation. No vacillation. No weakness.

"I actually thought he cared about me—about all of me, about the me beyond the beautiful. I was 27. I hit New York when I was 18—Mom's job money bought me the ticket, tuition at an acting school, a professionally shot portfolio and three changes of quality clothes so I could walk into an audition with all the other beautiful women and not look like I was straight off the farm.

"Turns out I'm not a very good actress," she said, shook her head. "I can play small scenes, impress community theaters, but . . . My best teacher took me aside once, told me I project better than any student he'd ever seen—up to a point. 'You hold back your core,' he said. 'You can't let go, can't stop protecting yourself enough to be a character who's vulnerable.'

"I wasn't good enough for quality acting on the stage, I wasn't one of the beautiful ones who couldn't act but got the right break and ended up on TV or in a movie anyway. But I had enough beauty to make print ads as a model, some runway work, 25 commercials. You've probably seen parts of me a dozen times. My agent kept me in three files: legs, hands, lips. I felt like a box of spare mannequin parts.

"Emmett started pursuing me the day we met. Not charging or pawing the ground like some other men, but quietly, firmly, as if *of course* he was meant for me. After a million creeps, after all the guys who wanted only one or two things from me, with all his charm, with the utter acceptance and confidence he showed, he seemed . . . I didn't want to be part of the commercial meat market any more and all that it entailed. By then Austin had just died, and I thought I'd been around, thought I knew all there was to know about . . . about romance, sex, men and women, and what was real behind all the corny songs and cynical pacts. Emmett seemed my best bet.

"Especially after he told me he understood how I felt about my mother, how he knew it was important that she not be given that one final kick into the gutter. He swore he'd take care of her, protect her, support her life just as it was. He was so clever. To prove that to me, he insisted on giving me a prenuptial agreement swearing he'd maintain her life-style as long as we were married, and if I died first—remember, I'd had a uterine cancer scare—if I died first, he'd still maintain her. That was so important to me I never worried about the things *I* agreed to—like never owning anything more than what I brought to the marriage, which was the clothes on my back, the *exact* clothes and their value. I've got all this jewelry he likes me to wear, just like he urged me to join the Hunt Club when all I wanted to do was ride horses. If I leave him, I can't take the diamonds, can't sell them to support Mom or myself."

"So what?"

She shook her head, whispered, "Not now. Not that part, Johnny. Not now."

I closed my eyes, nodded.

"It was never a romance," she said, perhaps to placate me. "Emmett's affection is all charm and no substance. Not that he's . . . We've . . .

"I've never been his lover, Johnny, not really. He . . . I think he went to bed with me in the beginning to establish he could, to mark his claim. I finally figured out that's what he wanted from me, a claim. I was Barbara Gracon Randolph. He wasn't giving me his name when he insisted I take it, he was nailing all that old southern society onto Sloan. I had a pedigree, was racy enough as a former actress to be interesting, a good drawing card for his social life, an enviable partner and hostess. My beauty mattered to him, but not the way I thought. It made *him* seem more charming, opened doors for him, just like my 'illustrious' heritage. I don't think sex matters to him any more than it does to that gelding he just bought. We don't . . . I'm not his lover, John. Even when I tried to be, when I thought I could be, when I wanted to become that because he was my husband and that's what . . ."

"It's OK," I told her, squeezing her hand. "It's OK."

Her eyes were wet, but she wouldn't let herself cry.

"So," she said, sniffled, forced a smile. "That's my life story."

"Only part of it," I said, smiled. "And until now."

"Yes, until now. But what about you?"

"There's not much to tell," I said. "Not much you don't already know."

"Of course there is!" she laughed. "John, you . . . Tell me! I want to know everything about you, all about you, all that . . ."

"Do you?" I hissed, unable to contain my frustration any longer. "Do you really? Everything? All I am, all I feel? All I want?"

She blinked, blinked again. The tears started and I reached for her, pulled her close, whispered over and over again that I was sorry, that it was OK, that everything would be all right.

April became May, May sailed into June. The world turned. U.S. and Soviet tensions made everyone nervous. In Prague, political rebels risked arrest by the secret police to spray paint John Lennon's name on the city's brick walls. Bobbi and I stood beneath an eclipse we sensed rather than saw, stole every moment we could. Her scent filled my life. She'd come to me, take me deep inside her, hold me close and my heart would beat against her chest.

Then she'd leave. Go back to him.

20

I WAS WORKING AT MY DESK ON THAT FIRST MORNING IN JUNE WHEN THE hall door clicked open and he strolled into my office.

"I say, John, isn't life grand!"

He wore a spotless white linen summer suit, with a light blue shirt and a natty tie, sported a blue silk handkerchief in his breast pocket. His black loafers were precisely the correct conservative touch. No one else could have worn his matching white hat and carried that black wood, gold-handled walking stick without looking like a fool. He struck a pose just inside my door: hip cocked, leaning on his walking stick while he closed his eyes, his head tilted back for a deep, invigorating breath.

"Nothing like a beautiful spring day in Washington! The air is clean, the sun is bright but not too warm. It's even a Friday. Makes me feel marvelous! Like a young colt. A stallion."

"I wasn't expecting you, Emmett."

"Yes, I know." He strolled around the office. The file cabinets, my framed license on the wall next to the pen and ink drawing, the stereo system, the couch, the view from my bay windows: his eyes skimmed over everything before he turned back to face me.

"Such a tidy little shop!" he said.

"Thanks."

His frown and the wave of his hand pooh-poohed my gratitude. He pointed his stick down the hallway leading back to my apartment.

"And that's where you live, isn't it?"

"Yes."

He leaned on his cane, thought a moment before he spoke.

"Kitchen. Bathroom. Probably, what—a storage or sitting room?"

"Storage," I said.

"Jolly good. I imagine you need one. You're the kind of chap who collects a few odds and ends in life."

"I'm not much for souvenirs."

"Really? How fortunate, though sometimes in our adventures we acquire more than we bargain for."

The cane swung up again, pointed back.

"Bedroom?" he asked.

"Of course," I said.

"Of course." He smiled down at me. "Bit cramped, isn't it?"

"It's sufficient."

"Of course it is. For your needs."

He strolled to the front of my desk, selected the chair on the left and gracefully lowered himself. He dropped his white hat on the empty chair. Every hair on his close-cropped head was in place. He draped one leg over the other. Casually, thoughtlessly, he played with his shiny ebony cane while we talked, sometimes holding it crossways in both hands as though he were a majorette in mid-routine, lightly rolling it in his fingers; once or twice he stroked his cheek with the gold L-shaped grip. Sometimes he rubbed the shaft against his shoe or one of his white pant legs. He was the perfect picture of relaxed, thoughtful elegance.

"Why are you here, Emmett?"

"No particular reason," he said. Smiled. "I was in the neighborhood, remembered your address . . ." He shrugged.

"I didn't know you spent much time on the Hill."

"Actually I'm up here quite often. Fund raisers, receptions, that sort of thing. Rendezvous."

"You have friends up here."

"I have friends everywhere, John."

"Lucky guy."

"Yes, I am—although I don't rely on luck. I believe in it, but I never bank on it completely."

"Really."

"I'm a gambler, John, but I'm not a fool. A fool plays whatever game lands in his lap. A fool doesn't know when to cut his losses and get out. A fool takes the wrong chances at the wrong time. A fool mistakes an exciting game for a profitable venture and is always shocked by the bill. And when life deals him a major risk, a fool loses his cool and his courage, makes the wrong play and blames bad luck for his ensuing misfortune."

"And you're no fool."

"No, I'm not. Are you, John?"

My smile was thin and hard. I said nothing.

"Of course you're not," said Emmett. His smile was wide, confident. I reached desperately for ammunition to shoot back at this man who'd ambushed me in my own office, anything to puncture his smug charm, divert him, regain my balance, control.

"You've been around Washington for a long time, haven't you, Emmett?"

"It's become my home."

"Lucky us. We must know a lot of the same people."

"This is a small town."

"Did you ever hang out here on the Hill?"

"I told you, John—I have friends everywhere."

"Yeah, well, I wonder. There used to be a guy like that up here, a guy who knew everybody and who had friends everywhere. Maybe you two knew each other."

"Maybe we did."

"He was a swell guy. Parviz Naderi. You probably called him Pasha."

"The headwaiter at the old Forum."

"Yes."

"Of course I knew him," said Emmett. "A popular chap."

"But somebody killed him."

"Well," he shrugged. "That shows you how dangerous this city is. Crime in the streets. One must be cautious— and smart."

"And lucky."

"Yes, and lucky."

"Were you and Pasha business acquaintances as well as friends?"

Emmett laughed.

"John! What kind of business would I have with a maitre d'?"

"You tell me."

His voice turned cold.

"Our . . . association was more personal than profitable."

"Pasha's name has come up in a case," I said. My blind shot had hit flesh, but suddenly I wasn't sure who was wounded or who might be in my line of fire: this man or the woman I was trying to protect. "I'm not sure what business he was really in."

"As far as I know, the restaurant business."

"But I've heard a lot of stories."

"There are rumors about everyone, John. Even you."

"Heard any good ones lately?" I asked.

"Why no," he said. "Should I have?"

Neither of us spoke for a moment.

"If I hear anything you should know," I told him, "I'll be sure to call."

We stared at each other, and I knew I was through. For now.

"I hope my asking about him didn't trouble you," I said.

"You're no trouble for me, John." Cold steel ran through his words. "Ever."

Then he was his charming self again.

"Such a lovely day! Pity we're inside like this. I hope Barbi is enjoying herself. She's at another one of those boring Club luncheons this morning, you know."

"No, I didn't know."

"Of course not! Why should you? It was just a figure of speech.

"Do you have plans for the weekend, John?"

"Not really."

"Shame. Should be lovely. Barbi and I will spend it together. Just the two of us. Except, of course, if she goes riding in the morning on our new horse.

"You know," he said, his voice sly and sweet, "riding can be such an exciting diversion for a woman. Stimulating. You should see her when she comes back to the house after a jaunt! She's so vibrant! So alive! So . . . eager and excited!"

I said nothing.

"She's so beautiful. So . . . spirited. Giving. Generous. I'm such a lucky husband. To have her, to be married to her, to enjoy all those . . . rights and privileges."

I didn't speak.

"I must confess," he said, friend to friend, man to man,

"I've been neglectful of my duties to Barbi—so much business to attend to, so many . . . pitiful, small problems to deal with. You know what I think, John, old man?"

"No, Emmett, I don't know what you think."

"I think that I'll devote this weekend to her. To Barbi. To making up for all the neglect I've shown her lately. In fact, I'll start tonight! Maybe this afternoon. I've got the time, all the time in the world. Tomorrow, tomorrow night. All day Sunday. Sunday night. And next week, too. The week after. As much as I can. As often as we can. Doesn't that sound marvelous?"

I said nothing.

"Well," he said, reaching down, picking up his hat, putting it on as he stood, "I mustn't keep you from your work—or waste any time dawdling with you. By the time I get home, Barbi should be there. What a surprise for her!

"I hope you have a nice weekend," he said before he sauntered out the door. "I'll be thinking of you. And I'll be sure to tell Barbi about our little chat. She'll be so pleased."

He rattled my doorknob.

"You know you really should be more careful, John. I walked right in! You're so easy! A man in your kind of life can't afford to be that easy.

"Good-bye, old chap. I'll be seeing you soon—though I'm afraid I can't say when. Barbi and I are going to be rather busy. Don't bother looking for me, I'll be there." He rattled the knob again. "You'll never know when or where I'll pop up!"

Then he left.

Summer rolled into town that Wednesday, brought temperatures in the nineties. The afternoon was humid, sticky. My air conditioner hummed for the first time that season. Cool air fell on us from the ceiling vent above the bed.

189

The blue sheet over our flesh absorbed sweat we'd earned the hour before.

"But what did he want?" asked Bobbi, though we'd already talked about his visit. "Did he expect to find me here, or . . ."

"He knew where you were."

"He wanted to rattle your cage," she said, corrected herself. *"Our* cage."

"Probably."

"Then he knows," she said.

"Of course he does—or at least he believes," I said. Something in her tone bothered me. "You sound relieved."

She shrugged. I felt her tense up, try to control it.

"No, I . . . Well, at least now we don't have to worry about *if* he finds out."

"You sound funny," I told her, frowned.

"Really?" she said, suddenly too calm, too matter-of-fact. "How?"

"I don't know, like . . . like maybe you weren't worried about him finding out."

"Of course I was. Why wouldn't I be?"

"You got me," I told her.

"You're just hearing things that aren't there," she said. I let it go but didn't believe her.

"What will he do?" I asked instead.

"Let it play out—*assume* it will play out. Figure out a way to jerk our chains if he gets bored or angry."

"Bobbi, we can . . ."

"No!" She put her hand over my mouth, pressed her cheek hard against my chest. "I know a thousand things you want to say, a hundred suggestions you have, but . . . not now. Not today. Please!"

"When?"

"I don't know, but please, *please,* John: not today."

I didn't reply.

"What did you talk about again?" she asked.

"I told you," I said, repeating my lies of omission. "A lot of nothing. The weather. My office. His . . . His *plans.*"

Her hands squeezed my shoulders.

"How . . . how was he . . . afterwards?" I didn't want to know, couldn't stop from asking.

She whispered, shuddered. "Like Emmett. Just like Emmett. That night over dinner he casually mentioned your name, that he'd 'dropped by' to see you. His damn smile dared me to say anything, ask anything. Do anything."

We pulled each other closer. A minute, maybe two, then she kissed my chest, raised her head and smiled at me.

"If you could be anybody else, anything else besides who and what you are, what would it be?" she asked.

"What?"

"Come on—dream a little, who . . ."

"I dream a lot."

She kissed me again—hard, to forestall any answer she hadn't wanted.

"Not that," she said, "not that stuff." Smiled. "Other things. Fantasies."

"From a down-to-earth guy like me?"

She laughed.

"Johnny, you've never been down to earth!"

"You're wrong."

"Maybe so," she said. "Probably not. Come on: who would you be?"

"A rock 'n' roll star," I said, and she laughed again, her nipples brushing my chest.

"Not just any star," I told her. "Not just famous or rich or popular, I don't want that. I'd want to be somebody who was worth something, whose songs were worth more than just dollars and sound on the radio. Somebody like

Springsteen or Dylan, Lennon—hell, even Mick Jagger. They're our poets. I'd want to write my own stuff, sing it my way. Rip through this world with my guitar. Never stop. Be so truly good, be . . ." I shrugged. "Like Springsteen."

"I like you just as you are," she said, kissed me softly, sweetly.

"How about you?"

"What about me?" she asked: still playful, but cautious.

"You've already got a dream name. Who do you dream about 'Bobbi' being? What would you want to be?"

"Safe," she said, her answer escaping before she could stop it. She tucked her head into the crook of my neck, her face flushed.

"Bobbi . . ."

"We don't need dreams," she said, her words muffled.

"Of course we do."

"Really?" she said. She pulled away from me, sat up in the bed, pulling the sheet with her. She clutched its blue cloth over her body as she stared down at me.

"Let me tell you about *real* life, Johnny. Those romantic *dreams* running around inside your head count for nothing. In real life you take what you're given and try to survive. That's the deal. That's it, that's all there is."

"You sound like your father, whining through the bourbon bottle."

"Maybe he wasn't such a fool after all."

"He died a drunk."

"But he lived well."

"Bullshit. All he did was wallow in self-pity. He couldn't have done that if he hadn't had a world of crutches like you and your mother, some friends, all that *society* and all those myths to lean on. He couldn't enjoy the love you gave him. He couldn't give any love either, not even to himself. He survived in spite of himself. If he'd have

192

had more guts, he'd have ended it all a lot sooner. But he didn't, so he sat in his goddamned swing and waited until he drowned.

"You think you're so tough, Bobbi. So practical. So real. And I'm a romantic fool. Well, look where I am, look where you are. Tell me who's better off."

"We're together."

"Yes, because we *choose* to be. That's what life is: choices, fighting to make a chain of hard bargains. That may not be fair—you can't choose anything your heart desires or your mind can imagine, you can't predict everything your choices will mean, you might fail when you try what you choose, you might do the right thing only to have the world dump all over you—but at least you've got a shot, especially if you're born healthy and not too poor and in someplace like America."

"But . . ."

"No buts!" I snapped. "No buts. You get choices. And responsibilities. Most people don't recognize all that they have of either: they're too blind to see. More 'n likely, they don't want to see, want to pretend they're 'free' from needing to choose, from the consequences of choosing. But the choices are there, the bargains are always struck. Nothing else is certain, not even the ground under our feet, but there are choices and consequences. They shape our lives.

"That's where dreams come in. They guide you through the choices you must make. That's why you better dream the big dream, the best one. You gotta be gutsy, keep it right and true and honest, not cheat it to make life sweeter or easier, not settle for something less. You better want the bargain you make. Better not deal in bullshit. Better not sell yourself a fraud—and better hope you never get tricked into buying one. Do any of that, you can get lost in your own life. Dream small or wrong, and even if you win your dream, you lose. Maybe there's some justice in that, I don't know. Don't look for much mercy. What I do know is that whatever happens, you always pay the price."

"Don't lecture me about *the price*," she said, cold and mean. "I've been paying . . ."

"For *what?*" I said. "You're paying with your *life* and getting back *what?* What in the hell did you choose? What was your bargain and what did it get you? Why . . ."

"Stop it!" She jerked her head to one side, squeezed her eyes shut.

"How can you judge me?" she whispered. "How can you . . . You don't even know, you don't . . ."

"Bobbi!" I reached out to touch her face, but she jerked away. "Bobbi, I'm . . . I'm not condemning you, or . . . I don't know, but that's not my fault. Damn it! I've done everything I could to know, but you won't let me, won't tell me!"

"I can't," she sobbed. "I can't."

"Oh bullshit!" I yelled, sitting up in bed, unable to contain my anger any longer, not knowing that anger would turn the first key.

"Don't you . . ."

"Don't what?" I said as I saw anger fill her too. "Don't call you on your little game, don't . . ."

"This is no *game!*" she hissed. She coiled herself into a tight ball, her back up against the wall.

"Then what would you call it? You play-act your Cora McGregor routine so I won't know who you are, run your theater on me and lie and disguise your past with your sleazy good friend Naderi. . . ."

"He was no friend of mine!" she snapped, shooting from the hip at every target I gave her. "I only met that greasy son of a bitch two or three . . ."

She stopped, but it was too late.

"You only . . . Bobbi, what the hell are you saying?"

Her face first froze over, then paled, and the tears returned.

"If you only met him *two or three* . . . Then what the hell was he to you? Why the hell do you care if he lived or died, let alone whether the police . . ."

"We agreed no questions." She wouldn't look at me.

"No we didn't," I told her, my mind racing. "Not for forever, not for now, not after you've told me . . ."

"I've told you nothing!"

"Bullshit," I said again, only softer. She hugged her knees to her forehead, hid her face from me.

"Talk to me, Bobbi!" I urged. "Please! You've got to tell me. . . . Don't you realize all the things I've wondered about? Imagined? Who you were, what you did, how Naderi and you, whether or not you . . . Can't you guess . . ."

"You and your damn imagination! Your questions! Can't you just leave it alone, take . . ."

"No I can't! You're too important, this is too . . ."

"Please stop!" she moaned, slid down the bed until she lay curled in a ball on the pillows.

"Talk to me, Bobbi!"

"Talking won't do any good."

"Nothing will do any good if I don't know the truth. That's all I want, Bobbi: let me know the truth!"

"The truth doesn't change a thing." She raised her head, pressed it flat against a pillow; opened her eyes but wouldn't look at me. "Besides, you don't just want the truth."

"If we don't start there, how can I know what I want? What I can have? What we can do?"

"Trust me," she said, then tucked her head back down into a fetal ball. Her words were empty of all emotion save desperation. "Just trust me."

"That's a two-way street," I said.

"Please," she said, "please, just . . . just let me . . . I'll . . . Please, not now. Not *now!*"

Maybe I should have pushed her more then, but she hovered at the edge of a blackness she'd fall into with the slightest wrong touch, a blackness that would swallow her up forever.

"OK," I said. "It's OK."

Slowly, carefully, I moved beside her, unbent her limbs one by one, stretched her straight on my blue sheet, then laid down alongside her; slowly, gently enfolded her in my arms and held her close.

"OK," I said again, felt her tremble, sigh with relief. "OK. Not now."

She shifted, held me back. The sheet tangled round her. She lay curled against my chest. When she spoke, her voice was flat, hard, bottomed out.

"All my life I've done what I had to," she said. "I got what I've got. You're the best thing that's happened to me since . . . since I was born, since my mother. I didn't choose for either of you to come into my life, but I couldn't . . . I don't want to lose you, lose this. I know that's not fair to you and I'm sorry, but I can't help what I want and what I've got. Please—*please* stay with me! Don't . . . ."

"I'm here, Bobbi!" I whispered. "I'm here. I'm not going anywhere."

She raised her head, her hands cupped my face and she kissed me: lightly at first, tenderly, then deeply, deeper and longer, with a frenzy. She kissed my lips, my cheeks, my forehead and eyes, my neck. She rose up on her knees, untangled herself from the sheet and flipped it to the bottom of the bed. My left hand stroked her thigh, her stomach, my fingertips gently reached out and pressed against her pink nipple, felt it stiffen as she moaned and I cupped her whole breast in my hand. She shook her head, her auburn hair swirling, floating, her face turned up as she licked her lips, moaned again. She took me in her hand, held me, held me; bent and kissed my lips, my neck, my chest. She kissed my stomach and my fingers tangled themselves in her hair as she kissed me and moved down my body. Her lips encircled me, her tongue caressed me and I called out her name.

"Inside me!" she cried. "I want you inside me!"

She rolled on her back, never letting go; pulled me on top of her and gripped me with her thighs as she guided me into her. We rocked together. She bent her knees, then straightened her legs into the air. Her arms went around me as I held her and she grabbed her thighs, pulled her legs higher, wider, her hips arching and bucking up to match my thrusts. I remember the sounds of our flesh smacking together as time and place became lost in our rhythm.

21

JUST AN ORDINARY TUESDAY NIGHT.

WASHINGTON SWELTERED BENEATH a six-day heat wave while the Pentagon rejoiced in its latest missile and the Iran-Iraq war escalated another notch. That week I'd finished routine witness location cases for two law firms, spent the rest of my time researching a patent infringement case and working up Freedom of Information requests to federal agencies for Art Dillon's toxic poisoning suit. In the almost two weeks since Emmett's surprise visit I'd devoted no more than a few phone calls to mover-and-shaker sources about the life and times of Parviz Naderi. I'd surpassed my contract with Murray the trucker, but still hadn't billed him—nor had he called for a progress report. Bobbi met me that Sunday for coffee at a suburban chain restaurant full of post-church breakfasting families. We held hands, spoke little. She had to go. Monday afternoon we made love without much laughter. She left, promised she could see me again maybe Thursday. There were so many things we didn't say, so many questions we didn't ask. That ordinary Tuesday night my apartment was oppressively empty, so I drove across town to see an early movie in a once grand cinema palace that had been chopped up into five separate theaters: one decent-

sized auditorium and four screening rooms slightly bigger
and far less comfortable than the average American living
room.

I can't remember what movie I saw; I only went to fill
up my hours, override the facts of my life with the fictions
flickering on the screen in that cool, anonymous darkness.
The audience was small. I was the last one to leave the
theater. There was no one on duty at the door, and strangely
enough, no cashier sat inside the glass ticket booth. The
sun had long since set. I stood alone under the huge marquee out front, the smell of popcorn drifting out into the
humid night and mingling with the sweet grass scents of
summer. The white glow from hundreds of marquee bulbs
showed the digits on my watch at 9:52 and counting, suf-
ficiently late for me to drive home, go to bed, another
evening killed.

A car whizzed by over the sticky pavement: red-dotted
taillights and throbbing engine disappeared around the
road's curve as I walked the four blocks to where I'd parked
the Porsche. This was a residential neighborhood, with a
narrow grass boulevard dividing the wide main street,
houses with lawns set back from the sidewalk. Half these
homes were dark, perhaps because children lived there and
children should be home safe in bed at an early hour, even
in the summer. A few of the homes had porch lights, but
only a few; their dim glow added little to the faint cones
of luminescence falling from tall streetlights at each corner
of the long blocks. A dog barked somewhere off to my
right, a metal garbage can clattered to the pavement in an
unseen alley, rolled a few feet, was still. A television bab-
bled from one of the houses. Parked cars lined both sides
of the street: I'd glance in each one as I neared it, find
nothing in the glass but the dark shapes and diamond flick-
ers of reflected night. My footsteps were cautious, as quiet
as I could make them, yet they echoed off the concrete,

sounds lost in the trees to each side. The crickets in the lawns to my right fell silent as I passed them, started their song again when I was safely out of range.

The silver Porsche was solid and secure, with no one hiding in the cramped backseat. Another car whizzed by me as I unlocked my door, some woman with long hair behind the wheel of a snazzy late model Mustang. Her brake lights glowed before she took the curve, then she vanished into her future and my past. For a fleeting moment I tried to imagine what life with her would be like. Was she beautiful and smart, did she laugh, was she free, alone in her life and able to take the chance with me? Where had she been in 1967, and where was she going in 1984? I told myself she'd glanced into her rearview mirror as she drove by, seen me standing there. I wondered if she'd thought of me too, imagined something—*anything*— or was I merely another face she hadn't consciously noticed in the crowd of strangers cast as the backdrop of her life.

The Porsche's rear engine growled to life, the tachometer needle jumping to 4,000 rpms, then settling down beneath 2,000 for a low, strong idle. My oil gauges were fine, I had half a tank of fuel. The speedometer needle pointed to the zero on the far left of its three-quarter circle dial; I'd never pushed it much more than halfway to its 150 mph end point. I'd automatically rolled my window down before starting the engine, a habit which (theoretically) would have served me in good stead if someone had planted half a pound of plastique under my seat and wired the bomb into my ignition. I kept the window down, turned on the air conditioner. The idle jumped to 2,100 as the engine labored to cool the car's interior. I waited for the hot air to blow out my window, turned on the radio.

The progressive rock FM station I loved had too weak a signal to reach this part of the city, so I pushed the 'station signal search' button, ordered my reception past the soft pop, classical, disco and crazed DJ top forty stations until I locked onto an oldy-goldy outfit and heard the announcer say, ". . . sure you will recognize this as one of the Beach Boys' biggest hits." He was right: those familiar lyrics keyed memories of eternities in my parents' dirty white, '64 Chevy sedan, cruising the streets of my hometown where life seemed bleak and dreams of ever driving a vibrant city's streets in any kind of cool machine felt more impossible than flight and far less likely than the steamy jungles of Vietnam. I rolled up my window, turned on the headlights, put the Porsche in first gear. My side mirror showed an empty road behind me; nothing but rows of parked cars lined both sides of the street before my windshield. I cramped the wheel, engaged the clutch and rolled off into just an ordinary Tuesday night.

The grass boulevard dividing the street had a turnaround slot about 20 yards beyond my parking place. I nosed the Porsche into that gap, slowed and looked both ways before wheeling the car back the direction from which I'd come. As I straightened the wheel after the turn I saw a pair of headlights wink on in my rearview mirror. Someone who'd been parked down the street and on the opposite side from me decided it was time to move too. I hadn't noticed anyone enter a car down there. *Must not have been paying attention,* I thought. The headlights pulled out behind me, twin yellow snake eyes riding low to the ground, hanging back behind me a block, block and a half—no doubt for safety's sake, or perhaps to let me set the pace and pick up the speeding ticket. The chain link fence surrounding D.C.'s huge water reservoir drifted by our right side; darkness cloaked that lake. The other car and I rolled through the blue black night, an accidental parade headed toward the heart of the city.

My mind was paying attention to the music and my memories, not my driving, so when the road split, instead of taking the proper fork to the right which would have dropped me down into Georgetown and from there home to the Hill, I went straight, realizing my error in time to curse, flick my eyes up to the mirror to see if I'd also run the traffic light. I watched it turn red just as the snake-eyed headlights passed beneath it.

Cutting it close, Mister, I thought. *Lucky for you there's not a cop around.*

The error put me in an unfamiliar residential neighborhood, a middle-class warren of one-way streets and dead-end drives. I knew the direction I wanted to go, but I wasn't sure how to get there, which streets led to one of the main traffic arteries. Those snake-eyed headlights glowed in my mirror: one of the neighbors, headed home. No doubt he knew exactly where he was going and what he was doing.

You should be leading me, I told him in my mind.

He sent me no reply.

"Satisfaction" by the Rolling Stones came out of the radio and I turned the volume up, felt my energy surge to their rhythm. The Porsche seemed to flow with the music. After four years under my hands this car that had cost blood of both the innocent and the guilty drove as if we were one. The Stones sang about the man on the radio and I remembered the *Post*'s surprisingly negative review of Springsteen's just released album, a record whose songs seemed deeper each time I played it again. The Stones were driving around the world when I took a left, headed down another dark street to where I thought there might be an intersection with a major thoroughfare. Five seconds later I glanced in my rearview mirror—and saw those same yellow snake-eyed headlights.

Gotta be a coincidence, I told myself. But my stomach turned cold.

No need for paranoia, I insisted to my instincts. My headlights showed the entrance to an alley leading off to the left. I downshifted to second (without touching the brake pedal and flashing its warning light), waited until the last moment, then cut the wheel hard, hit the gas and scooted down the alley, my eyes flicking from the narrow path before me to my mirrors.

Those headlights swamped me with their yellow glow before I was halfway through the alley.

"Shit!"

The tach and speedometer needles jumped as I pushed the gas pedal down. The mouth of the alley raced toward me, faster, closer. The yellow lights behind me didn't fade. 20, 30, 40 miles an hour. We shot out of the alley, flew across a narrow street and down the opposite alley. I flicked my headlights to high beam; so did he—not that he needed to: he was close enough (God he was close enough!) to use my light. The glare behind me bounced off my mirrors, stung my eyes. When I'd look back, all I could see was a fireball burning up my shadow.

My headlights cut the world into a narrow tunnel of eerie light, a pale yellow river rushing toward me with sickening speed. 50 miles per hour. Images flicked by me: huge green rubber garbage cans on wheels parked against tan wood fences, swollen black trash bags waiting by backyard hedges, the rear end of a car sticking out from an open garage. Tree branches drooped down into my headlights' beam. The alley floor was a half-paved, half-brick roadway covered with diamonds of broken glass that glistened in the electric glow. Chuckholes slammed into my tires. I missed the unbroken beer bottle, crushed a fallen tree branch beneath my tires. A cat leaped back into the shadows before my wheels got him.

The DJ on the radio prattled a commercial in soothing tones. My hand jumped off the wheel, flicked the knob and turned him off: the noise jangled my concentration. We shot out of that block, crossed another regular street and roared down another alley. I risked one-handed driving again, killed the air conditioner: full power to the engine. My shirt clung to my back, and beads of sweat dotted my forehead. The leather-padded steering wheel grew slick inside my grip.

The parked car loomed at the far end of the tunnel, a blockade of steel and glass waiting for our crash. For a moment I panicked, then realized the car was parked opposite the mouth of the alley: the exit was clear. I had to hit the brakes, warn my pursuer with the flash of red light as I downshifted, rode the brake pedal hard and wrestled the wheel to keep the car straight: 50, 40, I stopped looking at the speedometer, glued my eyes to the edge of the alley—coming, coming . . .

There! I shot out of that tunnel, cramped the steering wheel, skidded sideways into a full 90 left-hand turn. The tires screamed and my rear end spun around, slid to within an inch of the parked car before the rubber held. I jammed my foot down on the accelerator. The Porsche surged forward, roared down a wide, well-lit street. A red stop sign rose from the corner. I pushed the gas pedal lower. I flew through the intersection, crossed what seemed to be a major thoroughfare, heard a car horn honk off to my left but made it safely to another block.

And found those glaring, snake-eyed headlights still locked on me.

The hunter had all the advantages. He needed only to react, not decide. I would hit all the obstacles first. I was disoriented, only vaguely aware of where I was, fleeing blindly with no sanctuary expected or in mind. He knew precisely where he was: on my trail. Close on my trail.

Who was he? Didn't matter. He was the hunter. Victor Landell, the fish-faced lawyer with his army of sophisticated soldiers? The guys who'd shadowed Nick? I remembered the Washington fixer who'd known Naderi and died in a car wreck. The hunter could be anybody. If I was lucky, he was alone, forced to devote as much attention to driving the chase as I was. If I was unlucky, some gunman sat patiently in the passenger seat, a professional waiting only the proper moment to use his silenced pistol or, worse, his sleek hand-held Uzi machine-gun, his sawed-off shotgun. Maybe they wouldn't opt for gunplay, maybe instead I'd be a car accident too: lose control of the Porsche with or without their help. There are so many ways to die.

That major intersection must have been Massachusetts Avenue—the neighborhood looked right. I skidded through a right-hand turn, circled back, too intent on making it round the corner to scan my pursuer, identify his car. He made the turn too. His brights still blinded me in the mirrors. Five blocks passed in almost as few seconds. A major road cut cross my path. Again I ignored the stop sign, skidded through a left-hand turn.

It was Mass Ave.: upper Mass Ave., just below American University. I knew where I was, where I wanted to go. I wanted my turf. Live or die, I wanted this fight on my home ground. At least there I might find a chance. Those headlights loomed behind me, locked on me again.

"Come on!" I yelled above my roaring engine as I hit third gear and ran the yellow light at Wisconsin Avenue. "Come on you son of a bitch!"

Those headlights flew beneath the red light, fast on my trail.

Time shifted into a new tenor, a new texture: the world flew past me with our furious pace, but I lived in slow motion, an intense, disassociated effect in which I was aware of so much in excruciating detail. I was adrift, floating in a river of madness and mayhem, fully cognizant of a million terrible possibilities, processing an endless flow of data, functioning automatically, unable to feel more than intellectual resignation and a furious compulsion to perform. Fear, anger, hundreds of emotions crackled outside my flesh, surrounding me like a tingling electric aurora I sensed but did not heed.

That four-lane, downhill mile of Massachusetts Avenue is called Embassy Row. Hunter and hunted, we shot past centers of diplomacy.

A guard at the gate leading to the vice president's mansion swiveled his head as we roared by; I could only hope he'd report two lunatics racing toward downtown.

A battered, red-bodied, Plymouth sedan with a white vinyl top chugged placidly toward its destination ahead of me in the road's right lane, while a white van filled the left lane no more than three car lengths ahead of the passenger car. My headlights suddenly engulfed the Plymouth, turning its inside from night into day; its startled occupants whirled, looked back toward my specter. The driver was a pretty woman with dark curly hair; a cute, curly-haired blond girl of about 12 sat in the front passenger seat. No more than six feet separated my front bumper from their trunk when I whipped the Porsche into the left lane, shot past them as their brake lights glowed, then cut back into the right lane through the gap between the Plymouth and van.

As I roared past the British Embassy's statue of a cigar-chomping Winston Churchill, leaning on his cane and raising his hand in the V for Victory salute, my mirror showed that snake-eyed hunter shoot the Plymouth—white van gap too.

The Metrobus blocked the right lane, a yellow Toyota filled the left. As we reached the mammoth, futuristic black glass and steel box Embassy of Brazil I whipped the Porsche over the double-striped yellow center lane. Two sets of headlights rushed up the hill toward me. A horn blared and I floorboarded the Porsche, shot back into the far right-hand lane, fighting the fishtail, nausea. I roared across the bridge above Rock Creek Parkway.

Those snake-eyed headlights glistened in my mirrors again.

There are nature tours of Rock Creek Parkway in the fall when October's golds and reds color the forest of trees along that scenic route that winds through the city, separates Georgetown from downtown and leads commuters to and from the better northwestern and Maryland neighborhoods. There's a bike path that parallels the road, takes joggers, strollers and cyclists to the zoo, past a series of exercise stations where chin-up bars and balance beams await the energetic. There's a cemetery in the trees. Only the foolish or the deadly inhabit the park at night. In the morning the Parkway is one-way traffic headed into the city, in the evening it's one way headed out. During the day and at night, two lines lead each direction.

The night made all colors shadows as I downshifted, turned the Porsche onto the curving Parkway entrance road. The yield sign blew past me in a wink as my tires spun onto the thoroughfare. Traffic was light: car lights shone in one lane or the other every 50 feet or so. I wove in and out of them like a needle sewing a pattern between electric buoys.

Behind me, like a tail of thread, came those yellow snake eyes.

Past the Watergate complex, past the Kennedy Center, the ivory dome of the Jefferson Memorial glowing off to my right. The Parkway ended with a choice: through town or freeway. I chose the city, bright lights and the chance that a cruising cop car would chase the speeders, save the hunted.

But I had no such luck. Fluorescent crime lights bathed Independence Avenue with a surreal glow. I'd gained a block, maybe two on my pursuer. We roared through a city ablaze with eerie artificial luminescence, but the distance that protected me from him was also too great for me to see more of him than those hungry headlights.

Past the Department of Argiculture, past the Air and Space Museum, the Hirshhorn sculpture museum, weaving in and out and around law-abiding cars we raced toward the base of Capitol Hill.

If he knew me, knew his prey well, he'd know I was headed home. What did he think I'd do there—*What would I do there?*

The Botanical Gardens slid by on our left; the Capitol dome, floodlights shining on its white marble, waited at the top of the Hill.

I desperately tried to formulate a plan. Maybe I should cut left at the Library of Congress, blare my horn the whole half mile to the Capitol Hill police headquarters and hope that would summon armed guardians of the law to surround me before my hunter rolled up my backside.

Maybe I could bail out in front of The Eclectic, desert the Porsche where it stopped in Pennsylvania Avenue, have time to race to the side door, unlock it and run up the stairs before the hunters got there. If I made it inside my office, I had a chance, a big chance the hunters probably didn't know: in the middle drawer of my desk, hidden under old files of canceled checks, lay a .357 Magnum revolver, no doubt dusty, and no doubt as deadly and serviceable as it had been when I fired it on a range six months earlier. If all was as it should be, six live cartridges waited in its cylinder.

If all was as it should be.

Where are the police? I thought as I topped Capitol Hill. Independence changed to Pennsylvania Avenue, a major boulevard with cherry trees planted in the wide grass-covered median strip. Six blocks from home. As I passed the new Library of Congress building I saw those headlights roll over the Hill's crest behind me. I kept my eyes on the mirror for a second longer than I should have, saw the car was black and sleek and . . . and then sensed danger dead ahead, looked in time to swerve around a line of cars double parked in front of the Hill's late-night convenience grocery store.

Brakes squealed as some innocent citizen driving with the light on Fourth Street narrowly missed broadsiding me. I glanced back, saw the headlights just beginning to swerve around him. Another car loomed ahead of me, forced me to slow.

White light exploded all around me. My vision burned, blurred as the hunter roared to within inches of my rear bumper, flicked on his brights.

Sixth Street is a one-way thoroughfare cutting from right to left across Pennsylvania. My refuge in The Eclectic building was at the next corner. A small turnout lane cuts through the median strip from Pennsylvania to Sixth Street, a lane engineered to ease the angle for a left-hand turn. I didn't brake, didn't even downshift as I whipped the Porsche into that turnout lane, tires crying, inertia sucking me to the right in my car seat and why hadn't I fastened my seat belt when I started?

My move was too quick for my pursuer, who shot straight past the turnaround, roared down Pennsylvania Avenue. I had a vague impression of brake lights flashing on his car as I fought to regain control of the Porsche. My silver car careened across Sixth Street, down C toward the dead end of a deserted tennis court. I rode the brake, fought the steering wheel and somehow kept the car in the middle of the road without bouncing off the parked vehicles to each side on this quiet, residential street.

A 1972 Ford station wagon surged out of the blind alley between the concrete blockhouse municipal swimming pool and the old red barn of the Eastern Market. By the time it smashed me I was traveling a legal ten mph. The exhausted carpenter who'd been renovating a row house was too tired to anticipate a silver bullet sliding in front of him seemingly from out of nowhere. His front bumper smashed into the Porsche just above the left rear wheel well, crumpled the rear quadrant, skidded the car sideways with such force a suspension arm snapped in the rear axle. My hands flew off the steering wheel and I bounced against the car door. The engine died.

I staggered out of the Porsche, my eyes frantically searching the darkness for headlights. I saw someone emerge on their front porch, drawn into the night by the collision of metal against metal.

"Hey, gee, buddy, are you all right?" called the workman as he hurried from his car. "I'm sure sorry, it was all my fault, I . . ."

"Get down!" I called to him, my arms outstretched and waving him back.

"What?" He was 50, maybe 55, worried and scared, concerned for this craziness he saw but couldn't comprehend. "You OK? You got a bump on your head?"

"Get *down!*" I yelled again. If he hadn't nervously stepped back toward his car my waving arms would have pushed him.

"Hey, Mary!" By the glow of a porch light a man called back into his house. "There's been an accident! Call the police!"

"Call the police!" I shouted, my echo far more urgent than that stranger's command.

"It's OK, buddy, it's OK!" soothed the workman. He reached hesitantly toward me. "Here, why don't we walk over here and sit down. Are you . . ."

"You don't understand!" I shouted.

"Sure I do," he said, "sure I do."

"You've got to . . ." I started to say.

Then from behind me, from Seventh Street, which bordered the dead end made by the empty tennis court, came the sound of tires slowly rolling over pavement. I saw headlights swinging toward us on the gray cinder block swimming pool. That light cast our shadows against the wall, then bore straight at us as I turned, faced those yellow snake eyes ready to run, to dive, to die.

That car crept toward me. I shuffled forward a few steps, put distance between myself and that innocent workman. Long and black and low, the car turned right so it was broadside to me in the street, blocking my advance as surely as the wreckage of the Porsche and the station wagon blocked my retreat.

The driver's window slid down with a low electric hum. The dark shape inside moved, and suddenly there was that pale face, a death's head leering out at me with taut skin, high cheekbones and forehead, hair so flat as not to be there at all, a skull with a wide, ivory grin.

"Hello old chap," Sloan hissed. "Seems like you're in a spot of trouble. I warned you, didn't I? Told you these streets weren't safe, warned you to watch what you did and where you were going. All kinds of . . . accidents happen to all kinds of chaps when they don't mind what they're doing. When they get in the way. When they're not where they belong."

His eyes flickered deep inside those sockets, took in the baffled workman standing behind me, the couple waiting and watching on the porch.

"Looks like there's nothing I can do here," he said. His smile widened, "Not tonight. You're a very lucky chap. You get to walk away. From this one. But remember what I said: you're living in a rough town. Watch what you're doing, where you're going. I wouldn't want anything . . . bad to happen to you."

Then he laughed. The electric window hummed closed

as he backed his black Mercedes convertible around, rolled away toward Seventh Street, took a right and was gone.

A police siren wailed in the distance, grew closer.

"Hey buddy!" the workman said, stepped close behind me. "Hey buddy, are you OK?"

The whirling red light on the police car drew nearer behind us. They turned off the siren as they stopped the car, but left the spinning light on. We stood there, the pulsating crimson flashing on us through the darkness.

"Hey buddy," said the workman one more time, "are you OK?"

22

I'LL SEE IF MR. SLOAN IS IN," SAID THE PRETTY SECRETARY IN THE FANCY reception room.

"He's in," I told her.

She smiled nervously at me, slid from behind her desk and disappeared behind the door leading to an inner office.

"Please go right in, Mr. Rankin," she said when she returned.

He was leaning back in his executive's chair, a pile of letters neatly stacked before him on the huge oak desk. His gray suit was conservative but cut with a flair accented by his blue shirt and striped tie.

"Well, old man, I certainly didn't expect to see you first thing this morning!"

"I bet you didn't."

"That's a nasty bump you've got on your forehead."

"Could have been worse."

"Yes, it could have. That was quite an accident you had last night."

"What accident?"

Emmett laughed. "Don't tell me you've got amnesia!"

"Let's just say my vision of events needs clarification."

213

I eased myself into one of the padded leather chairs in front of his desk. "I want to hear your story."

"There's not much to tell," he said. Smiled.

"Oh, I doubt that."

"Don't be so certain, John. Overconfidence gets people into trouble."

"Other people, right? But not you."

He shrugged. "I'm not in any trouble, John. I never have been."

"I forgot. You're J. Emmett Sloan, model citizen." I swept my hand toward the framed documents and photographs that covered his walls. "You've got the credentials to prove it."

"We all do what we can."

"What did you do last night, Emmett?"

"You mean besides coming across your misfortune?"

"And chasing me across town."

"Chasing you across town? John, I have no idea what you're talking about. I went out for a drive last night. I go out driving almost every night—it's a hobby of mine. But *chasing* you? Never."

He laughed. "What makes you think I'd want to catch you?

"Of course, I saw you—driving rather irresponsibly, I might add, tearing up Independence Avenue. . . ."

"You locked onto me earlier than that. You were waiting for me when I came back to my car."

"Was I? Does anybody else besides you remember that, old chap? Say some reliable citizen who saw me *quite coincidentally* cruise past your parked car, decide to park down the road a piece and wait to see when you'd turn up, where you'd been and where you were going. Maybe just haunt you a trifle, like you've been doing me. Maybe do something more."

"Something more like what?"

"Well, if that was what happened, the something more was being too far behind you to witness your accident—although I did find you again, make sure that you were all right."

"Oh, *that's* what you did."

"Just the last part, John, the helping you. I can even prove it—if for some strange reason I'd need to. And that is precisely all you can prove too.

"Actually," he said, "I should be interrogating you."

"About what, Emmett?"

"You have been haunting *me*, old chap." He shook his head, smiled. "I didn't realize that until a few days ago. A friend told me you've been asking questions around town, questions about me and poor dead Pasha. Some vague case you're supposedly working on."

Emmett smiled, leaned across his desk.

"Really, old chap, all this time I thought ours was a . . . *personal* relationship.

"But now it seems you're trying to involve me in your sordid profession." He settled back in his chair. "And that I would strongly advise against—friend to friend, of course."

"What do you do here, Emmett?" The nod of my head took in his office. "What's this all about?"

"You know what I do, John. I'm a businessman. A manager. An entrepreneur, if you will."

"Where did you get the money?"

"Not that it's any of your business, but much of it was mine. Of course, when I first started out, I relied heavily on my clients for investment capital, but now the pot contains mostly my own funds. I've done rather well."

"So I hear. How much money did you and Pasha make together?"

"What makes you think we did any business together? I told you, I knew him personally."

"What business did you two have?"

"*My* business is just that, John. Mine. I have no need to tell you or anyone about it. I'm a private citizen—though perhaps not for much longer."

The bump on my forehead ached when my brow furrowed.

"Don't look so surprised," Emmett told me. "It's no secret that the life of public service has always attracted me."

"Hah!"

"Don't laugh at me!" The hiss I'd heard before cut through his charm. "Don't you ever laugh at me!

"Someday—someday very soon—I'm going to be somebody, Rankin. Somebody very important, somebody everybody knows, somebody with respect and a reputation."

"*Reputation?*" I hissed. "What the hell is that?"

"It's everything! Your reputation is what you're worth—but you wouldn't understand that, Rankin."

"I know about names, Emmett. You make your own, no matter what you call it or other people think."

"That's what I said."

"No it isn't," I told him. "But never mind, that doesn't matter. I'm curious, though. What will you do with . . . your reputation? What will it get you? What will it make you in the real world?"

Emmett smiled. "Who can say?"

"But you've got some ideas," I told him.

"Of course," he said. "More than ideas. I have a plan.

"It's all woven together," he said. "Who you become and what you do—but not like you believe. You're so naive.

"I'm not the kind of man who does well running for office, Rankin. Shaking hands on an equal level with some ordinary person in a supermarket. . . . Besides, elections are too chancy. There are easier, safer ways to become important. I've spent a lifetime becoming somebody, making connections, opening doors, serving on committees, doing good deeds in the public spotlight. Putting money in all the right pockets.

"I have friends everywhere, Rankin. Some of them owe me. Someday they'll be in a position where they'll need to fill a job with someone they know, someone respectable they trust and can sell to the public. Maybe just a small post, sub-Cabinet. Maybe an ambassadorship. The first job always leads to a second, one higher up the ladder. Who knows what? Politicians die in office, and their replacements usually don't have to face re-election until after they've had time to solidify their image.

"But even if I don't go that route I'll be somebody. Everyone will know my name. I'll have a reputation long after everyone in this town has forgotten some sleazy private eye named Rankin. I *will* be somebody! I *will* have that reputation! Nothing and nobody—not you, not the wife I selected like a show dog, not . . . not any petty, greedy fool like your Pasha will stand in my way!

"You wanted to hear a story, old chap?" he said. Passion burned deep in his eyes. "I'll tell you a story before I throw you out. Let's say it's a fairy tale someone else told me. Nevertheless, do try to pay attention—even fantasies like this one have a point for those who want to profit in life.

"Once upon a time a man named Pasha forgot who he was. He'd achieved some degree of success by being a stepping-stone for smarter, tougher people. But he wasn't content with that, no, not Pasha.

"Suppose . . . Just suppose, back when he was the Prince of Capitol Hill and all the hustlers used him, back when he attracted all the bright young men who needed a stepping-stone to get ahead, to jump into circles where they could see how things worked, maybe get a piece of the action, suppose Pasha got too greedy.

"Let's say there was this one bright young man—the

best and the brightest, to borrow a phrase from this town. This bright young man tried out Pasha's circle to see what he could get from it. Maybe this bright young man had some money he could lay his hands on, some cash for a quick deal or two, something profitable but probably not popular with the people whose cash it was. Let's say our young man and Pasha did some business, made some money together. When it was all over, everybody profited, even those who didn't know how their money got used.

"But let's say Pasha was a fool. He gambled he could make more than money from the deal. He knew a bright young man when he saw one—though even Pasha underestimated this young man. Pasha decided he could use this clever chap as *his* stepping-stone.

"So Pasha made his big play. 'You're with me all the way,' he told our hero. 'Either we're partners, or I'll make sure your friends who trusted you with their money find out about our business deals.'

"Poor Pasha. He overestimated his strength. By then, anyone could see that his days were numbered. Two of his cronies had died violently. He'd gone from being well known to notorious. The crowds he ran with were extremely rough and volatile. Even if he survived all the games he was playing Pasha was bound to turn into an albatross, a millstone around anyone's neck. If you were stuck carrying Pasha, there were limits to how far you could rise.

"What happened to Pasha, John? Among all the ruthless people he knew, who was smart enough, bold enough, to seize control, engineer the chance to be rid of him? Who knew something about guns, who could get one, who knew where he lived and was the kind of man who was patient, who would stall Pasha's threats and wait for the right dark night . . .

"No one will ever know, will they, old chap? At least, not so as the police can do anything about it. There were no witnesses. So many powerful groups and ruthless people had a motive for killing Pasha the police can't even begin to sort through them, let alone see the footprints of one bright, respectable young man. That gun, the only concrete proof . . . What happened to it? Thrown in the Potomac or Chesapeake Bay? Dropped into a junkyard car press, crushed into a ton of scrap steel, melted down and poured into God knows what shape by now?''

"What happened to the bright young man, Emmett?''

"What bright young man? That was just a story. But if he was bright enough, he went on to get what he wants. He's the kind of man who always gets what he wants because nothing else matters. He's the kind of fellow smart men don't cross."

"There's always someone smarter, Emmett."

"So what?''

"So . . .''

"So you control your own game, old chap. You're careful, you're patient, you know the players and you know the rules. You don't overstep yourself—like Pasha did. And when someone interferes with you, you don't hesitate or equivocate, worry about nuances or any sentimental nonsense between you and your goal."

"And that works?''

"Yes, old man, it does. I'm the ultimate pragmatist."

"There are other words for you."

"Your *opinions* mean nothing to me, but your actions are becoming a bit of a nuisance."

"Glad to oblige."

"Don't be so sure. I've had enough of your nibbling at me—both personally and professionally. You're in violation of all this town's rules, and I'll use them to nail you to the wall."

"Is that a threat, Emmett?''

"It's a promise, Rankin. Stay out of my affairs—all of them—or suffer the consequences."

"What consequences?"

"Whatever the rules allow." He smiled. "I have attorneys, other . . . options I can explore."

"Like you did with Pasha?"

"Get out, old chap," he said without losing his smile, "or I shall call the police and let them take care of you. The law is on my side."

"He's right," said Nick Sherman after we listened to the tape the second time. He nodded to the palm-sized tape recorder on my desk.

"Not a bad idea, but it didn't do us any good. He didn't say a damn thing incriminating. Hell, on the basis of that tape I couldn't even get the captain to give me the time to rework Naderi looking for Sloan's footprints—not that I'd find any. Any of the business shit they did was buried deep enough that I didn't find it the first time. Now, seven years later . . . Sloan's clients maybe could have complained back then about misuse of funds if they'd have caught him in the middle of it, but now nobody cares. Forget about statute of limitations: they're probably happy with what they got. When you pointed Sloan out to me this morning as he walked inside his office building, I remembered seeing his face in a picture of a party at Pasha's house, but that proves nothing he won't admit freely—they knew each other.

"Do you think he had one of those gizmos on him that tells you when you're being bugged?" asked the homicide detective who loaned me the tape recorder.

"What difference does it make?" I asked.

"Just curious." He shook his head. "Crafty son of a bitch, ain't he?"

"He's going to get away with murder, isn't he?"

"I gave up believing in miracles a long time ago," said Nick. "Of course, we do have one more chance."

I stared at him.

"You know who I mean."

My friend stood up, walked to the door then stopped, turned back and stared long and hard at me.

"You took a hard shot, cowboy, but you're still walking. This is a big old swamp you're in, and you better watch your step. Our friend is right: he can nail you half a dozen ways from Sunday—harassment suits, invasion of privacy . . . infringement on marital affections or whatever the hell his lawyers will call it. He can wipe you out with the law. Maybe he won't do it because he'll want to avoid the publicity, but maybe he'll figure in the long run it will be worth it and he can profit from the martyr role. He doesn't score the game like you and I.

"He's also the kind of guy who won't let the law set his limits. Lord knows what he was planning for you last night. I figure maybe even he didn't know, maybe he did just stumble on you and decide to spook you. Or maybe he thought he had himself another opportunity to play it out like he did with Pasha. He'll do that in a heartbeat if he thinks it will help him. I don't want to see that shit. I promise you he won't have a free ride if he does it, but that's the kind of promise that does neither of us any good."

"What do you suggest?"

"If I were you, I'd take a long, cold, hard look around. I'd make sure where I was standing and where I wanted to go, how I could get there. Then I'd grab all I could and start walking. Keep my head up. Get on with things. And maybe, just maybe, someday you'll get a shot. If you do, make it good. If you don't . . . got to keep on walking.

"What *are* you going to do?" he asked.

"I'll call you," I said.

23

S HE OPENED THE DOOR, HER EYES
WIDE WITH FEAR AND SURPRISE.
"John! I didn't recognize . . ." She glanced over my
shoulder to Rich's green Volkswagen station wagon; I'd
screeched to a halt in the center of the half-moon driveway
directly in front of the mansion's door. "I . . . What happened to your car? Why are you here? Don't you know
. . . What's wrong?"

"Come out of there!"

"What . . ."

She glanced back over her shoulder: the Latin maid saw
who it was, decided her mistress didn't need her, smiled
nervously then disappeared into the recesses of the house.
The tangy smell of lemon furniture polish on fine wood
sweetened the cold river of processed air that flowed out
of the house.

"Come out of there!"

Bobbi looked back over her shoulder again, then stepped
onto the grand southern porch, pulled the door closed behind her.

"What are you doing here?"

"I came for you."

"John, darling, this isn't the time or place . . ."

"You don't even know what time or place you're in."

"Please, this isn't . . ."

"This isn't a stage, Bobbi. You're not in control, you never were. Now there's no more time for acting."

"What's happened? What have you done?"

"Started playing it straight. But there's one piece of the puzzle I can't figure out."

"What puzzle?" She clasped her arms tightly across her stomach; her shoulders rose and fell as she fought for breath.

"Emmett knows, Bobbi."

"Of course he knows! He knew before we did! He knew when he watched us that first day you showed up here, the day Molly . . . Of course he knows!"

"He knows about Naderi. That I've been investigating him. That I know Emmett killed him."

"Oh God!"

She hugged herself tighter; seemed to cave inward, trembled as though she would crumble into pieces and fall to the pavement.

"What have you done? We were . . . He didn't know! I know he didn't know! He thought we were just . . ."

"We were just what?" I yelled at her. "He thought we were just lovers? Is that why you did it? Is that why you . . ."

"Why?" She yelled; her hair floated from side to side as she shook her head in rage and desperation. "Why did you do this?"

"Why did *you?* Did you end up in my bed to cover yourself? Cover your tracks? Sleep with me so Emmett would think that was what brought us together . . ."

"No!"

"Then what were you doing?"

"I was just . . . I didn't . . ." Her hands almost touched her face; she chopped the air with them, as if they were

223

twin hatchets with which she could define and justify her intent, carve her will out of the chaos. "Maybe in the beginning I tried to fool myself into believing that I was . . . that what I wanted and what I was doing . . . that it all served the grand scheme: give Emmett the lie he already believed to hide . . .

"But I couldn't do it! Believe me, oh God believe me, John—I couldn't do it! Not with you, not for that!"

"For what, then? For what did you . . ."

"For me," she said, sobbed. Her arms wrapped back around herself, she couldn't look at me. "For us. For you."

"Sure," I said, kept my voice hard and cold; kept *my* control. "Sure you did."

"Believe me," she sobbed. "Please believe me!"

"After everything else? *Sure,* I'll believe you." The sneer sounded through my words.

"What do you want?" she said.

Her tone was flat, seemingly casual. Torturers know her tone well: there comes a point where the will disintegrates from pain or pressure or the erosion of time. What is left within the body is honest and totally accessible, though bereft of personality and the human perspective.

"I want to know the truth," I told her.

"About what?" She started off across the open meadow where she and Molly used to ride.

"Parviz Naderi. Pasha."

"I only met him a few times—three, maybe four. Before Emmett and I were married. When I came to D.C. and Emmett would take me out—dinner, the Kennedy Center, parties. He never cared if we spent time alone, though he did that enough to . . . to *convince* me. We'd go to the nightclub Naderi ran—the Forum? They were old friends. Emmett liked to show me off. Back then, I didn't mind. Didn't understand all the motivations. Naderi was a creep.

But Emmett seemed to like him, so I stopped trusting my judgment, accepted him.''

''Where were you when Naderi died?''

''New York, probably. Our family friend mentioned it when I called her once. She knew I'd met the guy who ran that nightclub. Emmett didn't tell me about it until . . .''

''Until when?''

''Until this year.''

Her tone grew stronger, deeper. Torturers know that sound too. After the pain, the humiliation, the defeat of the will, after the absolute, dehumanized honesty there comes a rebirth, a resurgence of the human spirit. The scars never go away, the pain is never forgotten, but the flesh gives itself another chance. At least in the lucky and the strong. For some, the resurgence takes only minutes; for others, years. Those who never find that resurrection live out their time as zombies who've lost their soul.

''What happened this year?''

She grunted, tried to smile.

''I tried to leave him. After Christmas. After New Year's. I realized I couldn't stand to tear another page off the calendar if it meant I had to cross off the days beside him.

''I thought maybe I could cut a deal. For years I'd been his beautiful wife, his well-bred mare who attracted a few trophies and colored him with her blue blood. But the currency for that had been mostly spent. There'd always be some, but he'd gotten all the mileage out of it I thought he could use.

''This is civilization, right? Modern times. Emmett is the ultimate sophisticated, charming man. Urbane. Long ago I learned he was a hypocrite, but I never imagined . . .''

She smiled, shook her head; her gaze was distant as she remembered.

''That night . . . I tried to pick a night when he was in

a good mood, but with Emmett that's impossible. He always wears that smiling mask.

"He's not complicated," she said. "He seems more than he is but that's just his mind tricking yours. My friend Tresa says he's primal, a savage in a three-piece suit. All he feels are fear and hate, envy, greed. Hunger.

"We were in his upstairs study. A little before midnight. He'd just returned from cruising the dark city.

"He'd been expecting me. Since his vision isn't clouded by normal emotions, he reads humans like a book. He knew I'd been building to something, that my diversionary flings and the Valium and the Scotch and the days I'd ride Molly until both of us were ready to drop weren't keeping me in check. I knocked on his door. He told me to come in. I remember clasping my hands in front of me, pressing them against my stomach so they wouldn't tremble. He sat behind his desk, smiling that awful mask smile while I played out my speech in front of him. I'd rehearsed, worked out the points with Tresa. Thought I'd anticipated all his counter-arguments, all the ploys and power plays he'd try or threaten. He's utterly ruthless, but this is America, right? The twentieth century. Society was on my side. So was the law.

"You know about the pre-nuptial agreement, how my mother is utterly dependent on him. I didn't know what I'd do about her, how to . . . to keep her where she belongs, but I figured I'd find some way. I couldn't take it anymore!"

She shook her head.

"That was not my best performance. I stammered through it, waiting for the explosion. He just sat there, smiling. After I finished he let me sweat for at least a minute.

"Then he *laughed!* God it was awful. At first I thought he was forcing it, another one of his acts, but it was like he'd heard the punch line of a grand joke. The laughter grew wilder—hysterical. He stood up, circled around his desk toward me. Like a jackal, a hyena. Put his hand on my shoulder. It was the first time he'd deliberately touched me when we were alone in . . . it had been almost four years since we'd had sex. In public he was always affectionate, stroking me, directing me with his hand on my elbow, my arm. But as soon as we were married, as soon as he *had* me settled in, *trained* . . . he ignored me, never bothered with any unnecessary contact of any kind. That night, he reached out his hand, laid it on my shoulder. . . . It felt like ice burning through my dress.

" *'Sit down, Barbi,'* he said.

"And I did.

" *'You're such an amusing little treasure,'* he said. *'And such a fool.*

" *'You've forgotten your bargain. You forgot who you made it with. My deals are forever, Barbi. I decide what they mean. They may not be signed in blood, but that's their bottom line.*

" *'Do you remember Pasha?'* he said—and I swear to God, I didn't! He had to remind me. He paced circles around me, he *strutted*. Towards the end he sat on the edge of his desk. Always looked down at me, always talking in that charming, clever, well-paced oh-so *British* voice.

"That's how he told me about our bargain, and about Pasha."

"What about Pasha?" I asked her.

"Emmett killed him. Pasha tried to outsmart him, turn a deal they had into something he never explained. Emmett told me how he stalled Pasha, how they acted like best friends. How he stalked him for weeks. When we met, Emmett did business with crazy Latins—not revolutionaries or terrorists, but middlemen. Merchants. Businessmen who sold death's tools. In my naivety I found that exciting. Not connected to the real world, to real people who'd be backed up against brick walls to face those guns. Such intrigue made Emmett even more charming. Those shadow men seemed fascinating, so much more 'real' than the fashion people and Wall Street types, the drama crowd I knew in New York. I didn't realize then that they were all after the same things, they just perceived different limits. Emmett's friends were always giving him things, guns. He still has some around the house, one in his office. Emmett shot Pasha with one.

"That laughter, the way he talked, the pride he took in his Pasha story . . . I knew it was absolutely, totally true. For the first time I saw him *complete.* I've never been so frightened.

" *'I'll tell you when our arrangement changes!'* he said. *'I'll give you your role—and you'll play it like I say!'*

"Then he told me what would happen if I . . . displeased him too much. Stopped being his blue-blooded asset. Tried to leave him, divorce him.

"He read me a shopping list from hell. He controlled all my assets. He'd see my mother thrown out in the cold, stripped of everything. He'd leverage all his money and power against us. But that was just for openers. For the amusement of watching us suffer. He leaned against his desk as casually as if he were talking about the weather, and he told me he'd kill us, both of us. And anybody else who mattered to me, any . . . man I'd choose for my next savior.

" *'And I promise you, Barbi,'* he said, his face all screwed up and snarling, *'you'll be the last one to die.'* "

She closed her eyes, started to hyperventilate.

"Then he . . . he smiled again. Stood me up. Pushed me down on his desk. Raped me."

"Oh Jesus, Bobbi, I . . ."

"When he was done," she said, "he looked down, smiled.

" *'Now don't bother me with your nonsense again. Remember to stay in line. You've got your bargain.'*

228

"I looked back at him as I stumbled out of the office. He was sitting behind his desk. Reading *Time* magazine."

"Get out of it, Bobbi!"

"What could I do?" she said, as if she hadn't heard me. "I believed him, but there was so much I didn't know. Before I could do anything, I needed to know all I could. I went to the library, looked up all the articles on Naderi. Nothing was being done, but I thought that maybe the police might have something up their sleeve. I needed to know! Maybe something still could happen. That's why I made up that story, that Cora McGregor person who could have been . . .. There were all those hints about women at the Forum in the articles. You were an audience waiting for the character to appear. All I had to do was fill the role."

"Why me?"

"I got your name out of the phone book, drove by your office. Your business looked too small to give me any trouble."

"Thanks."

"Don't you see what you've done?" she cried.

"Yeah, I see. I've exploded a bunch of lies and illusions."

"They were safe!"

"No they weren't, Bobbi. Illusions are never safe, lies are the greatest danger. Now you can . . ."

"Can what?"

She glared at me, then smiled, cold and cynical.

"You talk about illusions and lies, what would you have me do now?"

"Go to the police. I have a friend . . ."

"I hope for his sake he's smarter than you are, John. What do I tell the police? 'My husband said he killed a man, but you've got no evidence of that and neither do I, so it's his word against mine.' Solid, respectable, popular J. Emmett Sloan, rising star of the city. His word against his dizzy wife's, the one who takes Valium with her Scotch and refuses to see a shrink and is believed to have slept with ten times the number of men she has. The actress who couldn't make it so she married a rich man who's taken care of her family for years.

"How long would I have, huh, John? How about my mother? How long before she has an 'accident,' some unknown fiend breaks into her house, kills the little old lady? Happens every day."

"That's so lame! 'The way things are' is no excuse. We make things happen—sure, you might fail, but if you fight . . ."

"If you fight—what? What do you get?"

"A reason to believe, to keep on going."

"A reason to believe?" She laughed. "You talk about illusions!

"Look around you, John. Look at this city you say you love. You call it your town: it's made for the Emmetts of this world."

"Bullshit! *We* made it!"

"Well, then they stole it from you. It's like every place else. They own it. Guys like Emmett, if they're as smart as he is, as lucky . . . You can never beat them."

"So what are you going to do?" My question was far more nasty than curious, and she knew it.

She turned away from me, stared across the meadow.

"I . . . I'm not sure," she said, shrugged. "Try to . . . figure something out, find some line to walk that will keep my mother alive, that will . . ."

"But what if she dies? She's getting old, she'll die and leave you with no reason but yourself to stay trapped in this prison you've built. That's what you've done, Bobbi. You thought you were building a fortress, but instead you built a prison. And now you're locked in there with a killer for a warden."

"And no way out," she added.

"There's always a way out," I insisted. "You've got to find the key, turn the key yourself to get out. Hell, make yourself the key."

"I wish it were that simple."

"Bobbi . . . What will you do? If your mother dies—
when she dies—with all the years ahead of you? What will you do?"

"I don't know," she said. Shrugged. "Try to survive."

"Why bother?"

I'll remember that silence all my life. She shuffled a few paces away from me, leaned against one of those white columns. When she finally spoke, she didn't look at me.

"What was it you called me? Lame?" She shook her head. "You think I'm crippled, don't you? Broken."

"I think you've made yourself a prison and locked yourself inside. I think you're too afraid to step out."

"Of course I'm afraid! You know what he'll do if . . ."

"I think you're more afraid of getting free than you are of losing when you try."

"Nobody is ever free, John. Ever."

"Don't play with the words, Bobbi. That doesn't change what they mean and what's going on. Don't treat your life like a . . . a character on stage you move around according to the director or the producer or . . ."

"Maybe I am a cripple," she said. "But I have to . . . There's only so much I can . . ."

She was like a rag doll when I turned her towards me, wrapped her in my arms. Her forehead pressed against my chest.

"Come away now, Bobbi. Don't worry about what it means other than it's a chance. No demands, no deals, no bargains, just a chance, that's all I can give you."

"That's not enough," she mumbled.

"That's all I got. That's all anybody has."

"Then nobody has anything worth having."

"Stop it, Bobbi! I'm in this too. I'm not asking for anything from you, I don't want anything. Just take the chance!"

"What are you going to do?"

"Fight!"

"How? When? Where?"

"I'm here. That's the most I can do now. I don't know about later."

"He'll kill you."

"He'll try."

"I can't do that to you."

"You won't be. Emmett will. I know what I'm doing."

I felt rather than saw her smile into my chest.

"No you don't, John. You just think you do."

"Bobbi . . ."

She pushed herself away from me, reached out, touched her hand to my cheek and left it there while her eyes searched my face.

"I can't," she finally said.

"Damn you!" I whispered.

"Too late," she said, heard the desperate sea of emotions behind my words. "Somebody beat you to it."

I turned, walked away; stopped at the top of the porch steps.

"We're in this together, Bobbi," I said. Turned back, stared at her as she leaned against a white pillar, her auburn hair floating in the hot, humid breeze, her sapphire eyes wide, moist. Her lips trembled. "I don't know . . . I don't know what happens next, what . . . I'll stay close, as close as I can. And no matter what, you know . . . you know my door never closes."

She started to cry.

"Take care," she said.

And I drove away.

24

SOME GUYS GET ALL THE BREAKS," HE SAID.

A green haze rimmed the city's horizon outside this air-conditioned room. The government proclaimed our pollution level hazardous to human health. A frowning, bearded crusader walked our downtown streets wearing sandwich board signs that asked: *"Is your mind controlled by silent radio?"*

The man sitting across the table from me continued:

"You get to leave this swamp for the cool, clean Pacific Northwest. None of the interviews should be that hard—though it's always rough talking to victims about their pain. The documents you're after should be routine retrieval. The other lawyers will like meeting you so they know who's helping them spend the clients' money."

Art Dillon sighed, lifted his glasses off his nose; he cradled them in front of him with both hands on the table while he continued.

"Sorry to spring it on you first thing on a Friday morning, but we just got wind of that proposed merger. We aren't sure how it will affect the case, so we'll want to file sooner than anticipated."

"I think I can make it," I told him.

"Busy?" he asked.

"You wouldn't believe me if I told you—and I can't tell you."

"You in trouble?"

I didn't answer.

Art sighed.

"Look," he said, "we need the stuff soon and they're expecting you out West, but that doesn't mean you can't take time for yourself, sort out whatever mess it is you're in. Some woman, I suppose.

"But as of Monday, you're on the road—which, given your state, is probably a great idea. That's a classic American solution to trouble: hit the road. Get out of this damn town. Get some perspective.

"Besides," he added, smiling, "you're getting well paid for this trip."

"I'll earn it."

"If we didn't know that, we wouldn't hire you."

"Mind if we go off the client's time for a few minutes?"

He frowned. "To go where?"

"On to my time—and I insist on a bill for it. I need a lawyer, and I need it on the record."

Art shrugged, glanced at his watch. "Sure."

"Call in Beth, would you? And have her bring her notary stuff."

Art buzzed for his secretary, relayed the proper orders. She walked through the law library doors a minute later, smiled and sat at the conference table with us.

"Rankin is the client for a few minutes, Beth," said Art. "He wants this formal."

"Of course," she said. Her smile said nothing.

I pulled the sealed envelope out of my pocket, pushed it across the table to Art.

"That envelope, the contents of which I previously prepared, is to be opened in the event of any death, incapa-

234

citation or . . . major crisis I suffer. I've typed up a letter to that effect that I'd like witnessed by you, Art, and notarized. The envelope contains instructions to you . . . in the event of.''

"I'll accept it," said Art stiffly. He gingerly lifted the envelope off the table. "Beth, witness that I'm marking this envelope with the date and the purpose. And . . ." He pulled the letter across the table, read it, signed it, then pushed it across to her. "Go ahead and read this, notarize it. Make him a receipt for it too."

Those formalities took a few minutes. Beth left the room. "I'll stick this in the firm's vault," he said. "Let my partners know it exists."

"Thanks, Art."

"We'll bill you for a quarter hour—low rate."

"It's worth it," I said, smiled.

Art tossed his glasses on top of a stack of rust-colored accordion files.

"This is on my time," he said.

"I've known you . . . what? Seven years? Back when you were muckraking for Ned Johnson. We created this 'New Wave' private investigator concept in '79, remember? Our smart idea. Straight out of the D.C. experience, the investigative committees. Create a job for the right kind of person, somebody who knows his way around government and private institutions, somebody who can hunt through bureaucracies rather than bug some poor housewife who's getting a little on the side. Somebody who can sort through a complicated package and add up the real score. No domestic work: no child custody fights, no divorce. White-collar crime and, yeah—we knew that spilled over into the organized boys, but no targeting mainline crooks, no hard-core criminal stuff. No tough guy nonsense. Political investigations, corporate wars.

"We didn't know if it would fly. Kept you in-house

when the firm was just a letterhead of five attorneys who were tired of working for somebody else. Six months later, with our blessing, you're out on your own and doing fine. Now there's a couple more of you New Wave types around the country. But you're still the first, and for my money, the best."

"Thanks, Art."

"This isn't selfless praise: it was my idea too, remember? And I taught you a trick or two.

"A few things in life give me pleasure. One is watching my theory take on a life of its own. This New Wave investigator concept is an extension of the practice of law. You keep getting it confused with justice, but that's your problem. Your career is my baby too, so I've kept a close eye on you, even when you started taking on all those other clients.

"Another thing I like is baseball. My favorite player has been Lou Piniella. Yankees. The paper today said he's retiring at age 40. He was smart, tough, the best at what he did. He knew enough to get out when the game he started playing got beyond what he could do. If he'd have stayed in at that escalated level, he might have ended up hurt, humiliated. Maybe worse.

"Lou is only five years older than you, Rankin. Like you, he was playing a sport with minimal dangers, maximum challenges, adequate rewards and acceptable risks. The kind of sport where he never had to give his lawyer a sealed envelope to open *in the event of*."

Art picked the envelope off the table, turned it over in his hands and then let it drop.

"If your game has switched out from under you this much, maybe you ought to think about retiring too."

Her message said call before noon.

"I have another of those Club luncheons," she said when I did. "You know."

"Yeah, I know."

"John . . . I'm so . . . Are you OK?"

"Sure. How about you?"

"I'm fine."

We gave those polite lies a moment of silence.

"I think we're safe," she said.

"For a while."

"I know you're upset, angry. I . . . I just . . ."

"We can talk about it later."

"Oh! OK, I . . . I can't see you until Monday."

"I'm sorry, I have to leave town for a couple weeks. Business."

"Really," she said.

"The toxic waste case. You remember."

"Yes," she said, a chill replacing the nervous tremor in her voice. "I understand."

"I'll be gone at least a week. Maybe two."

"Well."

"If there's any trouble, if you need anything, you can leave a message on my machine. I'll be retrieving them on the road."

"Don't worry," she said. "I'll be fine."

"Bobbi . . ."

"Will you call me when you get back?"

"Of course! Didn't you think I would?"

"Have a safe trip, John. Take care of yourself."

"You too."

We hung up.

On the road.

"Get out of town," Art said. "Get some perspective."

In Portland, Oregon, I spent a week interviewing former dockworkers, meeting them in lawyers' offices or coffee shops where their gnarled hands gripped tan mugs as they told stories of the strange sickness their work brought them.

So many of them were unemployed or unemployable because of their malaise. In ordinary homes on quiet streets I'd sit in an easy chair, stare at wives and children perched across from me on the sofa, their eyes full of dread they didn't dare voice. They waited for me to dispense some conclusive judgment as to what would happen, to tell them how bad it could be, confirm or deny the nightmares about cancer, about the fate of children yet unborn. I had only questions. After those interviews, searching public records and questioning the company and union officials who would talk to me was a relief.

An old college friend who'd led Vietnam War protests let me sleep on his floor. He'd spent a year at Harvard graduate school, then returned to our home state and fought the railroads for a citizens' coalition group before gravitating to D.C., where he became a wheelin' and dealin' number one staffer for first one, then another senator. He kept his bosses out of bar fights, got them to most of the recorded votes on time and prodded their consciences more often than they liked. After three years he said the hell with such nonsense, headed west to rediscover life beyond the Potomac. Now he used his savvy and style to shepherd a four-state Northwest regional commission regulating environmental planning. His wife practiced law in another state, they saw each other frequently.

His apartment building rose from the side of green hills encircling Portland like the lip of a bowl. The tops of twin western red cedars were eye level outside my window, 20-story-tall giants still growing after centuries of life. The city sprawled beneath his living room's wall of glass. Most mornings, gray clouds covered the sky and hid the horizon. By midafternoon, the sun burned the clouds off and revealed Mount Hood, a snow-covered pyramid with blue mist enshrouding its base. On a good day you could see what 1980's volcano eruption left of Mount St. Helens;

sometimes a wispy white steam plume rose from that shattered cone. The air was cool, clean, sweetened by Oregon's damp pines and free from pollution though Portland and its suburbs held as many people as D.C.

Everything fit in the view from his rooms. The Willamette River and freeways curved through the city. Ornate turn-of-the-century white stone five-story buildings nestled amidst giant modern glass and concrete skyscrapers. The rustic Jack London Hotel shared a neighborhood with clever, cheerful cafés that served fresh strawberries and yogurt. No one looked ugly or tense. Sturdy loggers walked peacefully beside mousy CPAs who'd calculated the decline of the timber industry. A millionaire once bequeathed dozens of free-flowing, four-spigot brass drinking fountains to the city so that no one need ever walk the downtown sidewalks thirsty. Many Portlanders were 1960s success stories, achievers who'd moved here for a quality life that meant more than money, fame, power or a monastic spiritual existence. They had good jobs, drove sensible Volvos, ate salmon. On weekends they hiked along mountain streams or strolled the packed-sand Pacific beaches a two-hour drive away. Their children went to fine public schools, learned about computers. Neighborhoods organized to restore old bridges, and a tavern owner beat an experienced politician in the mayoral race. This city has a stadium for minor league baseball, a symphony hall, an art museum, a zoo, a Japanese garden. Months of rain are a bargain price for life in Portland, where summers are bright, winter is gentle, and even the lonely lead wonderful lives.

It wasn't my town.

In San Francisco, merely being there seemed reason enough for life.

Art Dillon's associate picked me up at the airport and turned his guest bedroom over to me for my stay. We'd known each other for four years, mostly through telephone conversations. Only 33, he'd earned a national reputation as a tough litigator, but the identity he treasured was Johnny FarI, a name he carved for himself out of the Jamaican reggae music that had seduced his soul away from rock 'n' roll and the days when this son of Brooklyn Jews had been known as Spanish Johnny. His legal practice was booming, but his heart belonged to a small recording business supported by his law firm victories. So far the five reggae bands he'd recorded hadn't had a hit, but that didn't matter to Johnny FarI: he was part of the music, *mon*. The part of his life that wasn't reggae or the law was Maria, a black-haired fawn woman in her second year of medical school who shared her spare minutes with Johnny. Her golden retriever, Shira, who they claimed was a spiritual being and not a dog, made their household complete. They didn't know about tomorrow, but today was fine. As we pulled away from the airport in his old Chevy, Johnny slipped on his shades, slapped a cassette of Springsteen's "Born in the U.S.A." into the tape deck (out of deference to my passions), lit a joint and said, "Welcome to San Francisco."

All my life that city by the bay meant magic to me and the distant pulse of its streets had shaped my soul, yet I'd never truly been there. Once, between planes, I caught a taxi into the city, rode the cable cars on a round trip to Fisherman's Wharf, then taxied back to the airport and flew home with my enchantment basically untouched by experience. Now I slept in one of the small row houses jammed in a West San Francisco neighborhood called the Richmond. On a chilly summer Sunday morning I lay in bed listening to foghorns play a backbeat to church bells.

According to the bill I submitted to Art Dillon, Johnny and I spent 22 hours sorting through the complicated case, figuring out strategy, procedure, what to do *if*. I actually worked longer than that, spent hours in dusty public record halls and interviewed a dozen more workers and two dissident executives who'd since left our targeted company, but time and schedules lost much of their importance in San Francisco.

When I wasn't working, I hiked those legendary hills that were home for so much of America's history that never makes it into the pablum of high school textbooks or the slogans chanted at press conferences.

Coit Tower rose from the highest hill, a hollow stone finger pointing toward heaven. The view from its parapets encompasses most of the city and the bay where Alcatraz waits, a prison free of prisoners. On a clear day, Marin County is visible, though it's too distant to pick out the grand homes in that trendy suburb where the natives drive their Mercedeses to the town square for free Sunday wine tastings. The wealth of modern Marin County is present only as an implied cloud in the murals that decorate the curved walls inside Coit Tower's first floor. During the grim days of the 1930s, a government works project employed artists to adorn this public landmark, a magnanimous gesture to both starving artists and patriotic, civic pride. The results scandalized the city, for the artists created what critics call social realism with a decidedly revolutionary socialist twist: bold images of workers oppressed by a machine and money-ordered world, graphic street scenes of the hard life, heroes brandishing books by Reds, grim capitalists watching over all. In America, such representations barely qualify as art, but the paintings still adorned those San Francisco walls in 1984.

In Chinatown, it was the Year of the Mouse. What had once been a shunned ghetto for imported, third-class coolie laborers was now the city's most popular square mile. The buildings were squat and gaudy, with gilded gold Oriental characters painted on green and red walls.

Hundreds of restaurants and gift shops lined the sidewalks. Banners of Oriental calligraphy crisscrossed narrow streets where thousands of tourists, their cameras slung around their necks, rubbed against singsong jabbering "locals." The tourists' faces glowed: this was it! "Come on, Mother!" a 40-year-old man in black and white checked pants called to a stout, gawking gray-haired lady in a pink polyester pants suit. A pretty housewife from Iowa or Anywhere Like It amiably yelled, "Hey, monkeys, don't put your hands on the windows!" to two blond children staring into a shop filled with scrimshaw and jade figurines of divine beings they neither recognized nor understood. Lean, shaggy-haired teenage Chinaboys in rock 'n' roll T-shirts and blue jeans chanted, "Need any fireworks?" next to a movie theater where the soundtrack of the untranslated Japanese cinema epic being shown inside blared out over potential customers. The pungent odors of soy and other cooking oils, ginger, mustard, fresh fish and obscure, sweet scents no Caucasian could name floated through the streets. Bakeries sold almond cookies for 75 cents each.

North Beach grows out of Chinatown. Once this Italian neighborhood sheltered the West Coast bohemian movement, California's answer to New York's Greenwich Village, where the self-proclaimed intellectuals, beatniks and wandering rebels of the 1950s tamely turned up their noses at the men in the gray flannel suits society held out as models of exemplary American life. North Beach still had its coffee houses, its famous bookstore, but now sexual commerce dominated these streets. I saw no prostitutes plying their trade under noon sun, but dozens of entertainment centers offered every kind of theatrical sex show imaginable. The nightclub named the hungry i, once the mecca of folk song groups who shaped music in the late

1950s and early 1960s, now advertised "Male & Female Sex Act" on its marquee.

America's rebels left North Beach for another San Francisco neighborhood in the mid-1960s, crossed town to the Haight and became what the media, with its worship of labels, clichés and categories, called *hippies* and *flower children*. When I was in high school Haight-Ashbury was the spiritual crossroads for my generation. The address implied words reverently sworn to move mountains and cheaply bandied about in every commercial and con game: *Peace. Love.* Haight-Ashbury meant rejection of the straight life, no more business as usual, no war in Vietnam, free-flowing hair, music with lyrics and rhythms spun out of psychedelic drugs. All that died so quickly, became heroin madness and feeding ponds for human sharks. I found a pay phone at the corner of Haight-Ashbury. I had a dime, but no one to call. The free clinic was still there, but all around me were chic shops selling knickknacks, stylish clothing. Three self-absorbed teenagers decked out in the elaborate aggression of 80s "punk" style stalked my way, all black leather jackets, chains, engineer boots; well-greased spiked Mohawk haircuts on the two boys and dyed purple chopped locks for the girl. Their look cost money, and bought them only superficial strength. They lacked any depth of vision (no matter how naive). A street dude or advertising executive from any era could have crumpled the trio like fast-food burger boxes and dropped them in the gutter.

Rebellion soured in the 1970s, twisted inward on itself, and moved yet again in San Francisco, this time north from the Haight to Geary Boulevard, where Jim Jones established his Peoples Temple and proclaimed himself messiah before leading hundreds of his disciples to their death in the jungles of Guyana. No trace of that madness showed on the boarded-up tan stone mansion he'd used as a cathedral the day Maria and Shira took me there. Once I'd worked a case involving Jones's legacy, and I'd wanted to see what remained of that monster's legend: just a skeleton, a boarded-up castle. Shira sniffed, but didn't bother to pee on the wall. On the scruffy brown plywood covering one window a nameless vandal with a black marker had scrawled, "Rebel Truth."

Rebel truth, whatever it might be, seemed impotent in 1984's America. San Francisco was scheduled to be the site of the year's major political show: the Democratic Party's convention, where party faithful from across the land were to nominate an orthodox politician and the first woman vice presidential candidate from a major party to face a conservative Republican giant named Reagan in November's presidential election. When I'd left Washington, "the convention" and "San Francisco" drifted through thousands of conversations. In San Francisco, no one mentioned politics or the coming circus; all interest and excitement centered around the cable cars that were running again after more than a year's absence for repairs.

San Francisco's spirit smiles from the eyes of its citizens: they look at you without the paranoia, guile or anger that burns deep within so many other cities. People waiting at the bus stops calmly, curiously met my hungry stare as Johnny and I cruised the fashionable downtown financial district in his Chevy. The same smile, the same openness lit the faces Maria, Shira and I passed the day we shopped the teeming Mission district with its wide boulevards of cut-rate appliance stores, furniture stores, hardware stores, shoe stores. Every business had that musty, well-used look. Wares were displayed in an unguarded jumble on the sidewalk outside the shops. Every block had its cheap hotel. Like the entire city, the neighborhood seemed incredibly, completely integrated. Black, white, Mexican, every kind of Oriental. Young and old. The rich seemed to be the only missing group, though some of the bohemians in a chic corner café sported the deliberately dressed-down look. Everyone had that smile in his eyes, even the winos and the *cholos,* the Hispanic hoodlums who prowl the Mission sidewalks three abreast, white tank-top T-shirts, tattoos and heavy biceps that make them just as monstrous as any Times Square gorilla.

That look took me three days to get used to, four to figure out. It's not naivety or ignorance. It's a reflection of the city itself, a joyous celebration of life. *We're here,* the look says, *and isn't that wonderful?*

It was, but this wasn't my town either.

The silver airplane carried me back East, skimming through the sky like a bird headed to roost. The wing dipped over rolling green fields, acres of suburban tract housing in Virginia as we glided into Dulles Airport. So little had changed that I could touch, yet my world had shifted.

Perspective, Art had said. Perspective.

The sun hung a hand's width above the hills as I stepped out into the sticky evening. A line of taxis stretched to my left along the sidewalk out front of the airport. I nodded to the tall, balding man with a trim mustache leaning on the first cab in line while he talked with two other drivers. My man was neatly dressed in slacks and shirt; his olive tan complexion came from more than the summer sun. He tactfully detached himself from the crowd, slid behind the wheel and pulled his cab in front of me. I threw my bag in the backseat, closed the door and said a thankful prayer that his cab was air conditioned.

"Good evening, sir. Where are you going?"

"Home," I told him, then gave him my Capitol Hill address.

"Very good, sir."

The cab rolled toward Washington at a smooth, steady pace. My cabby drove as gracefully as he'd moved. His vehicle was spotless, inside and out. He had the radio turned to the public radio station, and classical music floated softly back to me. I complimented him on his driving.

"Thank you, sir. I used to be a pilot."

"Really?"

"Yes."

"Commercial?"

"No. Military."

"Here or . . ."

"I'm Iranian. I was in the Air Force."

"Oh. What kind of aircraft did you fly?"

"All kinds."

"You must have been an officer."

The mirror showed him smiling unconsciously.

"I was."

"Ah . . . Captain?" I asked. "Major?"

"I was a general."

"Really?"

"Really," he said, and I believed him.

"You would be surprised how many former Iranian generals are now driving cabs at Dulles Airport."

"How many?" I asked, taking the bait.

"Nineteen—from all branches of the service."

"That's quite a lot."

"We had a lot of generals back then."

"You were lucky to get out."

"Everyone has a certain amount of luck in life." He shrugged. "I was fortunate to be able to use mine at a crucial moment. It's a pity that many people squander their luck."

"A pity," I agreed. "Did your family get out too?"

"Yes, we were most fortunate."

"Things are different there now," I said.

"You know what happened?" he said. He assumed I

knew the media-delivered facts of the coup that threw his Shah out of power, the anarchy, the rise of the religious fanatic who now ruled his homeland with a fist as bloody as the Shah's. The Savak had metamorphosed into a new secret police, but basically only its name had changed.

"We lost our confidence," he said. "That's what happened."

"Well . . ." I said, then thought better of presenting other historical analyses.

"But," he said. "Iran is still Iran."

"Your English is excellent."

"Thank you."

"Did you pick it up when you fled over here or . . ."

"I was posted to the Embassy in Washington not long before the changes. For several years."

I felt like asking him if he knew Parviz Naderi, but didn't.

"How do you find America?" I asked.

"America?" He looked at me in the mirror. "I find America . . . complex."

"Yes, it is."

"Also . . . America is opportunity. Here, a man can do . . . anything!"

"He can try."

"Indeed," he said, nodding to affirm this faith. "Indeed."

We rode in silence for several minutes before he spoke again.

"Tomorrow is your Fourth of July."

"Yes."

"Happy Independence Day," he said formally, as if that were a sacred and common greeting.

"Same to you."

He nodded, smiled. Drove on.

* * *

Rich had piled the newspapers inside my office door, stacked the mail on my desk. I'd read the news on the road. None of the letters seemed compelling enough to open immediately. The dial on my answering machine indicated many people had telephoned, let the tape run. I left the answering machine on, didn't rewind the tape to hear who'd called. Ignoring my telephone messages and mail bought me a slice of time, postured to the world that I was in control and would answer its demands when I chose to. That petty decision pleased me far out of proportion to its importance. I felt as though I'd crossed some invisible border to a familiar yet uncharted frontier.

My jet-lagged body said it was only 6 P.M., but the clock on my wall said 9. The phone rang five times during the hours I stayed up, sat staring out the window while Springsteen played on my stereo. I heard my *"This is John Rankin . . ."* announcement answer the bell, heard the click as whoever called hung up without leaving a message. My mind drifted with the music, with feelings rather than thoughts as I found my balance in this strange world.

Perspective, Art had said. Perspective.

By the clock, I went to bed at 11, waited for probably another hour before my body agreed it was ready for sleep. The streetlights' glow in the polluted darkness hid the stars beyond the skylight above my bed. Voices drifted to my room from the sidewalks as people walked toward the ivory Capitol dome, moved from bar to bar to conduct business and politics and pleasure, headed home. A police siren wailed down Pennsylvania Avenue. I could trace its route, guess its probable point of origin and likely causes for its destination, knew the sliding scale of what could happen when it arrived: miracle to mayhem to madness; tragedies, terror, triumph; I knew them, knew their price.

I'd been on the road.

And this was my city.

25

DAWN WOKE ME AFTER TOO FEW HOURS OF SLEEP. MY SCHEDULE was back in sync with East Coast clocks and my body wasn't happy about it. By the time she called at five minutes to eight, I'd showered, downed a couple cups of coffee, and read most of that morning's *Post* without clearing away all of the fog between my ears.

"Mr. Rankin?" she said, "My name is Tresa Hastings. I'm a friend of . . ."

"I know who you are," I told her. "I thought you were in Paris."

"I got back three days ago. Sounds like I should have come back sooner."

"Depends on who you've been talking to."

"I've been talking to Bobbi . . ."

"So I guessed."

". . . and I want to talk to you. I called three times last night and got your damn machine. I don't talk to those things. I want to see you."

"Curiosity?"

"She told me you'd probably taken a cynical turn."

"How would she know?"

"She knows you—though I hope not as well as she thinks."

"Look, I'm not sure . . ."

"If you're not sure, then don't you think you better see me and find out?"

"I . . ." I couldn't think of a simple and strong reason to say no. "OK."

"I'm staying downtown," she said. "I'll catch a cab up to your office—your apartment."

"That's fine with me."

"In about half an hour?"

"I'll be waiting," I said.

"I'll be there," she told me.

Sorting my mail and listening to my phone messages filled the hour. Tresa Hastings said she'd called three times without leaving a message, but there were more than a dozen such calls on my tape. I was about to start returning calls to my list of people who *had* left messages when I heard the street door open. Someone slowly climbed the two flights of stairs, then knocked on my door.

"Come in!"

Her outfit was tan, a chic foreign-cut slacks and pullover combination with low-heeled brown shoes. She looked better than in the photograph Emmett once showed me on his wall. Perhaps the camera was never kind to her, or perhaps she wasn't as desperate as she had been on that portrait day. Her dishwater blond hair was still chopped off close to her ears. The haggard look had left her face, though her thin-lipped mouth was firmly set and her blue eyes were hard and haunted.

She entered my office slowly, let her eyes roam first around the room: did she remember some story Bobbi shared with her as the couch came into view? Tresa turned her eyes on me; their judgment was studied and impossible to ascertain.

"Is this what you expected?" I finally asked.

"Is what? You, this place . . . that Bobbi would find someone like you, would finally . . . that she'd suddenly let me know she was in some God-awful mess with Mr. Snake Oil but won't tell me what. . . . Just what was I supposed to expect?"

"Hell," she sighed, "nothing in life is like I expected."

"You better sit down," I told her, smiled as I stood. I gestured toward the couch, turned one of the wooden captain's chairs around to face it.

"Hell yes," she said, walking to the couch, collapsing on it. "I better sit down."

"Want some coffee?"

"Up all night tossing and turning, on my feet pacing at dawn. I lied to room service, had them bring coffee for two. Bellhop thought the lady alone in 617 got lucky. Shit, both of those little silver pots barely got me moving enough to get here. My kidneys are probably going to O.D. on caffeine. Hell yes, I could use another cup of coffee."

"I've only got instant."

"That won't be fast enough."

Three minutes later she mumbled her thanks as she took a steaming mug from my hand. I sat in the captain's chair, faced her over my cup. She took a long, slurping pull of the hot liquid.

"Christ, and you can cook too. Are you always this nice?"

"Usually I shoot my visitors."

"I wish to hell you'd done that to Emmett."

"He caught me by surprise."

"Don't let that happen twice."

"Don't worry."

" *'Don't worry'*? My whole life has been either worry

or warfare. I thought I could get out of it, but . . ." She shook her head. Her eyes softened, she smiled at me.

"How do you do, John Rankin?"

"I've done better," I said. Smiled back. "How about you, Tresa?"

"I've done worse. Ask Bobbi. If it weren't for her, I'd have drowned in that mistake called a marriage. She kept my head above water. Wouldn't let go of me when I didn't give a damn and fought her. Held my hand when I walked out.

"All that time we were swapping woes, but it was never an equal trade. Bobbi'd only skim the surface of her trouble for me. I knew that even then, but I was too deep in my own shit to pull any more from her, to help her much at all."

"That's not what she says," I told her.

"Yeah, well, she's always been too kind for her own good.

"So what happens?" Tresa asked rhetorically. "I finally get out, get my life cleaner than it's been since they washed me off in the delivery room, pulled myself together in Paris and even had a little real fun for once, came back and found my friend, my best and only friend, up past her eyeballs in some shit river she won't tell me much about.

"Of course," she said, smiled at me again, "it ain't all bad. There is you. You seem to have done more for her in a few months than anybody has in years. Thank you for that, John Rankin."

"Don't thank me."

"Hell, if I don't, you'll only hear it from Bobbi. Nobody else cares. So what happens now?"

"What do you know?"

"Ah, it's going to be like that, is it? The professional detective. Hard-boiled heart. You show me your cards and maybe I'll show you mine, huh? Why not? She trusts you, so I do too.

"I know she wants rid of Emmett, she has for years, but she couldn't figure a 'best' way to do it. I figure now she just wants to do it, the hell with whatever is best. Good for her. There's nothing I'd like better than to see her free from that creep. But from what she told me when I got back, he's got some new hold on her—something big, something bad, something powerful. That scares the shit out of me, because Emmett would stomp a baby who crawled in his way. I know she went to you looking for some kind of help, that you wouldn't let go of her or let it drop and that that all somehow led you two smack into each other's arms. And hearts. From what little she says and the way she says it, the whole mess now seems stuck at the edge of some high cliff—you pulling one way, her holding on, and Emmett standing there waiting to shove everybody over.

"She won't give me any details, which drives me crazy. When I push her, she says no, telling me would put me in the circle too, whatever the hell that means."

Bobbi should have said "in the bull's-eye," I thought, then I told Tresa, "She's right about that."

"Wonderful! That makes me feel so much better! My best friend is obviously just *fine*!"

"So let's cut the crap," she said, the sarcasm falling from her tone, "and you tell me what the hell is going on."

"I can't."

"Bullshit. You *won't*."

"Call it what you like."

"I call it bullshit and I don't like it one damn bit! I've got some rights here, Mr. Private Detective, Mr. Johnny-Come-Lately-Lover! I don't know if you do or not, but I love that woman! She kept me alive, and now I can't even touch her to help when she needs it! That's not fair! That's not right! And she . . . she . . .''

Tresa trailed off, her mouth closed in a tight, frustrated line.

"I don't need to tell you about fair," I said.

"Yeah, I know—fair is what you pay for the trip they give you.

"Look," she said, "could . . . could you just tell me: is this all real?"

"Yes."

"And . . . it's . . . Somehow it's dangerous, right?"

"Yes."

"Ahh." She closed her eyes, shook her head. When she opened her eyes again, the anger had left her tone.

"You really know how to make a girl feel good, don't you?"

"I wish," I told her.

"What are you going to do about it all?"

"Everything I can," I said, "but there's not much I can do; it's up to Bobbi."

"Bobbi has never ducked anything she had to do in her life."

"Maybe—but she's not very good at realizing what's what, at deciding what it is that must be done, that can be done."

"That doesn't say much for her coming to you then, does it?"

I didn't answer her. Again she sighed, closed her eyes and shook her head.

"What can I do?" she asked at last.

"Get her the hell out of there."

"Out of where? It's her life."

"You know what I mean," I told her. "Get her away from him. Get her to get herself free, to do what she has to do."

"Where will she go? To you?"

"That's a good place to start, but that's not necessarily where she should plan on ending up. I could be just a safer port in the storm."

"Oh sure, I'll just bet you're the kind of guy who's really *safe* for a woman. You prepared for all that?"

"You don't even know what . . . I'm prepared enough to do enough. To do the most that can be done."

"Secret games," she said, shook her head. "I hate them."

"Me too."

She glanced into her cup.

"Empty," she said, raised her head. "Where's your bathroom?"

I nodded back toward the apartment. "Oh yeah," she said, as if she remembered she'd been told that before.

When she returned, she walked to the bay tower, stared out the window.

"It's hot as hell out there," she said. "Muggy too. Like the air is the ocean. Kids keep throwing firecrackers."

"Fourth of July. Independence Day."

"Yeah. Sure it is." She turned to look at me. "Big day. What would you do today if Bobbi had never come into your life?"

"Probably wander down to the Mall this afternoon, see if I can get close enough to listen to the Beach Boys concert at the Washington Monument. Later I'd hook up with my buddy Rich, have an early dinner. Walk up to the Capitol in time to find a seat on the steps for the National Symphony concert, watch the fireworks."

"Sounds great. Wholesome and all-American. What will you do with what today really is?"

"Wander down to the Mall this afternoon. Try to listen to the Beach Boys. See if Rich wants to have dinner, get seats on the Capitol steps for the symphony and fireworks.''

"Huh. What would you do today if Bobbi could be here, free and clear?"

I had no answer.

"That's what I thought," she said. "I'm staying at the Fairfax. I made Bobbi promise to call me about 11."

"I'd call her," I said, "but . . ."

"Yeah: *But*. But you don't know who'd answer the phone, right?"

"I'll be around until at least noon," I told her.

She smiled, headed for the door.

"That's good to know." She paused before she walked out, looked back at me. "I figure you'll be around anyway."

"Probably."

She smiled. "Good to meet you, John Rankin."

"Good to meet you, Tresa."

She left.

My phone rang at ten minutes to noon.

"It's me."

"I know."

"I just got off the phone with Tresa. She told me you were back. Told me she went to see you."

"That's right."

"What did you tell her?"

"Nothing more than you did."

"And nothing more than what you've already told me to do."

"That's right."

She sighed and I realized my grip on the phone had turned my knuckles white.

"How . . . How was your trip?" she asked.

"Fine," I said.

We ran out of easy words, were silent for too long. When she spoke again her tone seemed to contradict itself. She sounded light, almost casual, as if all the problems in the world had been resolved. Yet a steel ribbon ran through her words and connected to some deep and serious import.

"Well," she said, "here we are."

"Yes, here we are."

Another long, painful pause; her voice was halting.

"This isn't . . . I was afraid I'd miss you—I mean, not get to talk to you."

"Why?" I asked.

"Would you have called me?"

"Yes."

"When?"

"I don't know, when I . . . when things got settled. When . . . When I was sure."

"Sure of what? Sure that Emmett wasn't around and we could talk?"

"Yes."

"And what else did you need to be sure of?"

"What I wanted to say."

She made a sound like a laugh—there is no precise label for that mocking noise that held understanding, not joy.

"Oh Johnny, sometimes you're so transparent! You went away—and don't tell me it was for work! You left when you drove Rich's car away from the house. You were already on the road then, even if you didn't know it."

"I was alone. You could have come."

"Too late, Johnny. Too late."

"No it wasn't. No it isn't."

"What did you find on the road, Johnny? What did you learn on your trip?"

"Perspective."

"Was it worth it?"

"I don't know."

"I hope so, Johnny. Oh God, if I hope anything, I hope for you!

"You were right, you know," she continued.

"About what?"

"Not about everything, but about much of it. About me. That's what I discovered . . . on your trip. See? It's like we both went somewhere, only I never got to move.

"What have you done about Emmett?" she suddenly asked.

"Nothing anyone can see. Prepared myself for whatever as best as possible."

"I bet you have." She laughed—this time a genuine, full laugh. "Remember when I told you I was glad you were smart, that I needed a smart man but not one who was too smart?"

"Yes."

"I got more than I bargained for. You are so much more than . . . You are smart, Johnny. And good. And tough. If you've 'prepared,' I bet it's the best way. I trust you, Johnny. I trust your abilities as well as your intentions. If you've done it, it'll be the best anybody could. That's good. You need to be ready."

"Bobbi . . ."

"You were right, you know," she said again, interrupting me.

"About *what*?"

"About me. About me making myself a prison instead of a fortress. I even did more than that: for 35 years I've made myself a prisoner. Such a waste, such a massive waste. Even if the walls called Emmett came tumbling down, I'd still be a prisoner. I've locked myself up in my history, locked myself up in my life."

"You don't need to be there. People change."

"Do they really, Johnny? After a certain point, do they really? Can they?"

"It's up to them."

"That's another thing you were right about, Johnny. It's up to me. I'm a prisoner, but I'm also the key."

"That's right."

"See? We don't disagree so much after all."

"Have you been drinking?"

She made the sound that wasn't truly a laugh again.

"No, Johnny. I'm sober. Stone cold sober. And stone cold certain. I am the key."

"What are you going to do, Bobbi?"

"What makes you think I'm going to do anything?"

"You have to."

She laughed again.

"That's what *you* say, Johnny. Maybe you're right, but maybe you're wrong. You know me better than anybody ever has—what do you think I'm going to do?"

"I don't know."

For the third time she made the mocking noise that wasn't a laugh.

"Well, don't worry about it, John."

"I have to. You're important to me, you know that. And we're connected."

"Yes we are, aren't we?" That much is certain— there was a bond, no matter what we called it. Or didn't call it.

"Bobbi . . ."

"We're not lovers anymore, are we, John?"

It took me almost a minute to break the silence.

"How can we be?" I said.

"You left."

"You wouldn't come with me."

"How could I?"

"How couldn't you?"

"What future would we have had, John? What would he have done to you?"

"That's not the only reason."

"No," she said. "No, it isn't. I told you: I'm a prisoner."

"And you're the key."

"Yes. I'm the key."

"Bobbi . . ."

"Don't call me that!" she said suddenly. "That's a silly thing, an imaginary name from a dream, an illusion. No more illusions."

"What. . . What shall I call you?"

"Call me your friend. Your special friend."

"You can't fade away on me. You've got to stay close, stay in touch. Because of Naderi. Because of Emmett. We're linked together. Our survival."

"Yes, well, I'm not worried about that. That can be taken care of. Everything can. And you . . . I trust you. You'll do what you need to do."

This silence burned the most.

"Any . . . Any regrets?" she asked.

"Don't be . . . ! I have a million regrets! A million things we never got to . . . that I never got to . . ."

"Thank you!" she whispered. "Thank you for that—for that and for everything!"

"Do one more thing for me?" she asked. "Do one favor, something I told you not to do?"

"What?"

"Oh, John! You are back to being John, aren't you? Not my Johnny anymore. My Johnny wouldn't have said, 'What?' He'd have said yes. Maybe even no. But flat out, straight out, no cautious probe."

"I'll do whatever I can!"

"You can do it, John. You can do it. One more time, as you go . . . Call me Bobbi one last time."

"OK."

The word could barely leave my tight throat. She waited a moment. I heard her tears.

"Good-bye, Johnny."

"Good-bye, Bobbi."

I hung up.

Keep busy, I told myself through my numbness. *Play out a normal routine. Get on with it. Get over it.*

The city's sea of heat and humidity engulfed me as I drifted down to the Mall. At the Washington Monument the swirling mass of half a million holidayers became an impenetrable wall of human flesh. They wore halter tops and cut-offs, blue jeans and T-shirts, baseball caps and cowboy hats, carried coolers and blankets for the grass that was already covered with other picnickers hoping to enjoy the free, multi-artist "popular" music concert. Most but not all of them were under 40, rock 'n' roll children gathered for an afternoon of fun and sun. Once I smelled the pungent odor of marijuana. The throng stopped me several hundred yards shy of the stage. The music was loud, but barely decipherable, and I didn't know the band. I turned back the way I'd come.

Somewhere on the Mall between the Washington Monument and the Capitol I bought barbecued beef and beer from one of the dozens of outdoor exhibition booths set up by the Smithsonian's National Folklife Festival. I sprawled out on the grass, listened to the distant echo of the rock concert and voices in the passing crowd. No one discussed the Revolution or concepts of life, liberty and the pursuit of happiness.

Rich and I left The Eclectic for the symphony a little after five. I told him only that Bobbi—*Barbara* and I had split.

"No other choice," I said.

"It'll work out for the best," he claimed.

The air was thick, heavy and hot, the walk unpleasant from our environment and somber from my mood. He convinced me we "should" stop for expensive ice cream on the way.

"Since I haven't had any dinner," he said, "it's not like I'm breaking my diet."

"Doesn't matter as long as it balances out, right?" I said, not really listening to either of us.

"Right," he replied. "Besides, you could use something sweet in your life tonight."

We went to the same place that I'd taken her to see the eclipse: the West Front steps of the Capitol. A small park waited at the bottom of the steps, a wide apron of lawn ending at the symphony's covered stage with its empty metal folding chairs and music stands. Television cameras for public channels flanked each side of the stage; a third camera stared up from the pit at the conductor's podium. Boom mikes hung from bandstand rafters like snakes in the forest. All the lawn space between the stage and the steps had been taken by eager fans of classical music, fireworks—or perhaps just free entertainment. The crowd was also rapidly filling up the Capitol steps, so we took the first two empty spots we found, squatted on the marble steps and remembered that we'd forgotten to bring a blanket for a cushion.

This evening crowd was better dressed, older than the hordes who'd roamed the Mall during the day. The authorities quibbled on the count of the symphony crowd: one official said 100,000, another claimed 240,000. Whatever, someone filled every place I looked. The scent of baby oil and coconut suntanning cream drifted in the evening air. A few minutes after eight, the conductor came on stage dressed—like the seated orchestra—in a white evening jacket with black pants. From where we sat they all looked about three inches tall. He bowed to the audience's applause, mounted the podium, raised his baton: the music began.

The program included Beethoven's Fifth Symphony, a medley of songs from American pop composer Henry Mancini, and selections from John Philip Sousa. A famous Irishman played his flute. The fireworks following the concert were allegedly wonderful. I wouldn't know, I never got to see them.

She stepped out of the milling crowd halfway through the second movement of Beethoven's Fifth: they parted, and there she was, about ten feet away from us and at the bottom of our flight of marble stairs. She stood still to scan the crowd—much to the annoyance of the seated people whose view she blocked and the two streams of people moving past her in the narrow aisle between seated bodies. Her clothes were the same ones she'd worn this morning, though now she clutched a shoulder-strapped purse to her side. But her face, her expression . . . She looked like a survivor of a bombing raid searching the rubble for her family.

"Tresa!" I hissed.

She spotted me, pushed her way up the narrow path between people seated on the steps and the wide marble railing until she reached my side.

"Where have you been!" she said. Her words were excited, frightened—and loud.

"What are you doing here?" I whispered.

"Excuse me, ma'am," called a white-shirted Capitol policeman who'd been struggling to keep some semblance of order all night. "Please keep moving or sit down. You're blocking the aisle."

I pulled her down beside me. She barely noticed. I shifted to my left, forcing Rich and the rest of the people on our step to bump each other and shift too. One of the men sighed pointedly.

"You've got to come with me!" said Tresa. "Now! Something's gone wrong, there's something wrong, I just know . . ."

"What are you talking about?" I whispered.

"Hey!" called a woman's voice from behind us. "Would you people please shut up? Some of us are trying to enjoy the music!"

"It's Bobbi," said Tresa, ignoring the request. "She's not where she's supposed to be! Something must be wrong!"

"What do you mean?" I said. Nausea mushroomed through me; my skin tingled.

"I can't find her! I've been calling and calling and she said she'd be there but she's not. The last time I talked to her this afternoon she sounded worried like something . . ."

"Look, you two," whispered a man in the row behind us, "either shut up or take your troubles somewhere else—all right?"

"You've got to come with me!" said Tresa, her tough act dissolved into desperation. "Please! For her!"

I sighed, looked at Rich.

He handed me his car keys.

26

WE DROVE THROUGH DARKNESS, OUR FEEBLE HEADLIGHTS FADing into the road and the night.

"Tell me again," I said as I slowed Rich's station wagon to take a curve the Porsche wouldn't even have noticed.

"I've already . . ."

"Tell me again!" I interrupted Tresa.

"I talked to her right after you did," she said, her voice low and impatient, like a schoolteacher repeating a lesson the child should have already learned. "She called me from somewhere on the road, I think . . ."

"Why?"

"Because later she said . . ."

"Go back to what she said, as she said it."

"She was upset, been crying, I could tell. I asked her what was wrong and she said nothing, everything was getting right and then laughed that spooky laugh of hers. You know, the one . . ."

"I know. Go on."

"She said you two wouldn't see each other again. Said she wasn't . . . enough for you, right for you. Didn't go on much about that. Dumb me, I couldn't come up with anything smart to say. She said she called to tell me because she'd promised she would and she always kept her word. She said she didn't want to bother me with her, not to worry, more of that 'brave front' bullshit.

"I asked her if I could see her and she said no. To wait. She said she missed me, was sorry for being such a mess of a friend. Cried a little more. I told her not to worry, I'd done it to her too. That made her laugh.

"When I asked her what was happening tonight she said she wasn't sure. She said Emmett had plans. That he'd been in and out all day, that he obviously had something big doing tonight. I thought she meant some party or something, but now . . .

" 'What about you?' I asked her. 'You going with him?'

" 'No,' she said. 'I'm going home.'

"I told her I'd call her later; she said good-bye. That was that."

"You figure she was someplace else because . . ."

"Because she said she was going home.

"Only she's not there," said Tresa. "You heard the phone: 20, 30 rings and no answer. It's been like that since three this afternoon. At five, I started calling every ten minutes. I got panicky about six, called her mother in Charleston.

"Bobbi had talked to her this morning, like they do two, three times a week. Nothing big, the usual 'I love yous,' and 'take cares,' 'don't worrys.' I got her mom a little upset by asking if she'd heard from her since, but I smoothed that out. Lied or something, I don't remember.

"There really can't be anything wrong, can there?" Tresa asked me, desperately wanting to be proven overly imaginative.

I didn't answer her.

"Oh God!" she said again.

We reached the main road leading to the house. Less than a mile to go.

"What will we do if Emmett's there?" she asked.

"We'll say hello—and we want to see your wife."

"What if . . ."

"It's too late for what-ifs. Too late and too uncertain."

"Won't you tell me what this is all about?" she asked.

"This isn't the time," I said, and hoped she hadn't heard the clunk from beneath my seat.

She'd told me her story as we walked back to The Eclectic for Rich's car. I made her come upstairs. My answering machine showed no calls. She dialed Bobbi's number, held the phone receiver away from her ear so I could hear the unanswered ringing. She said she was scared and didn't question my command to go to the bathroom while I tried calling another number. While she was out of the room, I took the .357 Magnum from my desk. The revolver was too big to carry. No one could miss its bulge if I stuck it in the waistband of my jeans, tried to hide it with my maroon polo shirt. The toilet flushed as I bundled the gun in a gray nylon windbreaker. She didn't mention the crumpled up jacket I carried to the car, didn't ask why I put it under my seat. Maybe she didn't notice. Maybe she didn't want to know.

"There's the house," she whispered, as I turned the car down the private lane.

The porch light glowed. A few lights shone on the first floor, fewer still on the second. I slowly cruised into the driveway, parked the car parallel to the long front porch. No other cars were in sight. The doors to the garage on the right side of the house were closed. I shut off the engine. Rolled my window down.

The crickets started up again. Wind rustled in the trees beyond the whitewashed barn. A horse snorted inside the barn—the thoroughbred. Bobbi had told me the animal seldom stood silently in his stall. She'd ridden the beast only that first day.

"I don't hear anything, do you?" asked Tresa.

"Come on," I said.

I pulled the heavy bundle out from under my seat, led her up the porch steps to the front door. I rang the bell.

And rang it again a minute later.

"Does the maid live here?" I asked, sure I already knew the answer.

"No. She comes in every day, sometimes stays to cook or help with dinner, but . . . the two of them live here alone."

I rang the bell a third time.

"Do you have a key?" I asked.

"We can't go in there!" she said.

The doorknob turned in my hand, the door swung open.

"Sure we can," I said, stepped inside as I yelled, "Hello? Anybody home?"

The entryway was lit, empty. A light burned in the empty drawing room off to our left. The shadows of the railing for the stairs ahead to my right made gray lines like bars on the wall.

"Call her," I said to Tresa.

"Bobbi! Bobbi, it's me, Tresa!"

No answer.

"Sloan!" I yelled. "Emmett Sloan! Are you here?"

Still no answer.

"Is anybody here?" I yelled.

Nobody answered.

I shook my left hand, unfolded a layer of jacket from around my gun; it was still hidden, but not by much.

We glanced in the library, the dining room, the other big sitting room on the first floor. Nothing, nothing but highly polished furniture, neatly ordered crystal in glass cabinets. The chrome on all the appliances in the kitchen gleamed when we turned on the light, but no one besides us was there to appreciate it. An antique grandfather's clock ticked in the hall.

"Let's go upstairs," I said. "Stay a couple steps behind me."

The door to Emmett's study stood open, so we went there first. A floor lamp lit the room enough for me to see it was empty. I glanced at the wall, noticed a banquet photograph hung where once I'd seen the picture of Tresa and Bobbi. His desk was tidy and bare.

We checked five small, dark rooms: three guest bedrooms, a bathroom and another small sitting room. I don't know if Tresa understood why I stood clear of the doors I swung open, why I waited a moment before reaching around the corner, groping for the light switch and clicking it on. Why I entered the room slowly, my hands almost crossed.

There were two back "master" bedrooms. A crack of light shone between the carpet and the bottom of one door. I went to the other room first.

It was his: clean, neat, sterile, almost like a hotel chamber with many mirrors and vast closets. His smugness scented the air.

We paused outside the last closed door. Tresa was pale, her hands trembled.

"Should we . . ."

I opened the door.

Her bedroom. Also clean, also neat, also almost hotel-like in that it seemed to hold a person in transit who had brought only the baggage and belongings necessary to live within these walls. But her touch was here—in the colors, the photograph of a smiling older woman propped next to the dressing table mirror, in the junk and worthless clutter that wasn't there. Her brush lay on the other side of the mirror; when I moved closer I could see a few auburn strands caught in its teeth. The huge bed was made.

Her bathroom lights shone through the gap between the closed door and the carpet. If it were like his, her bathroom would be a brightly lit, elegant chamber with mirrored walls, handmade tiles and gilded faucets. To the left of the door would be an elegant shower tub, while an ornate marble sink and cabinet top would fill the wall to the right. The toilet would be against the far wall, centered in the entryway. I swung the door open.

She lay sprawled on her back between the closed toilet and the sink. Her scuffed black shoes must have been ten years old. The right shoe was half off. She wore old khaki pants, and her blue Levis shirt was sun-bleached. Her arms lay palms-up. Her jaw was slack, lips slightly parted. No lipstick or makeup colored her face. Those sapphire eyes were open, dry. An ugly red crease furrowed a raw but shallowly scraped line back from Bobbi's forehead into her hair where a left-sided part would have been if she'd worn that style.

But what commanded attention was the black hole of a third eye in the center of her forehead. A crimson star spread out from that brutal orb, with red tendrils snaking down to her temples, back into the crown of her thick auburn hair that was matted and crushed. The stain spread out from her hair, a sticky scarlet sea on the white tiled floor.

"What . . ." said Tresa, then she saw past me into the room of sparkling chrome and gleaming white porcelain.

"Oh God no!!" Tresa rushed forward. I muscled her back toward the bed, then stepped into the bathroom.

"Stay out of here!" I yelled as I shut the door with my elbow.

There was no need to touch her to know, but I did and

hated it. The flesh on her neck felt like rubber. No pulse beat beneath it.

The next thing I remember is the sound of Tresa throwing up in the bedroom. Slowly, slowly, that brightly lit world came back into focus.

A cocked, black automatic pistol lay on the floor by her feet. An automatic ejects the back shell casing of every bullet it fires; after the first shot, each new discharge recocks the weapon. One brass shell casing rested against the open plug of the sink; a second shell casing lay beside the sink bowl in front of makeup jars and an inverted seashell that held her ornate watch and rings.

A foul, red splatter about the size of a basketball marred the mirrored wall above the toilet. A quarter-sized hole dotted that stain, slightly off-center. A second, similar hole was punched through the glass maybe a foot above and to the right of the first. The mirrored wall had shattered into two cobwebs of jagged lines radiating out from those holes. My fragmented reflection stared back at me from the glass not covered by gore.

I left that room.

Tresa was sobbing face down on the bed, her breath coming in great gulps. She was limp, like a fish out of water.

"Oh God!" she cried. "Oh God! She's dead, she's dead, isn't she?"

"Yes."

Her sobs grew louder. I pulled her up, made her stumble beside me to the bedroom door. She didn't want to stand on her own, but I squeezed her shoulder, jerked her a few times until she had her feet firmly planted and her eyes as focused on me as they could get.

"Stay in here. Shut the door. Sit with your back against it. Open it only when I say, when I use your name. You'll be all right."

"Don't leave me!" she cried.

But I was already in the hall, shutting the door. I heard her weight slide down the other side of the wood, heard her sobs start again. I pulled my gun from its bundle. The Magnum felt heavy and certain in my grasp.

Room by room I tore through the house we'd already searched. The hell with caution: I threw doors wide open, stood silhouetted in their entryway while I flipped on the light, dared anything to move—bedrooms, bathrooms, his office. The first floor, running down the stairs two at a time. The drawing rooms, pantry, the kitchen and out the back way. The screen door banged shut behind me—I whirled, snapped into a marksman's crouch, the Magnum cocked and trembling in a two-handed grip.

Nothing moved. The crickets started up again.

Only her car waited in the garage.

The barn smelled of hay and horse. The beast locked in his stall snorted and pawed the floor in fury. He was a dark shape shaking before the sights of my gun. For one raging moment I started to squeeze the trigger—then I turned and ran.

When I stopped I was in the grassy meadow where I'd watched her ride Molly, halfway to the white rail fence by the main road. No traffic moved over its distant pavement. Trees along the meadow's flanks stood like shadows in this indigo night. The house glowed eerie electric white. Only a damn gun filled my hand. No bullet I could shoot, no target I could hit would bring her back. I staggered round and round, whirling in a circle like a drunk dancing beneath a quarter moon.

"Tresa?" I said after I knocked. "Open up, it's me, Rankin."

The door flew open. Tears still ran from her eyes, but her breathing was back to normal, her color less pale.

"Where did you go?" she whispered.

"I checked the rest of the house again," I said. "Come on."

She didn't protest as I led her down the stairs. The central air conditioning worked on my sweat-soaked shirt, chilled me, but I wrapped my gray jacket around Tresa's shoulders. She took it without comment, probably without noticing it.

"Sit here," I said, lowering her to a chair in the entryway next to a table and a phone. I picked up the receiver, dialed 911.

"Police."

"My name is John Rankin. I'd like to report a shooting."

"Where are you, please?"

"I'm at . . ." I blanked on the exact address. A neat stack of stamped envelopes next to the phone caught my eye: paid bills, from the look of their destination. Bobbi's graceful handwriting had filled in this return address. I read it to the police dispatcher.

"What's your phone number?"

I read it off the sticker on the phone.

"Do you need an ambulance?"

"No."

"What kind of shooting, Mr. Rankin?"

I paused, said, "She's dead."

"Who?"

"Mrs. Barbara Gracon Randolph Sloan. This is her house."

"Are you . . ."

"Another friend and I found the body a few minutes ago. Tresa Hastings is the friend's name. She's pretty broken up and I have to help her now. We'll be waiting outside."

"Units are on the way."

Tresa and I were at the door when the phone rang.

"Hello?" I said when I answered it.

"Mr. Rankin?"

"Yes."

"County Police," said the same voice. "Just checking."

We hung up.

Ten minutes later flashing red and blue lights appeared out on the main road, turned and came up the private lane. The white cruiser pulled to a stop behind Rich's station wagon. I hoped the law wouldn't look for the impotent Magnum stashed under Rich's driver's seat. The cop who climbed out of the cruiser couldn't have been more than 25. His uniform was brown, his head bare. His eyes took in Tresa leaning against the open front door, crying softly, then swung back to me. He walked toward us slowly, radio cradled in his left hand while he held his right stiffly against his leg so his wrist brushed the holster on his belt.

"Did you call about a shooting?"

"Yes. It's in there, second floor, back bedroom. The light is on."

"You're Rankin?"

"And that's Tresa Hastings."

"Why don't you show me?" he said. His gesture with the radio said that was a command, not a question. "Please come with us, ma'am."

He made sure we led the way. When we got to the bathroom, he had us stand several feet opposite the door while he entered it sideways. His eyes were just a flicker from any move we'd make. He spent maybe 30 seconds looking, then came out.

"Did you move her? Touch anything?" he asked.

"I checked for a pulse on her neck. Touched the doors coming in."

He grunted, radioed for detectives, a lab car. And told

the dispatcher to notify the morgue. Another uniformed cop strolled into the bedroom just as our man finished his report. The second cop nodded to his colleague, glanced in the bathroom.

"My," he said.

"Anybody else around?" asked the first cop.

"I looked through the house and the grounds pretty good," I told him.

"Before or after you found the body?"

"Both."

The cops exchanged glances, and the second one left the room. I heard him opening and closing doors in the house.

The three of us tried not to stare at one another. The unseen cop clumped down the stairs to the first floor. Our cop's radio crackled with calls for other units and other events.

"You're not her husband, are you?" the cop abruptly asked.

"No."

"Who were you to her?"

Tresa's eyes focused on us; I blinked at the cop.

"I was her best friend," I said.

He nodded, said nothing for a minute, then muttered, "Rough night, huh?"

"Yeah," I said. "Rough night."

"Good evening," said a husky man in a green polyester suit. He paused at the bedroom door, pulled a handkerchief out of his pocket and wiped his face. The uniformed cop stiffened, nodded and got a nod back from the man in the suit: somewhere in those civilian clothes he carried a badge.

"Was on my way back from break," he said, as if it mattered. His bass voice rumbled from somewhere deep in his barrel chest. "Understand we've got a shooting."

"In there, sir," said the patrolman, nodding to the bathroom.

The man in the suit spent 20 minutes in that closed room. During that time two men wearing uniforms and patches that said "lab technician" arrived. The patrolman told them, "The boss is in there. So is the body." They set their bags down, looked at each other, left. They returned with a folded stretcher. Tresa started to cry again. The technicians looked embarrassed, moved the stretcher into the hall and stayed with it until they were summoned by the cop in civilian clothes. They moved inside the bathroom with cameras and measuring tapes, jars of fingerprint powder. He came over to us.

"Terrible tragedy," he said, shaking his head. His face was kindly, his eyes soft and sympathetic. "I'm County Detective Dave Bechtel."

Tresa and I introduced ourselves.

"Do you mind giving me a quick idea of how you happened to find . . . What did you say her name was?"

"Barbara Gracon Randolph Sloan," I answered. "Mrs."

"Yes," said the detective. "Mrs. Sloan."

My version then started with Tresa and I being unable to reach her by phone, covered the drive out, finding the body, searching the house twice. Calling the police.

"You say you're a friend, Mr. Rankin?"

"That's right."

"Good friend?"

"Yes."

"Uh-huh. Live around here?"

"How can you two stand around *talking* like that when . . ." Tresa shook her head. Anger was replacing her tears. Bechtel and I glanced at her, saw no appropriate response. He turned back to me.

"No," I said. "I live in D.C."

"What do you do?"

"I'm a private investigator."

"Well," said Bechtel. Downstairs a door slammed. Feet

pounded up the stairs. "Isn't that something? We've got this peculiar shooting and who do I run into at the scene but . . ."

"I demand to know what is going on!"

Emmett Sloan stormed into the room, yelling as he came. His subtle British accent was gone: uncontrolled anger had stripped away his sophisticated veneer and he was once more just an American boy.

"And you're . . ." said the county detective.

"I'm Emmett Sloan, and this is my house! What in the hell are . . ."

For the first time since bursting into the room, Emmett noticed me. He blinked, saw Tresa.

"Mr. Sloan, I'm Detective Bechtel, County Police. I've got some bad news for you. There's no easy way to do this, so I'll just tell you flat out: your wife is dead."

"What?" Emmett's brow wrinkled and he frowned, as if he hadn't heard Bechtel.

"Your wife is dead," repeated the cop. "There's been some sort of tragedy, a shooting, in the bathroom. . . ."

Emmett bolted toward that door. One of the technicians moved to block him.

"Let him look!" called Bechtel. They did, though they held his arm.

He turned back to us, shuffled a few steps closer.

"Take it easy," said Bechtel. "I know it's rough. If you want to go into the other room, lie down . . ."

Emmett shook his head. His expression was dazed.

The cop stared at the husband, watched his reaction.

"Officially, this isn't how I'd like this," said Bechtel, "all of us together, but seeing as how we're here . . .

"Right now," he continued, "this is an inquiry to determine what happened. We'd like you to all cooperate, and if you have any questions . . ."

"I don't understand," said Emmett.

"Sir, your wife's been shot. It could be a suicide, but there are a few . . . problems we need to clear up. Where were you tonight?"

"At the Matthews' barbecue, of course," said Emmett. His eyes moved from the bathroom to Bechtel to me. He seemed disconnected, distracted. "They went to the fireworks."

"And you went with them?" asked Bechtel, a gentle, helpful prod.

"No, I went driving."

"Alone?"

The county detective's voice had a new edge. Emmett's eyes narrowed as he felt it. His answer was slow, drawn out.

"Yes." He jabbed his forefinger toward me. "What the hell is he doing here?"

"That was the question I was asking him when you came in," said the county detective. Everyone's eyes turned to me.

And in that moment I saw it all.

I knew the *problems* that bothered the county detective. Two shots for one suicide. Killing yourself takes nerve—less courage than staying alive, but nevertheless, suicide is not a timid act. To raise a gun, point it at your forehead, stare down that last black tunnel and squeeze the trigger with your thumb . . .

Two shots for one suicide. I didn't know then what Nick would tell me later, that yes, there are records of it happening, of some souls so desperate they took the first bullet that missed killing them and had enough strength left to fire a second. I didn't know that Emmett normally kept that gun in its original manufacturer's box, the box in the bottom drawer of his desk. They'd find Bobbi's fingerprints on the box, on the instruction manual included by the factory, on the box of shells given to Emmett at the same time he received the weapon from a grateful arms merchant he helped make rich. The fingerprints proved only that her fingers had touched those things—or been touched to them. I didn't know then how such facts would be found and stacked behind first one, then another conclusion. But I knew what I saw, and I knew what that county detective was thinking:

How could anyone have the brains, the determination and the guts to do all that? Forget about motivation: finding a reason to die is easy. For someone to try suicide is understandable, but to fire one shot from a heavy, unfamiliar gun, have that awful roar full in your face as the cartridge explodes and the powder flashes, sears your vision as the bullet rips a gash across your skull, *and then* to realize you're still alive, have the willpower and guts and physical grit to hold still, turn that gun toward your forehead again, tighten your thumb on that trigger again . . . ?

Especially a woman like the one lying dead on that bathroom floor. I knew that thought ran through the policeman's mind, and I also knew that thought was the answer to his doubts.

Bobbi's life played back for me, all that she'd done. The bargain she'd accepted with Emmett: hopeful on the surface, cynical and grim at its core. The calculated game she'd initially played with me. Molly, how she'd done what she thought necessary for the one she loved. That sexless monster now caged in the barn outside that she wouldn't let beat her. I played back all we'd said. *You're doomed*, I'd callously told her; why bother to continue the charade? *You're a prisoner*, I'd said. *You're the key.*

And she'd ultimately agreed. She'd set herself free, set all of us free too, for she must have realized Emmett would maintain her mother as long as he could rather than lose that last link to the echelons he envied. *I trust you*, she told me, trusted me to be good enough to survive Emmett after she was gone. She was a prisoner beyond redemption, stripped of all illusions, unable to justify her fate any longer, unable to change it, unable to bear it. She was the key. She set herself free. She said her good-byes, paid her bills, changed to her old clothes, took off the rings and jewelry that she wore as chains and turned the key.

That she killed herself I had no doubt, just as I had no legal proof.

There stood J. Emmett Sloan, murderer. Of that too I had no doubt, just as I had no legal proof. He was guilty for so much of Bobbi's life though not directly for her death. And the law could not touch him for his sins. He roamed free and unfettered in the world, devouring all who stood in the way of his insatiable quest for respect, adoration and honor, for a reputation, an image. In that moment, perhaps for the first time in his life, he stood scattered, out of control of the events around him.

In that moment I saw it all; my vision sickened me with rage and sorrow and guilt. I saw it all—and I saw a chance.

"Maybe," Nick had said, *"just maybe, someday you'll get a shot. If you do, make it good."*

"Let me ask you again, Mr. Rankin," said Detective Bechtel. "What made you come out here tonight?"

"I was concerned for her safety," I said.

"Why?" said Bechtel.

Emmett paled.

"I told you I was her friend. A very good friend, better than I ever planned on being. We met in January when she hired me."

"To do what?" asked Bechtel.

"She suspected her husband of murdering a man called Parviz Naderi. He was killed in Washington. Shot twice. In the head."

Tresa lunged toward Emmett.

"You murdered her, you son of a bitch!" she screamed.

Bechtel hooked one arm around her stomach, swung her off her feet and tossed her back my way. I held on to her as her anger turned back to tears.

The uniformed cop nervously fingered the snap on his holster; he was staring at Emmett.

"Ask D.C. Homicide Detective Nick Sherman about Naderi," I told the county man. "It was his case. He knows me and all about my investigation."

"I think we all better ride to the station," said Bechtel. "In separate cars."

"What are you doing, Rankin?" hissed Emmett.

"My duty," I told him. "I'm telling the law the facts as I know them and can prove them."

"You lying bastard!"

But I wasn't lying and I didn't. I told the truth—I didn't speculate, I didn't conclude, I didn't offer my opinions. I told the law what it wanted to hear.

There wasn't much the law could do. The county police spent weeks trying to determine if Emmett killed his wife or if she committed suicide. They went to the D.C. police with questions about Naderi, ended up with Nick, who even with his department's blessing to reopen his investigation found nothing new. Emmett got a great lawyer. He was never charged. Bobbi is still listed on the county books as "death by misadventure." The investigations eventually suffered a *de facto* demise.

But they were enough to destroy Emmett—or at least his dreams.

Bobbi's strange death made the papers, and the same bitchy *Washington Post* reporter who'd dined with me at Emmett's mansion wrote a scathing "analytical" feature story on him as a man in the middle of violent scandals. Without proclaiming either his guilt or innocence, she linked him to Naderi's death and notorious legend; to the strange, unresolvable gunshot death of his wife, mentioning the half-dozen times the police had questioned him, the fact that he retained a top criminal lawyer. Her piece noted that this man who'd once been everyone's friend was now shunned as the city's most prominent leper. She skated the boundaries of libel, but Emmett was in no position to sue.

I often think of her, and our conversation at that dinner party.

"Ain't life a bitch?" she'd said. *"You can't ever get what you want. There's no such thing as justice."*

"I didn't know those were the same thing," I'd replied.

"If life worked out perfectly, they would be."

"What can you expect?"

"Hell, at least a little excitement or something. Some scandal. Isn't that kind of thing your department?"

I'd told her *no*. History proved both of us wrong.

She got what she wanted: some scandal, a little excitement, plus the kind of story for which she was famous and amply rewarded.

So many of us got what we wanted; so much of life worked out perfectly. Rich lost weight. Nick wanted to know who killed Naderi. Emmett wanted a reputation. Tresa wanted her friend to be free of her husband. Bobbi wanted to be safe. I wanted to know the truth.

And we all paid the price.